Love &
Death
IN BURGUNDY

Love & Death
IN BURGUNDY

SUSAN C. SHEA

MINOTAUR BOOKS

NEW YORK

This is a work of fiction. All of the characters, organizations, and events portrayed in this novel are either products of the author's imagination or are used fictitiously.

www.minotaurbooks.com

Designed by Omar Chapa

The Library of Congress Cataloging-in-Publication Data is available upon request.

ISBN 978-1-250-11300-9 (hardcover)
ISBN 978-1-250-11301-6 (e-book)

Our books may be purchased in bulk for promotional, educational, or business use. Please contact your local bookseller or the Macmillan Corporate and Premium Sales Department at 1-800-221-7945, extension 5442, or by e-mail at MacmillanSpecialMarkets@macmillan.com.

First Edition: May 2017

10 9 8 7 6 5 4 3 2 1

For Alice and David, and for Tim, always

ACKNOWLEDGMENTS

This story owes its life to two American friends who intro- duced me to their tiny town in France and who, long before that, invited my family into the magic world they created with their music and art. What I observed over the years is that it is possible—not easy, but possible—to invent the life you dream of living. Their generosity of spirit inspired this story, even though Katherine and Michael are not them, and Reigny-sur-Canne is not a real town, hovering in the right place geographically, but only in the mists of my imagination, as do all the people who live only there.

My deep thanks to Ceil Cleveland, David Corbett, Glenda Burgess Grunzweig, Terry Shames, and Steve Shea, for their insights and early reads; Kimberley Cameron, for her steady encouragement; at St. Martin's, Alicia Clancy, for telling me she loved the characters, and Bethany Reis, who made it a better book; Anne Trager of Le French Book for connecting me with a real gendarme; and the people I met in the Yonne region of Burgundy, who were courteous and knowledgeable about everything from cheese to chocolate to the deeply mov- ing history of a place that suffered so much during the Nazi occupation and that fought so valiantly against it.

Life in a small French village is far more complicated than one might suppose, and memories are long. In the end, what happened couldn't precisely be blamed on the collision of different cultures, although Burgundians will tell you their wines, cheeses, and history set them apart from the rest of the world. The truth is, tragedies ultimately are individual, and this one was no different, except perhaps that the people involved were oblivious to the import of the thunderclouds gathering over their village. That someone would soon be dead did not occur to anyone.

—P. L. Vickers,
The Mysterious Death at the Château

Love &
Death
IN BURGUNDY

CHAPTER 1

Reigny-sur-Canne was hardly more than a crossroads in Burgundy's famous landscape of pastures and grapevine-planted terroirs on rolling hills, overlooked by tourists for the most part, which was fine with its residents. No shops selling souvenir tea towels and postcards, not even a wine *cave*, only a musty-smelling bookstore and a sleepy café. Katherine Goff had realized soon after she and Michael transplanted themselves to the village three years before that the only reason summer visitors with maps made their way to Reigny was to see the crumbling Château de Bellegarde, which had played a role in the medieval clash of titans that defined so much of Burgundy's history.

This July morning, the pear tree's shade was welcome. Katherine's two guests sipped *café crème* from ceramic bowls their hostess had found early on in furnishing the old house her husband bought for her on a whim. Katherine, still beautiful at fifty-five, was stationed at her easel, her graying hair gathered in a ponytail, her petite body wrapped in an old patterned apron, and her fingers smudged with paint.

"We're going to put on the best show Reigny has ever seen, darlings." She picked up a brush. "Michael will play guitar and sing, of course, and Emile has offered to join him in a duet."

Yves, the owner of the bookstore, slumped in a misshapen rattan chair and groaned. *"Mon dieu,* Katherine. This does not make me desire to be on the same stage, you understand? Your husband, he is *incroyable,* amazing, but Emile, he cannot sing well in any language." Handsome, fortyish, with a strong Gallic nose and dark, almost black hair and eyes, Yves spoke heavily accented English with a drawl, pulling his words out like taffy.

"Yves is right," the pretty American woman sitting near him said. "You can't count on Emile's performance to impress an audience other than Jean's nasty pack of dogs." She nibbled some *pain d'epices,* Dijon's famous spicy gingerbread, with perfect white teeth. "Someone should speak to that man about keeping the beasts in his yard. It's impossible to take a walk without them trailing along as if they were about to jump you. In Cleveland, they would be on leashes."

"You're not in Cleveland anymore, Penny," Katherine said as she spun back to her easel on red leather 1940s heels, a vintage find at one of the summer flea markets and only five euros. "I have a remedy for that. Not for the dogs, of course. They will be with us, like ancient curses, until we die. Michael says Betty Lou has agreed to do a set, and you two can sing one of those funny disco medleys you do so well. Perhaps we can convince Emile to give us an accordion number instead of singing."

She picked up a tube of burnt umber oil paint and squeezed a little onto her palette, wondering if she had been too blunt with Penny, who could go on about how things were done in the city of her birth, a city she had fled the moment her late parents' fortune had been settled on her. She wondered if Yves, who had never seen a reason to travel outside of his native France, even knew where Cleveland was. She jabbed the brush onto the canvas in an area that was going to be sky. In the foreground of the painting, two young women in long gowns appeared to be examining a lamb. The scenery behind them was what Katherine saw when she looked over her crumbling stone wall, a field of alfalfa still dotted with the last of the brilliant red poppies.

"I haven't sung in ages and I'd be embarrassed," Penny said, "especially if Betty Lou Holliday's going to perform. She's famous. People will be coming to hear her, not us." She paused to swat at a bug that had settled on her slender, un-covered arm. "Damn these horseflies. Why don't those new people from Belgium board their horses somewhere in the country?"

"My dear, this *is* the country," Katherine said. She would have to put the unfinished painting away soon and set up for her lunch party. "More black, do you think?" she said, half turning toward Yves, but really thinking out loud. Here in Burgundy, she had discovered after several years of full-time residency, unabashed blue sky days were as rare as uncom-plicated relationships. The heavy rains, chilly even in sum-mer, appeared seemingly out of nowhere. Skies darkened ten minutes after she hung the sheets, and the alfalfa danced in gusty winds.

"Betty Lou hasn't had a big hit record since, well, since they were records and not CDs," she said to comfort Penny. "Maybe I'm exaggerating. Country music was never my thing. Anyway, Michael's trying to persuade her to try a little rock. Her husband, J.B., is her producer, you know, and he's all for it."

"I don't understand why you offered to organize the

entertainment for this local thing," Penny said. "It's so much work."

"Well, to be the queen of the party, of course, admired for pulling off the best show in Reigny's history. I expect you to cover me with glory." Katherine laughed to disguise her hope that they understood how serious she was. "Everyone will say what a charming and talented woman Madame Goff is, and how lucky we are to have her in our midst."

"Have all the ladies coming to lunch today volunteered, or is this a recruiting event?" Penny said.

"No, not at all. I'd like Betty Lou to meet some local people. She's isolated in that house they leased so far out of town. Michael says it's elegant, but the real draw is the recording studio. The place is owned by a French actor, but he's never there."

"I am invited for lunch also?" Yves said, eyebrows cocked in what Katherine guessed he thought of as an appealing expression. "I don't mind closing for a couple of hours. Business, it is terrible. Yesterday was one customer, a tourist who wanted every book in the shop about the château, as they all do this time of year, but nothing else."

"I'm afraid not. Adele Bellegarde is coming."

"Why?" Yves said, his voice rising. "She tells tales about me and you invite her to your home? I am insulted." He abandoned his smile and glowered at Katherine, who was too used to his extravagant moods to pay much attention.

"Yes, I know. But that's only because you wooed her daughter before abandoning her for our adorable Penny," Katherine said. "Naturally, she is disappointed for Sophie's sake."

"Wooed? I do not know what that means," Yves said, not entirely convincingly. "Her mother put me in a position where I had to ask the unhappy thing to a film or two, but that was it. A bore, I tell you."

"Yes, well, unfortunately, Adele knows exactly how you feel about her daughter. I think you told everyone in town, which was a very foolish thing to do," Katherine said, "and now she will not break bread with you. I do understand how she feels, you know? It was unkind of you, Yves."

Penny looked at Yves and smiled, tapping his hand before leaning down to pick up her bag. "You are a bad, bad boy," she said in mock rebuke, making a face at him.

At that moment, a large black dog bounded up to them, pink tongue hanging out. More slowly, a man in a Stetson and a smaller, white version of the shaggy dog followed, the man dipping his head to enter the leafy green shade.

"Howdy," he said, pulling up a straight-backed chair from near the tree's trunk and swinging it around so he could sit backward on it. He took off his hat and ruffled his pale blond hair, clenching a thin, unlit cigarillo between his teeth.

Penny let out a small scream. The dogs had tumbled in her direction, and Gracey, who was roughly the size of a small black bear, bumped into her as it playfully nipped its companion.

"Down," Michael shouted. "Git, both of you." He waved his hat and both dogs ambled off, grinning and panting, to find their own shady tree.

Yves spoke into the quiet. "Your dogs, Michael, they do not know their place. Not like French dogs."

"I wouldn't have a French dog if you paid me," said the man in the cowboy hat. "Damn things piss on the furniture."

"Now, darling," Katherine said to her husband. "You know that's not true. It only happened once and it was not, thank heavens, an upholstered chair."

5

Michael Goff laughed. "Kay's the most softhearted person I know. Once is enough in my book. You won't catch my dogs doing that." He cocked his head in Katherine's direction and winked at Penny as he said it.

"I saw that," Katherine said, pointing her brush at him. "Stop teasing. Anyway, it wasn't a French dog. It was the ambassador's dog, which makes it a German dog by your logic." She gestured broadly with the hand that still held a paintbrush.

"Albert Bellegarde's no ambassador. He's a businessman who got an honorary job title because of his money, which I heard he earned by selling guns to mercenaries." Michael had pointed this out to his wife before, but Katherine chose not to remember it if the occasion called for a bit of dramatic emphasis. She understood that correcting her on small points was merely one of the running choruses in a long and comfortable marriage, and so she breezed past comments like this one.

Yves, however, took full advantage of the opening. "You see, he is a villain," he said, stabbing the air with his forefinger to drive home his point. "Me, I am surprised he has not been arrested or even assassinated."

"Oh, for heaven's sake," Katherine said, "he's an old man, maybe a bit full of himself."

"Michael," Yves said, changing gears seamlessly in the face of the irritation he heard in her voice, "you are going to sing in Katherine's little show, *non*?"

"Yup, I'm doing a set with Betty Lou. Got any requests?"

"Rock and roll, *mon ami*," Yves said in a loud voice, "that is what we want. Maybe you can get one of your famous friends to do a set, yes?"

Yves had probably started the rumor three years ago that

the new American resident was a rock star living incognito in Reigny. Their next-door neighbor, Emile, a cheerful man of small talent and high musical ambitions, had taken up the idea with gusto and had doubtless spread it far and wide, at least as far as the nearby market towns. Katherine knew it made Michael uncomfortable. On the other hand, it was flattering and, after all, her husband had been on the verge of stardom before things with the band went sour.

"What about you?" Penny asked her.

"Paint the stage set, of course, and make the champagne punch, using Crémant, since we only use wine from the region. The fête's in honor of the Feast of the Assumption, so the entertainment should probably be, well, decorous."

"*Non*, Katherine," Yves said with a burst of laughter. "I assure you it is not celebrated in Reigny as a religious festival. This is France; *vive la république*."

"In any case, I hardly feel I'm up to tap dancing in front of an audience." Secretly, she was torn, liking the notion of showing off her figure and dancing moves almost as much as she feared having people laugh at her. It was her exercise and she practiced in front of a mirror daily, in the wood-floored bedroom behind dense lace curtains, staring critically at the woman who looked back at her, scanning for inadvertent comedy.

Lately, to her annoyance, the voice in her head insisted on asking what Madame Pomfort would think. Everyone in Reigny-sur-Canne looked sideways at the widow who presided over Reigny's social life before deciding when to plant their dahlias or paint their shutters. Unfortunately, Madame shared the local prejudice against foreigners. Those few, mostly seasonal, residents who even noticed her snubs learned to keep a low profile when in her company, say, picking up a newspaper at the café. Most of them disappeared in the depths of winter anyway, irritating the locals who had to put up with cold rain, freezing temperatures, and poorly heated homes.

Katherine, however, felt the rejection of the local society keenly. When Michael surprised her by saying he'd found a house online that seemed to fit her dream of a simple life in the countryside south of Paris, he had assured her she'd fit right in with her command of French and her desire to please. But all her life, Katherine had lived with the equal terrors of being invisible and being seen by everyone as a fool, the legacy of an unloved childhood she had never quite escaped. The unease clung to her like a creeping fog at times, fended off by painting and flea market shopping, solitary tap dancing, and an extra glass of wine when the smell of rejection threatened to choke her. Mme Pomfort was the living embodiment of her fears, living five hundred yards away down the picturesque little road.

Charm, Katherine's only weapon, had not penetrated Madame's thick armor. Katherine's few friends were summer visitors like Penny or the outgoing Belgians who came for long weekends, and the Bellegardes, who lived in the château but were not quite part of the local scene either. The young Englishwoman who had moved into a dark little house at the other end of Reigny's main street was no relief, being somewhat reclusive. But the mostly elderly women and men who made up Reigny's year-round population followed Mme Pomfort's lead like courtiers attending a queen. All except Yves, who considered himself a communist except when it came to paying the annual commune tax for garbage collection.

"*Mais oui,*" Yves said now, jumping up. "Of course you

shall tap, my dear Katherine. I shall sing with Penny, and your husband and his American cowgirl-singer shall amaze us all with their duets. Emilc, well, I don't think so. We shall arrange to keep him busy at the *pétanque* court, yes?"

"Country music, Yves, and Betty Lou was big time," Michael said.

"Emile may surprise you," Katherine said. "He has apparently dug up an electric guitar. He told me he was in a rock band in Paris when he was a student. Admittedly, it seems a little strange given his fixation on the accordion."

Michael snorted. "Well, hell, we've all been in a rock band at some point or other."

"Not me. You were in a famous band, weren't you, Michael?" Penny said. "The Crazy Leopards? I went to see them when they played at Wellesley for homecoming. We were thrilled."

Michael unfolded his height from the chair, turned it back to face the little group, and slapped his hat on his leg. He squinted into the far distance and shrugged. "That was more than twenty years ago, and I left the band before they went platinum."

Katherine looked sideways at Michael. Would this never stop hurting? She had seen the slight twinge of his mouth before he answered Penny.

"Well, I've got to get on with the rehearsing," he said, and walked around to where his wife was standing and gave her a quick kiss.

"Darling, you will be gone until four, won't you?" Katherine said. "This is really a ladies' lunch. No one will gossip if you're here."

"Can't have that," Michael said, leaning in to snag a piece of gingerbread from the scallop-edged serving plate with the hairline crack only she could see, another of Katherine's flea market finds. "So long," he said, ducking under the tree's low branches. He ambled back across the uncut lawn toward the old stone house, accompanied by a yellow cat that appeared out of nowhere to trail along behind him. Katherine paused to admire his broad shoulders and the snug fit of his jeans. He had been a catch back in the day, five years her junior, which hadn't mattered a bit to either of them, and she still felt lucky. A few minutes later, the group under the tree heard his old Citroën labor up the little road next to the house.

"My dear husband has no idea if people are idly gossiping or plotting an overthrow of the European Union," Katherine said to Yves and Penny as the car sound faded away. "He has no French, and hand signals don't work in general conversation as well as they do when choosing croissants at the patisserie. Now, I must clean up and finish the ratatouille for lunch, so off with you both. Penny, I'll see you at one."

"My plumber's due in a few minutes, anyway," Penny said. She stood up and shook out her elegant linen slacks. "I don't know why he can't fix things the first time, or even the third. It's the same every summer, from the week I arrive until I close up the house. I'm beginning to think I'm his retirement fund."

"You probably are," said Katherine, coming to kiss her American guest on both cheeks.

"If you hear me scream, I've been attacked by Jean's pack of wild animals." Penny wafted off in a cloud of expensive perfume, picking her way down slate steps, through the tangle of roses and irises to the end of the garden and through the iron gate, which squealed as she opened it. Yves pulled his car keys out of his pocket and jingled them.

"I must be going also. Tell me, are the Bellegardes coming to the fête, do you think? I don't know if I will attend if they are."

"I didn't want to say anything more in front of Penny," Katherine said, putting her arm through his and leading him to his car. "But it was rather more than a couple of dates, Yves. You even talked about making her your partner in the book-shop once you were married. Poor Sophie has retreated to Paris and her father is furious."

"*Jamais.* I never said that, it is only the lies her mother tells. She is such a snob, and he, my god, he would like us all to believe his money makes him better than the rest of us."

"Well, it certainly makes him something," Katherine said. "I have a feeling he could buy this whole town if he wanted to. Someone told me recently—Betty Lou's husband, I think—that he's a very rich man."

"He's nouveau riche, which is not the same thing," Yves said with an audible sniff. "And he is German."

"A naturalized French citizen, Yves, and you know it. He took her family name when they married forty years ago. Now, stop arguing and go back to daydreaming in your little cubby," Katherine said, smiling up at him to take the sting out of her words.

"Ah, but you have not told me if Adele and Albert Bel-legarde will attend the big celebration. If they do, I will be forced to drink a great deal of punch and snub them com-pletely."

"I thought you said you weren't coming if they were. Never mind." She raised her voice and laughed as he started to explain his changing position. "As long as you don't run the old man through with a sword, I'm sure it will be fine. Sophie will probably stay holed up in her father's office in Paris. You've spoiled the summer for her, you know."

"Hah," Yves said with a snort. "She will be holed up, as you put it, counting her father's ill-gotten gains. She is a sharp little capitalist, you know." Yves folded himself into his battered car and in a moment was speeding down the narrow road.

CHAPTER 2

Katherine counted the forks again. She had been sure there were enough for the main courses, a salad, the cheeses, and the raspberry tart without her having to disappear into her cramped kitchen to wash them between courses. How annoying that she seemed a couple short.

"Drat," she said in a loud voice, which made the little white dog perk up its ears. "Drat" sounded at least a little like "dinner." But everything sounded a little like "dinner" to Fideaux. The aroma of garlic and tomatoes, of slowly simmering veal and carrots, of fresh bread and cheeses set out to reach room temperature in a hot kitchen all signaled good things to come to a small dog. Seeing that his mistress was making no move toward the refrigerator, he flopped his head back down on his paws in the center of the room. He knew his time would come, when the plates needed licking or someone would feel his fixed gaze upon them and slip him something from the table.

Katherine lifted her feet over the animal as she went back to the drawer in the armoire. Shuffling the contents back and forth, she finally found two more slightly tarnished utensils. "Eh, voilà," she said, and pivoted out of the kitchen and into the yard. She had arranged a long table spread with a lace cloth that had begun life as two curtains before catching Katherine's eye at a dusty antique store, a *brocante,* in Auxerre. Part of the adventure of moving to France had been the decision to sell their worldly goods in Los Angeles and start accumulating French everything. "At the *vide-greniers,*" Katherine had told Michael, "the village flea markets that are held in every town in Burgundy on some kind of rotating schedule. Nothing expensive." The only exceptions to their extensive moving sale had been some clothing, a few books she couldn't live without, and Michael's sheet music and guitars.

"Let's see," she said now. "Penny at the end of the table, Betty Lou across from that young woman who took over the farm at the other end of town, Adele next to me and across from Pippa, which will keep her as far from Penny as possible, although Pippa is likely to drive her crazy with nosy questions if she speaks at all. Such a strange strange young woman. Jeannette on my left so I can keep an eye on her. Oh dear, I hope she behaves herself. But honestly," Katherine said to the yellow cat, which had materialized as it was wont to do, seemingly from nowhere, "someone has to help her learn how to be grown-up. Her mother is dead, she's almost fifteen, for heaven's sake, and can't be climbing trees and scratching what itches her in public." A woman's voice called out her name from the road beyond the tall hedge. The party was beginning, and Katherine hurried into the house for the platters of ratatouille and the baguettes.

Penny was chic in what Katherine recognized as an Armani outfit. Penny, Katherine had noted on several occasions to Michael, "has major money. That's how she was able to tart up that lovely old house so it looks like a suburban Cleveland mansion."

Katherine wasn't jealous, although Penny's kitchen was large and had surfaces to cut bread and vegetables on without fear of upending the cutting board onto the floor. It also had a huge refrigerator-freezer and two—two!—dishwashers. "If I didn't love Penny," Katherine had said to Michael one night in bed after dinner at her friend's house, "I might say it was a bit vulgar." Fortunately, she acknowledged to herself, Michael had known better than to reply.

Next to come in through the gates and up the garden path was Marie, the new woman in town, a quietly pretty thing in her thirties, married to an earnest young man with large ears that stuck straight out from the sides of his face. His appearance was so striking that people tended to overlook Marie. Her dark hair was covered by a scarf tied at the back of her neck and she carried a ceramic bowl that she handed to Katherine with a shy smile. "Fresh cheese, *fromage frais,* you know? From our cows." Her smile broadened. "I made it myself."

Katherine was still exclaiming about the cheese when the gate clanged open again and a tentative voice wafted up. "Halloo, it's only me." First a nimbus of curly red hair, then the rest of a lanky young woman climbed into view. She was dressed in a voluminous skirt and an oversize sweater. Pippa—born Philippa—Hathaway was easily six feet tall, with pale porcelain skin, large gray eyes, and a generous mouth. She was British, and had moved to Reigny the previous year. Pippa was, she had explained to Katherine when they first met by chance at the café, a writer of murder mysteries. "Well, almost. I'm working on my first, but I intend to write for a living." Katherine had a hunch she was lonely. Reigny was certainly no place for a young woman in the best of times. She was, Katherine had said to Penny, an odd duck to choose to bury herself here. But she spoke English, which would be nice for Penny and Betty Lou.

As if on cue, Betty Lou Holliday rocketed into the driveway in her massive SUV and jerked to a halt, kicking up a cloud of dust that drifted slowly toward the pear tree. "Hope I'm not late," she called out as she slammed the car door behind her. "That damn husband of mine kept me rehearsing in that sweltering studio for hours. The man expects me to churn out albums every year. Hi, Kathy; hi, everyone." A teenage boy slid out of the passenger side of the car, his face blank, his torso curled slightly. For an instant, Katherine worried that he was going to join the lunch party, but Betty Lou patted him on the shoulder as he rounded the hood of the car and said, "I'll pick you up later, Brett. Try not to get killed on that damn thing." The "thing" in question was a skateboard, the kind of public annoyance Katherine had, naively, hoped to escape by leaving Los Angeles. The boy didn't respond, but turned back to leave by the driveway side of the property.

"What's for lunch?" Betty Lou was wearing what looked like a violently colored bedspread over her large form and at least twenty silver bangle bracelets on one arm. She billowed and jangled as she strode toward Katherine, manicured toenails in leather sandals peeking out from under her skirt.

Before Katherine could introduce her to the others, a black Mercedes sedan pulled into the driveway. The skateboarder was walking slowly down the center of the path, and the new car had to wait, its engine idling. The car's horn blared twice, then once more. "Brett, move your ass," Betty Lou said, and laughed.

The car edged forward and stopped. An elderly man opened the driver's-side door and began to berate the boy in a querulous voice with a trace of a German accent. "Where are your manners? Can't you see I needed to turn in off the street?" His voice was high-pitched and strained. "You're that American boy who came to the last château tour the other day. Well, young man, you're in France now, and you'd best develop some French manners."

To which Brett merely looked at the driver as if he were speaking Urdu, Katherine thought. Brett turned out of the driveway and immediately the loud racketing sound of the skateboard on asphalt signaled his departure.

"Kids," said Betty Lou, seemingly unperturbed. "I'd lend him the car, but lord knows when he'd remember to pick me up. He's probably off to find that cute girl who hangs around town."

"Jeannette? Not today. She's coming to lunch. But he's not old enough to drive, is he?" Katherine said. Even though he looked eighteen or nineteen, she thought Michael had mentioned he was younger.

"Here, no, but in Tennessee he had a learner's permit when he was fifteen, and now that he's seventeen, he already has his license and, God help us, a secondhand car my foolish husband bought him."

The teenager disappeared and the guests turned their attention to the woman who exited the passenger side of the car. She was large-boned, white-haired, and handsome. Although she, like the driver, must have been in her eighties, she carried herself like a soldier. Katherine, who prided herself on her own posture, admired the woman for not giving in an inch to advancing years. Adele Bellegarde was the hereditary owner of the medieval Château de Bellegarde, descended from centuries of Bellegardes who had inhabited and defended their castle. This day, she was dressed for lunch in a bourgeois neighborhood on the Right Bank in Paris rather than for a country meal under a tree in Burgundy in the middle of the summer. Her pumps were already a bit dusty, she had on opaque stockings, and she was wearing a navy blue suit with a pink silk scarf at the neck.

She patted the old man's forearm and said something to him, and he subsided slowly into the car. "Darling," she said in a high voice as she met her hostess and presented a bottle of chilled Chablis, "you are so kind." She bestowed two sedate kisses in the air near her hostess's cheeks as graciously as if she were knighting Katherine.

The Mercedes backed out of the driveway at a glacial pace. Everyone but the new arrival glanced over as it exited gingerly onto the roadway and saw the driver, Monsieur Bellegarde, lean out of the open window to watch his wife's progress onto the lawn. He appeared to disapprove of something. Katherine cringed slightly, feeling, as she always did, that he was criticizing her bohemian ways. He probably blamed her for Brett's sullenness since they were both Americans. It didn't help that if she had enough wine she sometimes ventured tap-dancing routines at the family dinner parties Adele occasionally invited the Goffs to join. Albert Bellegarde made her feel ridiculous, and she resented him for that. Perversely, she liked Adele, perhaps in part because Adele soldiered on in the face of what Katherine thought must be great and ongoing disappointment in her choice of a husband.

"This is Adele Bellegarde," Katherine said to Marie, the

young cheese maker. "And this is Betty Lou Holliday, the American singer," she said to everyone, raising her voice. "She and Michael will be performing together at Reigny's festival." Adele inclined her head in Marie's direction. Pippa lifted a long arm and waved a greeting. Betty Lou jangled her bracelets. Katherine poured wine for everyone to get the conversation started, but kept an eye on Penny and Adele.

After a few minutes, she realized she needn't have worried. Adele Bellegarde had spent her youth in Swiss boarding schools, learning how to behave in every situation. The set of her chin and the straightness of her spine made it clear she had no intention of speaking more than was necessary to the American with the horrible French accent who had the bad taste to be friendly with the shabby bookseller who had deceived her daughter.

Katherine held up the first course as long as she could, hoping Jeannette would arrive, but the flying bugs were beginning to sniff out the platters, and she gave up, disappointed in her protégée but unwilling to sacrifice the occasion. No sooner had the first dish been passed around than the teenager did arrive, bounding up the garden steps while shouting out a combined greeting and apology. She stopped at the top of the stairs, panting and pushing long, golden curls off her face with one hand while dropping the shoes she was holding in the other on the slate so she could hop into them. She wore a gauzy dress of some cheap fabric. It puffed and fluttered around her slender form when she moved. She looked delicious, as she did in Katherine's paintings.

"This," said Katherine, with a touch of steel in her voice, "is Jeannette. I thought it would be right to include her in our luncheon, now that she is a young woman."

Jeannette, the daughter of Reigny's disreputable family of

thieves, smiled broadly and looked around at the faces, which reflected varying degrees of welcome. If not everyone was delighted to see her, she appeared not to notice, but circled the table to bestow the obligatory kisses a girl gives to her elders, then took her seat like the hungry schoolgirl she was and immediately reached for a fork.

The party proceeded from there as Katherine had hoped it would. The women drank the chilled Petit Chablis that a small vineyard sold locally and Jeannette even had a watered-down version. The group nibbled happily through several courses, and talked about everyone—well, nearly everyone, since Yves and Sophie were by tacit arrangement out of bounds—with relish. Betty Lou asked if it was true that Pippa wrote something or other.

"I'm working on a murder mystery set in an English sea-side town, you know. Well, that is, I have been, although it's not going terribly well. I might write one set here in Reigny if I could think of something really awful."

"Awful?" Adele said, distracted from her plate, fixing the young woman with a stare. "What on earth do you mean?"

"Murder, you know, like a garroting, or someone being beaten to death. Only for my story, of course. Not for real. But I need inspiration, don't I?"

"Well, murder mysteries, that's cool," Betty Lou said, but no one else seemed interested.

To keep the silence from becoming awkward, because she already knew none of the French guests cared what the foreigners did and Penny didn't read if she could help it, Katherine chimed in, "You must love cats. I see several when I walk past your driveway."

"Mademoiselle has five," Jeannette announced to the table, her mouth full of veal. "Four black and one all colors.

They don't like to be petted. My brothers tried to catch them once."

Pippa looked unhappy, and Katherine, who had seen the cats sunning themselves in the sloping driveway that ran down to the house, had no trouble imagining Jeannette's younger brothers running at them and yelling at the top of their lungs. More than once during her winter walks, she had thought she might venture down the driveway and knock. But somehow it never seemed like the right moment. Perhaps it was the way the cottage seemed to lean back into the trees, sheltered from prying eyes. And Pippa was so much younger that Katherine wondered how much they'd have to talk about after cats and weather.

"Well, yes," Katherine said, and turned the conversation to the newcomer in Reigny. Soon, Marie was being bombarded with questions designed to help the others place her in her proper socioeconomic class as quickly as possible. Luckily for her, she was a graduate of the Sorbonne, even if she did milk cows at the moment, and her mother and father were a university professor and an attorney, respectively. She and her husband had bought the farm from a distant cousin whose family had owned it for at least a century. The project, a romantic, back-to-nature adventure paid for with her husband's inheritance, centered on making prize-winning cheese from their small herd of Jersey cattle.

Penny wondered, politely, why cheese as a career? Marie explained she and her husband were vegetarians. Wasn't that unhealthy, Adele asked. Betty Lou said America was full of vegetarians these days, so much so that the beef industry was "in the dumps." Jeannette said she loved "*le hamburger*" more than anything in the world. Katherine, on her third glass of wine, felt her feet twitch in a tap rhythm.

As she came out of the kitchen with the tart, she almost bumped into Michael, back from the Hollidays' studio, carrying his Gibson guitar in its case. He ignored Betty Lou's invitation to join them. "I promise, I'm not here," he whispered as he squeezed Katherine's arm and slipped inside. "See if you can save me a piece of that great-looking dessert, though."

At precisely four o'clock, Adele looked at her watch and rose from her chair. *"Adieu,"* she said to the table at large. "I must go." And, like magic, the black Mercedes pulled into the driveway again. This time, the motor shut off and the driver stepped out and walked toward the group. Albert Bellegarde was taller than his wife, well over six feet, which was underscored by his military bearing and the cut of his double-breasted jacket in a navy blue that matched his wife's suit. His face was mottled pink and he wore a blue ascot and the same disapproving frown Katherine had seen when he dropped off his wife.

"Madame," he murmured to Katherine in a slight German accent, bowing.

"Bonjour, Albert," Katherine said with as much pleasantness as she could put in her voice. She smelled port on his breath, a small warning sign to be careful. "Do you know Marie? Perhaps you've met her charming husband? They're fixing up the old place across the road from Jean's?"

"Enchanté," Albert said, taking Marie's hand briefly. "Although I do not know how you can be comfortable, living near that thiev—"

"And you know Jean's daughter, Jeannette?" Katherine broke in. Jeannette didn't get up from the table immediately. Katherine frowned and flapped her hand at the girl, and Jeannette reluctantly unfolded herself, staring boldly at Albert and fiddling with a spoon.

"I know Monsieur. He's the German in the château. He doesn't like our dogs," she said in a loud voice, ostensibly to Katherine, but with her eyes on Albert. "Even our pretty puppies, the ones Papa let us keep."

"Her father drowned the rest," Penny said in a sour voice to no one in particular from the far end of the table. "In a bag, Yves says. In front of the children."

A sudden awkward silence overtook the party. Jeannette stuck out her lower lip and glared at Penny, who merely shrugged as she lifted her wineglass and drank deeply. Adele looked daggers at Penny, presumably because her comment was so impolite. Pippa, who had been playing with her wineglass, looked up sharply. Betty Lou smiled brightly first at one person, then another, as if to encourage them to go on in this interesting fashion.

Albert chose not to speak, but turned to his wife and gestured toward the car. Adele took the hint smoothly. "Such a charming gathering, Katherine."

A man's voice from beyond the hedge interrupted her leave-taking. "Here I am, my dear ladies, come for *un café.*" Yves bounded through the gate and up the steps past the roses, a wave of hair falling rakishly over his forehead. "You see, I have brought you these little cakes, quite perfect for the dessert course, are they not?" Stopping at the same spot where Jeannette had put on her shoes, he gazed around him serenely and held up a patisserie box tied with a pink ribbon.

Katherine was not fooled. Her heart sank. Yves knew exactly what his appearing here would do, and he was delighted to have all eyes upon him, even if a few were hostile. Albert was glowering at him, pulling himself up straighter, his vein-ribbed hands clenching and unclenching at his sides and his pink face getting brighter. Adele had thrust her strong chin in Yves's direction and was squinting toward him as if suspecting a new trick from the scoundrel who had jilted her daughter.

Penny jumped up and came to him with her hand held open to take the box, a small smile playing around the corners of her mouth. Yves handed off the pastries with a flourish and, dancing over to Katherine, planted twin kisses on her cheeks before turning to the table. "Ah, but is there no demitasse for me?" he said in mock surprise. "Has someone stolen my cup, eh? How about you, my *petite* nimble fingers?" he said to Jeannette, who laughed heartily and raised both hands to show all she held was a silver spoon.

Yves turned, still smiling. "Madame, Monsieur," he said, clicking his heels and bowing to the Bellegardes, "it is interesting to see you at my dear friend's home. Katherine is such a kind person and she would not want—how to say this—for anyone to feel they were not welcomed in the social life, no matter what, would you not agree?"

Katherine uttered a small, involuntary cry, and signaled to Yves to be quiet. He ignored her and smiled blandly at the old couple. Albert's hand shook as he took his wife's arm and attempted to turn her toward their car, but Adele pulled her elbow away and drew herself up as tall as Yves.

"Your behavior, sir," she said in her best finishing-school voice, "is, as usual, boorish. You dishonor our hostess, but then I suspect you don't care as long as you are the center of attention. Good day, dear Katherine."

Katherine, who had been holding her breath, let it out in a rush. Good, the Bellegardes would leave and peace would be restored, no thanks to Yves.

But Yves wasn't about to let Madame Bellegarde throw

the last dart. He began to laugh theatrically, his head thrown back and his hands in his pockets.

Albert rose to the bait, suddenly lurching toward him. Raising his hand high in the air, the old man swatted Yves feebly across the cheek. "How dare you insult my wife," he cried in a quavering voice.

Jeannette backed away from the table, her eyes sparkling and her mouth making a perfect letter O.

Penny called out to Yves, "Oh, quit it, for heaven's sake."

Betty Lou cackled. "Oh dear," she said to the table at large, "I guess we're gonna see a real catfight."

Yves stopped laughing and grabbed Albert's arm. "Listen, old man, I will say what I like, since you and your wife feel free to tell lies about me to the entire village. My life is my own business, do you hear?"

As Yves turned away, Albert, much more quickly than Katherine would have believed possible, picked up a dessert plate and broke it smartly over the younger man's head. The sound of crockery falling onto the slate path was the only sound in the yard for a moment. Then Penny screamed, the neighborhood dogs started barking, and Michael came barreling out of the house.

"What's going on out here? Is there a problem?" He stopped when he saw Yves standing in some degree of shock, raspberry jam dripping down his forehead and a dollop of crème fraîche poking out of his hair. Albert grabbed Adele and force-marched her to the Mercedes without another word, Adele looking as stunned as Yves. The car started up and lurched out of the driveway with complete disregard for any traffic that might be rounding the bend.

"Damnation," Michael said into the silence. He looked a question at Katherine, who shrugged and made a helpless gesture, then tossed a napkin in Yves's direction. "Are you still fighting World War II? Wipe off your hair and let Penny take you home. Kay's had enough excitement for one day, I expect. You made a mess of her party."

Katherine sat down and pondered silently the precariousness of men's egos in general, and the loss of one of her beloved dessert dishes, part of a delicately gold-rimmed set that she had found in an antique store in the historic city of Beaune, always bustling with tourists, a few years ago. They had been much too expensive and Michael had asked if she was sure she needed them as he pulled out a roll of euros, although they both knew he would buy her anything if she made it clear she had to have it in order to be happy. Now, she could cry, really she could. Only eleven, and even if no one else ever noticed that there was an odd plate when they had a dozen people over to eat, she would see the mismatch and it would bother her every time.

She was angry with Yves, and she rarely allowed herself to get angry. He was spoiled and conceited and thoughtless. When he came over to apologize, she didn't look at him. By extension, and unfairly, she knew, she was angry with Penny too. They left quietly, followed quickly by Marie, whose cheese lay uneaten in a dish on the table.

Jeannette gave Katherine a noisy kiss and a rough hug before skipping down the steps, thrilled at the story she would have to tell at home. She was careful to hold the two spoons she had pinched so they wouldn't hit each other in the pocket of her dress and give her away.

Pippa had been leaning forward in her chair, as if to catch every detail. Katherine wondered how soon they would all wind up as suspects in a manuscript. The young woman suddenly shook herself, as if waking from a trance, and stood up. "Oh dear, I must go. So nice of you, Katherine, such an interesting party." Not being French, she didn't kiss Katherine, but shook her hand absently and scurried down the steps, holding up the hem of her skirt.

Betty Lou leaned back in her chair under the pear tree, smoking and fingering her wineglass. "That young man certainly got what he wanted. Handsome devil, but full of himself, isn't he?"

Katherine sighed. "What you must think of us," she said.

"Not you, was it? That Yves's got a bee in his bonnet, and the old guy flies off the handle pretty quickly. Reminds me of a couple of rockers I knew in L.A. back in the day. They'd get so stoned they could hardly see straight, then brawl 'til one of 'em passed out. Had a half-dozen albums go platinum, if you can believe it. Don't know when they had time to get into the studio and make anything decent. What is it with these two guys? Michael said something about a war. Was the old man a Nazi?"

"Oh, that isn't it. Albert's German by birth but his parents immigrated to Switzerland when the Nazis came to power. He took French citizenship ages ago, before he and Adele were married. But you're right to wonder. The occupation and French resistance to it was intense in this area and still ignites harsh memories and prejudices. Albert gets tarred with that brush behind his back, unfairly."

"What kind of work does the old guy do? My husband says he's rich as Croesus."

"J.B. knows more than I do about his money, then. I do know he used to deal in arms, you know, sales of guns to armies. But later, he was a French honorary consul of some kind for a few years. He must be close to ninety now, and I doubt he does anything other than escort visitors to Bellegarde around on the occasional tour. Sophie, his daughter, pretty much runs his business, I think. No, the argument between him and Yves is personal," Katherine said, sighing. "Yves dated Sophie for a couple of years, but when Penny opened her house this spring, he dropped Sophie to take up with Penny."

"Fickle, is he?"

"God's gift to women, you know the type. Sophie took it hard and the senior Bellegardes saw it as an insult. I'm afraid her parents have been badmouthing him, and he them, in the village and the entire area. In a small place like this, you know, gossip has consequences. Everyone's been forced to take sides. I hate it."

"But you had them both here for lunch," Betty Lou said, puffing smoke into the tree thoughtfully.

"I didn't invite either of them," Katherine said. "Albert was chauffeuring his wife, and Yves? He crashed. I'm furious. All that work to make a nice party and he ruined it."

"No," drawled Betty Lou, getting up and shaking out her dress. "It was a lovely lunch. Thank you, my dear. Must get back or J.B.'ll have my ass. He is bound and determined I'm going to get a new album ready this summer, whether my dwindling number of fans want one or not. I think he must have his eye on another of his investment properties. Some vacation this is. The man has expensive tastes and I must feed them."

She patted Katherine on the shoulder, called out good-bye to Michael, who had retreated back to the house, and pulled away in the SUV, leaving Katherine alone with the dregs of the lunch, a mess of broken crockery, and the beginning of a serious headache. As she brought dishes back to the kitchen she wondered uneasily if Yves and the Bellegardes would now call a truce, having had a shot at each other and relieved the pressure of their mutual resentments, or if the rest of the village would be treated to more histrionics. "I guess it could have been worse," she told Fideaux, who was happily licking the remains of the veal off a plate. "They could have decided to duel at sunrise."

CHAPTER 3

Jeannette smiled, thinking about the excitement at Katherine's party. It had been a much more interesting way to spend those hours than minding her younger brothers or stacking bricks in the front courtyard for her father's business. Living here was such a bore, she thought from her perch hidden in the tree. If she lived in Auxerre, say, or even in the market town a few kilometers away, there would be more traffic, more people walking around, people who didn't know her and wouldn't automatically yell "Stop that, Jeannette" when an apple or a hen's egg hit their windshield or the ground in front of them.

She dangled one long leg down from the branch and leaned back against the trunk. Two adult dogs lay panting at the foot of the tree, and she could hear her younger brothers teasing the puppies, who barked incessantly back at them. Summer afternoons were so dull, nothing but the sounds of the kids and her father's rock-cutting tools in the quarry, and Emile singing to himself as he fished under the bridge. The only part of the day she liked was hearing Michael play the guitar in his yard.

Michael, she had decided long ago, was sexy for an old

guy, with a way of looking at you that said he noticed you in particular. He dressed chic, in jeans and boots with a real cowboy hat and an Indian belt buckle with stones in it. Everyone knew he was a rock star, living here to get away from his American fans.

Katherine was okay too, and sometimes gave her little presents, although it was easy to fool her. Katherine thought Jeannette needed a mother, which was ridiculous since she was almost fifteen. Jeannette liked being free to come and go. Her father told her he didn't want the authorities coming around asking questions, so it was her job to make sure the boys had food, slept in their own beds, and wore shoes to school. Other than that, he didn't much care how she spent her time. She was used to having no mother. It hardly bothered her to hear her school friends talk about going places with their families, or how their mothers were always wanting to know what they were doing. Who needed that?

She heard the harsh sound of metal clunking against pockmarked pavement, a stuttering noise coming closer and closer until it rounded the corner. It was the American, Brett, on his skateboard. Was he coming to see her? She flushed and scrambled out of the tree, brushing crumbs of bark off her shorts and yanking at her tight T-shirt. Brett Holliday was the coolest, well, the only cool thing in her whole summer, a stranger who had dropped into her village when she thought she would go crazy with nothing to do. He was living with his parents in the fancy converted barn on the outskirts of town. Brett was the handsomest boy Jeannette had ever seen and the most sophisticated. It was cool that his father was a record producer and his mother, even though she was really old, was a famous singer. He was nearly eighteen, and she thought he liked her.

"Hey," he said, jumping off his still-moving skateboard and catching it with one hand as he stopped in front of her.

"Hey," she mimicked in the same bored tone, carefully picking the green polish off one fingernail. The dogs stood up slowly and padded back to the courtyard.

"What's up?" He spoke in a lazy voice that made her heart turn over. He flicked his long dark hair off his face and looked at her from under thick black brows.

"*Rien*, nothing," she said with a shrug. "It's hot."

"Wanna ride my board?"

"Sure. Where?"

"Same place we did last time, the castle driveway."

Jeannette hesitated. M. and Mme Bellegarde did not like them to play in the driveway, but it was the best place in the entire village for skateboarding, a long, curving slope with hardly any traffic and better paving than everywhere else. M. Bellegarde was rich and had the whole driveway paved last year, all except for the circle in front of the château's old wooden doors. Her father said it was a waste of good money and that M. Bellegarde had too much money for one man. But Jeannette knew he was mainly pissed that the old man hadn't brought the whole job to him, only the part he told her father needed to be reproduced with local quarry stone as close to the original as possible, the carriage entrance.

"We can look if they are home," she said, concentrating to get the English right. Brett had no French, and Jeannette couldn't wait to tell her friends how her English had improved because she had an American boyfriend this summer. They would look at her with respect and envy.

"The château is open for tourists only some days. Other days, they go for the lunch or for visiting the other châteaux, and sometimes all the way to Paris." If they were gone today, she and Brett could skateboard all they wanted. You could hear the old people's Mercedes coming through the village and hide in the little forest that started right next to the château and they would never know. Jeannette thought the forest was the best hiding place in the whole village, better even because it backed up onto the quarry, where you could lie on flat rocks on the hottest days and get a tan.

"Okay, let's go," Brett said, looking around. "Got your bike?"

"No, my brother borrowed it to do some errands for Papa," Jeannette said. "I can walk."

They set off, Brett riding slowly on his board, pushing off only enough to stay even with Jeannette. As she fiddled with her hair, she saw him looking sideways at her breasts. She knew they showed through her shirt. She was conscious of her bare legs. Did he think she was pretty?

Brett had told her he argued with his parents when they told him they were spending the whole summer in France and that he couldn't stay home by himself. His father had reminded him about a time last winter when Brett offered to sell marijuana to a man who turned out to be a *flic*. Brett laughed as he told Jeannette the story. Of course his father talked the cops out of pressing charges. "My dad's kind of a big deal back home," he said, shrugging. "I'm still a juvenile, technically, so the cops were more into scaring me, anyway." Until he ran into Jeannette, Brett said, he had done nothing but lie around the pool house next to his parents' recording studio, watching DVDs. He had looked at her in a special way when he said it.

Jeannette knew what boys wanted. They bragged about it in school. "Ooh la la," she could imagine Brett saying to his friends when he got home. "There was this French girl I did it with." Her face got hot thinking about the implications. Did she want to "do it" with Brett? She had a feeling she was going to have to decide one day soon, which made her heart—or was it her stomach?—flip over again.

A half hour later, they were sitting on a bench at the top of the driveway. Jeannette was spitting onto her finger and patting the moisture on the outside of her elbow, which was bright red and had a raw patch. *"Ce n'est rien*, it's nothing," she said. "Only the little sting, you know?" She smiled at Brett, who was checking his board for damage. "I think I did better this time, *non*?"

"Wanna go again?"

She wanted to do whatever Brett wanted, was floating and a little dizzy with the pleasure of having him hold her around the waist and push her hip out to show her how to balance on the board. When she fell, he grabbed her hand and pulled her to her feet after catching the board, and this last time, he bent his head down to look at her elbow and his hair grazed her chin. She breathed in the scent of him through her open mouth and was about to say yes when she heard the deep sound of the Mercedes diesel engine.

"We'd better get out of here. Come on, *viens ici*, this way." Jeannette scampered into the heavy brush at the far side of the driveway, waving her arm at Brett to get him to move quickly. They disappeared into the tangle of rhododendrons and walnut trees a few seconds before the Bellegardes' car rounded the bend and pulled into the gravel courtyard. From their hiding place, Jeannette and Brett could see the Bellegardes struggling with plastic bags from the *supermarché*, talking in low tones to each other as they crossed the courtyard, hauling the groceries in through the ancient wooden doors to the château.

Jeannette tried to guess what might be in the bags. They ate weird things, she knew from the time she found the sitting room's French doors unlocked and snuck into the pantry. Jars of bright red cabbage that had German-language labels she couldn't read. A tin of foie gras, which she knew was expensive and which she would have liked to take except it was the only one, and if they noticed it was gone they'd be more careful about locking doors and then she'd never get back in to look around. She had taken one of a stack of small tins of fish and had opened it with the little key that was attached to its lid when she had climbed back into her hiding place in the tree. But she spat out the fish, which was oily and pickly at the same time, and which looked like something that had been lying around in the mud by the river too long.

Jeannette became aware of how close Brett was. Their arms were touching and his skin was warm. Suddenly, he shifted his weight and leaned forward and across her, bumping her chest with his shoulder. She stepped back abruptly, looking quizzically at him and then in the direction he was facing. "I thought I heard something," he whispered. But the bold way he stared into her eyes made her blush for some reason.

"Where?" she whispered back. "I don't hear anything."

"Oh, it's gone now, I guess," Brett murmured. "Probably a cat."

"Ah," Jeannette said breathlessly, her breast still tingling where he had brushed against it. "We can go now. The sign on the driveway says they will be opening for tours in an hour, so they're probably getting ready."

"I went on the tour. Well, part of it. The tower sounded cool, but the stairs were shut off, so I bailed."

"The stairs are the best part; they're rounded, you know, and very steep. But the rest is boring," Jeannette said, not sure what "bailed" meant but confident that Brett hadn't enjoyed it any more than she had when her school group went. "Monsieur wants you to look at the stones and pictures of Madame's great-grandparents. There are some old guns and ladies' dresses that I sort of liked, but that's it."

"Yeah? Maybe they'll let me fire an old musket. Bam," he said, closing one eye and pulling a pretend trigger.

Jeannette started to laugh, but clapped her hand across her mouth. "Come on, let's go before they see us."

Brett tucked his board under his arm and the two of them ran lightly down the driveway. When they were clear of the Bellegardes' and walking back toward her house, Brett asked, "Do you spy on them or something?"

"I spy on everyone," Jeannette said, giggling. "I do—have done—it since I was a kid. It's the only thing to do here. You should have seen the way M. Bellegarde insulted Yves the other day."

"He yelled at me, too, for nothing. What happened? Were you spying?"

"*Mais non,* Katherine invited me to lunch and when we were leaving, M. Bellegarde hit Yves over the head with a plate. He broke the plate, too. Oh, it was so funny," Jeannette said, laughing out loud.

"Why'd he do that?" Brett said.

"I don't know, but I think Yves slept with his daughter. At least that's what Papa says. It was so funny to see Yves's face. I nearly died laughing."

"Weird," Brett said. "You'd think old people would be over this stuff. I mean . . ." He trailed off.

Jeannette snuck a look at him. His face was flushed and his lower lip stuck out. He was angry, which only made him look handsomer. For some reason, her breast tingled again, and she hit it lightly with her own arm to stop the sensation. "Your parents, do they fight?"

Brett snorted. "Well, yeah. All the time. About everything, it seems. Don't yours?"

"My mother died when I was a little girl. I'm sure Papa would get mad at her if she were here. He is mad at everyone. It is his way, I think."

Brett didn't say anything and Jeannette hoped telling him wasn't a mistake, that he wouldn't stop spending time with her now that he knew. Hurriedly, she changed the subject. "M. Bellegarde is a Nazi. Mme Pomfort, the lady who owns the church garden, she says so."

"Isn't that stuff old history?"

"Sure," Jeannette said, hoping she had chosen the right word in English. "He's German, anyway, and Mme Pomfort, she hates all Germans. She says the people who live next to her are German sympathizers, although Papa says she only says that because they are fighting about the church garden."

Brett picked at the plastic label on his skateboard, a cartoon of a Japanese boy with a cape. "I think we're going to the beach next week," he said. "Mom says we need a change of scene, or something."

"Lucky you. I've only been once, with my class. We were studying the war and went on a bus to Normandy. The water was so cold and the wind was blowing. *Zut*, but it was still fun."

"We're going south," Brett said. "You know, the Riviera?

My mom says it's like San Diego, really warm and sunny. My dad says he'll rent me a motorbike. It'll still be a bore. They don't have surfing, he told me."

Jeannette wasn't going to admit she had no idea what San Diego was, so she said, "Lucky," again and remembered photos of a beautiful blue sea with palm trees and women in bikinis sitting on beach chairs. It was an ad for somewhere on the Riviera and she had promised herself she'd get there someday. And here was Brett, about to go but not at all excited. She had to practice being not excited when something good happened. Sadly, she didn't have much opportunity.

A car engine sounded somewhere in the village and in a minute, the Hollidays' SUV pulled up alongside the pair. "Hey, kids," said Betty Lou, rolling down her window and washing them with cold air and the smell of cigarettes, "what are you doing outside on a hot day like this? Brett, I need you at home to help me with something. Hop in."

Without a word, Brett opened the passenger door, threw his skateboard over the seat into the back, and climbed in. "Bye, sweetie," Betty Lou called out to Jeannette as the car pulled away.

Jeannette stood in the road for a moment, unsure. Brett hadn't said good-bye or that he'd see her tomorrow. She couldn't decide if he liked her or not. Was she too young for him? Would he like her better if she wore makeup or a push-up bra? She wished her best school friend lived in the same town so she could ask someone. It was hard sometimes not having a mother, although she wasn't sure this was something girls talked to their mothers about in any case.

" 'Nette," a man's rough voice bellowed from somewhere out of sight. "*Vite*, come home and fix dinner, right now. The kids are hungry."

"Coming, Papa," Jeannette called, and, shaking off her confusion, she ran down the hill. Sausage and fries, and after dinner they would all watch the dubbed American police show on the new TV her father had brought home.

CHAPTER 4

Katherine peered at a gangly rosebush that was losing its battle for morning sun to an aggressive hydrangea. She bent a stem of the larger plant back until it snapped, knowing that she wasn't really solving the problem, but promising the timid rose more attention later in the month, after the *vernissage*, the opening party for her art exhibition. The offer of a solo show in her adopted country had been an extraordinary compliment. The gallery owners had spent several years in Los Angeles, which they felt created a bond between them and Katherine. Still, she had been taken aback at the challenge. Now, she was working hard to complete a dozen or so oil paintings of the Yonne countryside.

Still brooding over the loss of her plate and the quarrel that had led to it, she wondered for the umpteenth time if she had been too quick to bring Penny into her small circle. When Penny had arrived two years ago, Katherine had welcomed another American and someone who spoke English comfortably. She sometimes retired to her bedroom with a headache after a trip to the veterinarian or the pharmacy from the effort of always having to speak and listen in another language.

"We are interlopers, cat," she said as she turned her attention to the climbing white rose that was heavy with scent and spent blooms begging to be cut. "Not you, of course, since you could not have wandered in from too far away. You are the real thing at least, a French citizen. You even meow in French, don't you?" The cat rubbed up against Katherine's leg as if to acknowledge the compliment. As she worked, Katherine stifled pinpricks of doubt about Yves's ability—or perhaps it was willingness—to set aside his love of drama for the sake of harmony in the village after the debacle at the lunch party. The Bellegardes undoubtedly thought she had invited him to come.

Maybe she had been too optimistic, but after suffering through two winters of loneliness made bearable only by Michael's presence, Katherine had come up with a plan to be part of Reigny's annual summer celebration, to be, in fact, responsible for the best show ever. She had put herself forward at every opportunity since early spring. She had begun by bribing the mayor's wife with a shockingly expensive box of nougats from the best master candy maker, the *maître chocolatier*, in Avallon. Having gotten her to agree that it would be amusing to let Mme Goff organize the entertainment, Katherine had all but stalked her neighbors on market days in Ancy le Franc, Avallon, and Noyers. She had engaged in a campaign, with the anticipated victory taking the form of extravagant public praise and three kisses from Mme Pomfort when the event was over. Nothing else would do. Her future happiness in her adopted home depended on breaking through Madame's formidable disapproval, and the fête was her one chance. Now, she wondered if it was a lost cause. Word of the debacle at Mme Goff's house would be all over Reigny and it would especially shock the women who hadn't been invited, never mind that they would not have come in any case.

The phone rang. Michael might be out, bringing the garbage to the big bins in the village *poubelle*. She pulled off her thick gloves and hurried in the kitchen door, which flapped noisily behind her. Only nine o'clock and the flies were out. If Jean ever came back to finish repairing the roof, she would ask him to work on the doors so they stayed closed. Jean was a hard man to pin down, however, unless he wanted payment in advance, in which case he was there every day.

Michael was sitting on a battered rococo sofa she had found at another flea market, one of the endless summer *vide-greniers* that peppered the landscape and attracted steady crowds to villages and towns all over Burgundy to examine bits and pieces from other people's attics and storerooms, everything a potential treasure beyond price. He was leaning forward, reading a score propped on his music stand as he strummed a guitar. The phone was within reach, perched on a round table with intricately carved, if chipped, legs.

"For heaven's sake," she said as she skirted the music stand and a sprawling dog, "why don't you pick it up?"

"What good would that do?" he said with a sheepish look. "I feel like an idiot because I have no clue what they're saying. Anyway, it's always for you."

"Except when it's J.B. for you," she managed to say as she banged into the table's edge and yanked the receiver off its plastic base. She was tempted to let it ring, fearing it would be someone who had heard about the melodrama at the other day's lunch and wanted a full account, perhaps one of the Parisian families that came down to their houses during the summer months.

"Mme Goff ici. Oui, c'est moi. Is it you, Adele? Wait, I can't

understand. Slower, please." As she listened, she began to flap her free hand faster and faster at Michael, signaling him to stop picking out chords and pay attention.

"How could this be? Are you sure? Are you alone?" Her questions appeared to be shoehorned into slight pauses in her friend's rapid speech. Michael sat back, laid the guitar on the seat next to him, and watched his wife's agitated movements. "Have you called the police? Yes, of course we will. We'll be right over. Five minutes, I promise." She hung up and stood there, silent.

"What's the fuss about?" Michael said. "Somebody stole the ancestral silver?"

"Michael, it's awful news. I can hardly believe it. Albert's dead. Adele wants us to come over right now. Honestly, she sounds like she's falling apart."

"Poor guy, did he have a heart attack? He sure was riled up at your party."

"Adele says he fell down the stone stairwell. But then she seemed to be saying he was murdered. Of course, that might be my French failing me."

"Why'd she call you, I wonder?" Michael said. "Why not her daughter? I assume she called for an ambulance?" He sat with his hands on his knees, watching as his wife darted around the room, alternately scooping up and dropping sweaters and scarves appropriate to the changeable weather of a Burgundian summer day. She grabbed first one then another half-filled string bag, examining the contents of each.

"Because we're her friends. And she did call the mayor, and he's sending Henri. You remember him, the sheriff?"

"Don't they have to call the regular police?"

"I presume it's Henri who calls the police or the firemen or whomever you call if someone has fallen down the stairs and died. It may be the mayor who calls in the gendarmes. I don't understand the way the French handle these things, but it's not as simple as it might be. And if he was killed . . . I really don't know."

"Slow down, sweetie, you're going to trip over an animal if you don't take it easy."

Katherine did stop, pivoting in the center of the room. What was she looking for? she wondered. She needed to concentrate, but to do it quickly. Then she darted over to a hulking armoire under the stairs. "She needs us now. For all I know, she has called Sophie, but Sophie's in Paris, and that means at least two hours, even if there's a fast train leaving the moment she gets to Gare de Lyon. For heaven's sake, what are you doing?" She stared as Michael ambled toward the kitchen doorway, which was framed by age-stained beams. Dusty bunches of dried leaves and flowers were suspended over the doorway, decorated by drifts of cobwebs.

"The dogs have to eat if we're going to be gone for a while. And I expect we won't get out of there for hours once that woman gets going."

" 'Gets going'? Michael, her husband is dead. What can you be thinking? Let the dogs' breakfast go."

"It'll only take a minute. Anyway, I'm sure he wasn't murdered." Michael's voice was muffled because it was coming from inside the open refrigerator, where he and the two dogs were searching for a bag of fresh bones from the butcher.

"How can you be sure? You don't like him. Yves doesn't like him. I'm not sure who in Reigny does in particular, other than his wife, and I only assume she does. She's not very demonstrative." Katherine fluttered around the crowded room with its stacks of dusty art books and eccentric, mismatched furniture, looking for the belongings she needed in order to

44

make this decidedly unsocial call on her neighbor. Michael didn't answer, which could have been because her point was well taken, or, she had to admit, because disliking someone wasn't much of a motive for murder. She stuck first one, then another straw hat on her head, unpinned the silk flower from the discarded model, and stuck it on the one she wanted to wear. She stuffed a scarf, a plastic packet of tissues, and a sketch pad into her bag, muttering, "One never knows."

A few minutes later they were in the car, backing out of their driveway at great speed. Katherine never quite got used to the abandon with which Michael careened backward into what might have been a horrible car crash. For his part, Michael said he had supernaturally good hearing that would warn him if a car was hurtling toward the bend in the road right before the entrance to their driveway, screened at this time of the year by masses of tall hollyhocks and a quince bush as tall as a tree. Theirs was an uneasy truce in all matters of driving, and Katherine twitched as she always did and held her breath until Michael ground the Citroën's machinery into a forward gear and whined noisily down the lane.

The scene at Château de Bellegarde made Katherine's heart lurch against her ribs. It wasn't unusual to have a handful of cars parked on the gravel circle at the top of the paved driveway on summer weekend days, but the uniformed gendarme standing at the door next to the old portcullis was a first. So was the police car, which was parked at an awkward angle nearby. In addition to Albert's car, she recognized the sheriff's battered van, which was always present at official occasions in Reigny.

"I was hoping that Adele was, well, perhaps imagining all of this. But if that man is here, it must be real."

Michael only grunted as he backed the car up against a

stone wall that barely held a wildly overgrown shrubbery garden at bay. Katherine flung her door open and headed to the entrance before he turned off the engine. When the policeman saw her coming, he tossed his cigarette to the gravel, ground it out, and held up one arm.

"I am Mme Goff. Mme Bellegarde called and implored me to come," she said in French. "She said she needs me."

"Sorry, Madame, but there is police business here."

"Michael," she said, drawing herself up to an imposing five-foot-three inches and speaking in the most imperious tone she could muster as he came up behind her, "tell him we're expected."

Michael gave her an odd look, perhaps a reminder that his French was not up to much, but tried anyhow. *"Nous sommes amies*, friends, okay?"

The policeman looked pained but pulled a radio from his shoulder harness and spoke into it rapidly. Katherine couldn't catch more than a few words. She was afraid he would turn them away, but after getting some staticky message back, he waved them in. She pushed her hat, which had slid to one side, down on her small head firmly. "Adele, darling, we're here, we're here," she sang out as she stepped into the chilly darkness beyond the door.

CHAPTER 5

Had the door to the courtyard not been open, she would have had to stop and let her eyes adjust to the gloom. At that point, had she looked up, she would have barely made out a huge tapestry on the far wall beyond a stairway that split in two at a landing. She didn't, having been given the grand tour and an excruciatingly detailed interpretation of the tapestry the first time she and Michael had visited the château. Everyone who took the tour knew the tapestry was a Gobelins, albeit shredded and faded by centuries of neglect, and that the staircase was not original to the château although the cavernous hall was. Parts of the cluster of structures predated the Hundred Years' War, but others had been added when that conflict left the original duke's property partially in ruins. The Bellegardes had researched every inch of the building and every season of its history as the stronghold of a Burgundian fiefdom. It was one of Albert's chief pleasures, she recalled, to personally conduct tours most summer Saturdays, expounding on the glories of his wife's family. Their portraits sat on easels or were mounted on the walls in almost every room, uniformly prim and severe in their expressions. Poor Albert, he would miss this.

Katherine entered the sitting room with its ridiculously high ceilings and perpetual chill, and saw Adele sitting on a sofa near the monumental fireplace. A handkerchief covered her face. Abandoning her bag and hat on a chair, she raced over to the new widow. Tears stung her eyes. She reached for her neighbor and hugged her as best she could. Adele was taller and wider than Katherine and was sitting ramrod straight, so it was a little like hugging a tree, and after an awkward moment, she loosened her grip and sat forward on the edge of the sofa.

"How could this have happened to my poor Albert?" Adele said from behind her handkerchief, choking off a sob. She lowered the covering and Katherine saw that her eyes were red-rimmed.

"Oh, my dear, we are so sorry." Katherine turned to include Michael, who was standing in the center of the room, rolling an unlit cigarillo around in his mouth. He did look miserable, but she suspected it had nothing to do with Albert's death. He was a Montana cowboy and had no clue how he was supposed to act in a French castle where no one spoke English and women were crying.

The duties of Henri Soral, Reigny's sheriff, were usually of a minor nature, mostly telling drunken *pétanque* players to be quiet when their late-night arguments wafted over Reigny, or suggesting in an offhand way to Jean that someone's new gardening tools might be slipped back into their shed, from which they had disappeared a day or so before. Now Henri was frowning deeply, talking fast on his cell phone, while making little chopping gestures with his free hand. In the doorway, another uniformed policeman appeared, stared at them briefly, then marched toward the outer door, his hard soles clacking on the stone floor.

Katherine heard a car slide to a halt on the gravel, a car door slam, and more footsteps. Before the noise could resolve itself into a person, another car arrived, more doors slammed, and more steps came purposefully toward the sitting room. Henri snapped his phone shut, Michael took the cigarillo from his mouth and turned, and Adele clutched Katherine's hand.

Katherine recognized the mayor, a prosperous man who gave off an aura of having been happy with his last meal. The other man, narrow-shouldered in a black suit, was a stranger to her, and apparently to them all, as the men, except for Michael, exchanged names and handshakes before turning away as a group to confer.

"Who are these people, and what are they doing in my house?" Adele said to no one in particular. Katherine was sure Adele knew who Henri was. He had twice been called to the château when beer-bottle-throwing young men from out of town had decided to celebrate someone's upcoming marriage in Reigny's run-down café, probably so their womenfolk would not see them in such a disgraceful condition. "You"— Adele raised her voice enough that everyone in the room turned, as if individually tapped on the shoulder with a strong finger—"introduce yourselves, *s'il vous plait*. I am the widow and the owner of this château."

Adele also knew the mayor, Katherine understood, even if she chose to pretend otherwise. He hurried over, an oily mask of concern on his face, to pay his respects and refer to the unfortunate business in one rushed sentence. The château and the attention that Reigny-sur-Canne received in guidebooks for having such a venerable site would have been enough, but there was also the wealth of the inhabitants, people who might be persuaded to invest in one of the mayor's land-purchasing schemes or agricultural projects,

Katherine thought as she watched him pay his exaggerated respects. He was explaining to Adele that Henri had called the gendarmes from Auxerre, who had requested the aid of the *gendarme brigade de recherche*, but that it was a formality only, and he begged her not to concern herself.

He swung an arm toward the thin man in the black suit, who came over to the sofa, bowed to Adele and Katherine, and introduced himself as Lieutenant Decoste of the brigade, the head of the investigation. A formality, he said in a soft tenor voice. Madame would understand. A few questions. At that point, he looked at Katherine, who chided herself for feeling slightly defensive. After all, she had not intruded, she had been sent for. Surely, Adele would make that clear to the policeman. Adele wasn't looking at her but up at this new authority figure in some confusion.

"But my husband's death is a simple thing. He was old, you know, and I expect he lost his balance and set foot on those wretched old steps by mistake."

Katherine knew about the steps, back stairs that wound down to the old kitchen wing of the château. She had almost fallen herself on the tour, since there were no handrails to help, and the steps were steep and twisted and had uneven depressions in them from at least six hundred years of booted use. They were part of the usual tour, mainly because there were wood and glass cases set in the alcoves that displayed the Bellegarde armory of old guns and swords, and Albert loved talking about them. Katherine started to say something in support of Adele's protest, but the policeman held up one hand in a "stop" gesture. Really, she thought, one would think the police wanted relevant information. Adele had let go of her hand and Katherine edged off the sofa and over to where Michael stood, chewing on his cigarillo.

"Ready to go, Kay?" he said in a low voice. "Doesn't seem like anyone wants us right now, and I got to check out one of my guitars before I head over to Betty Lou's."

"She might want us in a minute. Adele looks ready to collapse." She smoothed her hair, which she had pulled into a little bun, pushing stray strands back under the rubber band, unsure of her position in this drama, only that she surely had one. After all, she was Adele's dear friend, or at least thought so. Adele's coolness at this hour of crisis disappointed her, although she would never say a word about it.

"Just ask her, honey, does she need you or not?"

Katherine wasn't sure she wanted to put it that directly. What if Adele brushed her off? She crept back toward the men standing over Adele. "Darling," she said hesitantly at their backs, peering around the mayor, "is there something I can do? Coffee, perhaps a tisane? Have you eaten?"

Lieutenant Decoste's shoulders moved and his sigh was audible. Henri and the mayor ignored her. Adele peered at Katherine blankly for a moment before reaching out her hands. "What shall I do? I am alone? Where is my dear Sophie? Is she coming?" And she began to weep.

Katherine circled the mayor, pulled the packet of tissues from her pocket for her friend, and, ignoring the silent watchers, put her arm around Adele again. "You've called Sophie already? Is she on her way?"

Adele nodded. "*Oui*, by the first train, but she won't get here for hours. And poor Albert is left lying on the stairs." This brought on a loud wail and more weeping.

"Surely not," Katherine said, turning to the circle of men and forcing herself to speak in the clearest French she possessed. "You have moved him to his bed, have you not?"

"He will be moved, Madame," Decoste said stiffly. "In an

instant, *bien sûr*." He switched to English. "But I ask you please to absent yourself from this interview so I can collect the facts without delay, yes? If you wish to stay to tend to Madame, you can sit in the room across the hall until police business is done."

Adele looked up at Katherine and nodded, then blew her nose. "The sooner the better." She sniffed. "And we can deal with things in a more dignified manner, as Albert would wish." She straightened her shoulders, wiped her nose one more time, and waved Katherine away, but with a small smile this time.

"We can go?" Michael said.

"Not exactly." She wasn't ready to leave and for once Michael's lack of French allowed her to skate over the policeman's dismissal. "We can wait across the hall. I'll explain."

"I can't figure out what's going on with everyone jabbering away like that."

She was about to remind him that this was, after all, the jabber of the host country, when a loud voice from the reception hall boomed, and in English.

"What the hell. Of course I'm going in. Mike, what's going on here?" A heavy man, whose excess fat seemed to move independently of his frame, hurried into the room. He was somewhat taller than he was wide, and he was dressed for someplace other than rural France in a loud, short-sleeved print shirt that drooped halfway to his knees. The design appeared to be a picture, repeated over and over, of a water scene in which a white motorboat rode high on neon blue seas under a nightmare orange sky. The shirt was paired with wide-legged tan shorts and brown boat shoes with no socks. Michael was used to Betty Lou's husband and his idea of a vacation wardrobe, but the shirt, or possibly the man himself, momentarily paralyzed the group clustered around Adele. They stared at him wordlessly.

He rolled toward them and stuck out his hand. "J. B. Holliday," he said to the policeman. "Record producer, visiting your fine country. Hey, Mike; hey, Kathy. Everything okay?" The last after a double take and a hard look at Adele's face.

Before anyone could answer, Decoste raised a hand, palm out, in a stop sign. "Monsieur, might I ask why you are here?"

"I have an appointment with Albert. What's going on?"

"Monsieur," he said, bowing slightly toward Holliday. "I will speak with you, but," he said, lifting his hand again as J.B. opened his mouth, "in a few moments and in the other room, if you please. I am busy at the moment. *Merci,* Monsieur," he added in a louder voice when it appeared Holliday might not go quietly.

With Katherine's not quite audible explanations leading the little parade, the three of them filed out and across the hall to the anteroom where tourist groups normally waited on wooden benches. An amateurish painting of a French Renaissance woman hung prominently on one wall. It never failed to set Katherine's teeth on edge when she spied it coming into the château. Done in the late nineteenth century, she had explained to Albert, not medieval at all, doubtless copied from a costume book, and yet the artist had managed to screw up the perspective so badly that the woman's feet looked as though they'd been grafted on from a giantess.

There was no sound from upstairs, which wasn't surprising given that the floors were separated by a foot or more of solid stone. J.B. sank onto a hard wooden bench. If he was uncomfortable, it didn't show. "Talkative lot, aren't they?" he said with a wheeze. "I dropped by to see old Albert for a few minutes. Business. What's going on anyway? Someone rob the family jewels?"

"Albert's dead," Michael said. "Not sure why the cops didn't just say so."

"You're kidding me," J.B. said explosively. "Goddamn, that's bad news. He and I were about to do a deal."

The young uniformed policeman they had first seen in the doorway of the sitting room came clattering down the formal staircase and into the anteroom, stopping abruptly and putting his hands behind his back. "We wait for the lieutenant," he said in hesitant English, gesturing for Katherine and Michael to sit on the benches.

"We wait for a few minutes and that's it," Michael said, walking over to the slit window in the wall and peering out at a shaft of sunlight. "Kay, honey, I know you want to help, but if your friend's got to focus on all these people"—he waved an arm to include everyone seen and unseen within Château de Bellegarde's walls—"we should leave. You can come back later."

"Of course," Katherine said, sinking down, realizing she was beyond tired, aching with tension. There was too much happening and yet nothing happening, and no one cared what she thought. She felt useless and invisible, two of the worst states she could imagine.

J.B. wanted to talk. "The guy was a little rigid, and Betty Lou told me about him breaking a plate on the head of that arty-farty bookseller the other day, but still, dead is dead, you know what I mean? Hey, you don't think the guy he argued with—"

"No," Katherine jumped in, alarmed. No good stirring up gossip.

"What'd he die of?"

"Adele said she found him on the stone stairs that go down toward the back side of the building from the bedrooms. They're quite uneven, and they circle down at a steep pitch. More for atmosphere than everyday use, I would have thought, although they must be a quick route to the kitchen. I don't know why they even include them in the tour except that they're original to the château and Albert gets to show off his collection of antique guns."

J.B. shook his head. "I didn't even know there was another set of stairs. The main ones are damned impressive, though."

The young cop had been looking back and forth with increasing unhappiness, and tried out his English again. "No talking. *Silence, s'il vous plait.*"

"Whatever you say." J.B. looked up at him, chuckled when the cop said nothing, and took a copy of the *International New York Times* out of the satchel-style briefcase he carried. "Young man, why don't you set yourself down? I'm not going anywhere and neither are you, apparently, until your boss says so. What's your name anyway?"

The policeman said nothing and appeared to be studying a small oil painting that hung next to the door. It was a faithful representation of some earlier generation of Bellegarde cows lounging in a field. Katherine had a hunch the policeman might not have much English and was choosing not to start a conversation in which he would be at a disadvantage. J.B. looked at the gendarme for a moment before shrugging, winking at Katherine, and burying his head in the newspaper.

Her husband, she knew, was itching to leave. He got impatient waiting in line at the butcher's shop in Avallon while customers chatted happily with the white-aproned man behind the counter, seeming to make their choices of roasts and chops into epic stories to be told in shrill, high voices while each cut was carefully and slowly wrapped in white paper and tied with string. And while she loved the feeling of sharing common space at a restaurant, Michael wondered how anyone could spend three hours on a plate of beans and sausage.

Sure enough, he straightened up from the wall he had been leaning on and flicked his hand in farewell to J.B. "I'll come over later for rehearsals. I want to play with a different guitar for one of the songs. Betty Lou's sounding good."

"So she is," the producer said, looking up again and beaming, "especially with you doing harmony and lead guitar on that fine Stratocaster of yours. I like the material you're trying out. This could be a big deal for all of us, Mike."

Katherine felt a flutter in her chest. Wouldn't it be the most wonderful thing if Michael became a star at last, if he had a concert tour? He could thumb his nose at that sneak Eric and the others who had let Michael think he was going to be part of the band right up to the week of signing their contract.

"We're thrilled, J.B., really we are," she said over her shoulder as she hurried to catch up to Michael, who had already opened the door. Of course, he didn't feel comfortable talking about music deals and would fight against his own hopes. It would be her job now to smooth over his apparent lack of gratitude and be happy enough for both of them until success was a sure thing.

J.B. pointed at her and barked, "Barbecue. Soon. Betty Lou will call you."

"Did you introduce J.B. to Albert?" Katherine said, standing next to their car. "I didn't realize they knew each other. One doesn't, somehow, think of them as the kind of people who would be drawn to each other by mutual interests. And they're from different generations."

"He dropped by the studio one day to see what we were doing. J.B. seemed to know who he was. I got the idea J.B. was hoping he could convince the old man to invest in one of his projects, but we didn't talk about it."

"I'm confused. Albert had an arms business of some kind."

"Decades ago. J.B. said he sold that and is now a private investor, pretty successful too. Has shares in all kinds of businesses and in a lot of countries."

"And J.B. thought he'd like to buy a rock music studio? That sounds bizarre."

"Yeah, well, not to J.B. He was probably here today to ask for something."

A breathy voice from the edge of the driveway called out, "*Bonjour*, Mme Katherine; *bonjour*, M. Michel," and the bushes parted. Jeannette bounded out and across the gravel, her halo of curly hair aglow in a sunbeam, her long tanned legs flashing. "You saw the body, yes? Was there the blood everywhere?" The girl's eyes were alive with curiosity and her smile was guileless.

"Where on earth did you come from?" Katherine said. "How long have you been here?"

"Shoo," Michael said, with mock sternness. Katherine knew he thought Jeannette was a good kid overall, although he insisted she had Katherine wrapped around her little finger with her angelic looks and her Frenchness.

"There's nothing to see, and if some of the old ladies in town see you poking around, they'll have fits," Katherine said. It was true that Jeannette and her siblings were the collective black sheep of the village, a pack of wild things who stole the cherries off the trees and teased other people's dogs to distraction. Michael had sent them home a half-dozen times when they came to see huge Gracey, *"un ours noir."* A black bear, they tried to convince the littlest boy, whose mouth gaped in a combination of fear and wonder.

Jeannette slid her eyes to Michael for an instant but threw an arm around Katherine and nuzzled her.

"No, no," Katherine said, trying to disentangle herself, caught between impatience and sympathy for the girl, who obviously wanted to be involved in any drama that might add excitement to her otherwise too-predictable days. "You're too much, child," she said with a laugh. "We have to go home, and no, we did not see M. Bellegarde. Now go away."

"I saw him," Jeannette said in a stage whisper. "I saw him last night, from my hiding place." She pointed back to the wooded area.

"Well, it happened later. The poor man fell in the night, long after you were in bed, *cherie.* Now, let me go. We have to leave."

Michael, already in the car, signaled his intent to leave as he normally did, by starting the engine and putting the car in gear. As it chuffed to life, Jeannette backed away, grinning, and raced down the driveway.

"Where does that child get her energy?" Katherine said, piling her hat and carryall on her lap. "Although, I suppose what really worries me is what she does with it all."

Michael had a hunch, but he was sure Kay wouldn't like it, so he didn't mention J.B.'s hotheaded son, who seemed on the prowl for something or someone to relieve his boredom.

CHAPTER 6

Finally, something exciting. Jeannette could hardly wait for the boys to fall asleep, exhausted, hot, and sweaty, in their beds. Her father was sleeping in front of the television. She knew he wouldn't wake up until the middle of the night, and then only to stumble to his bed. He wasn't a bad father, she thought as she snuck down the stairs and slipped through the door into the darkness. She had read about fathers who bothered their daughters or whipped their sons, and her father did nothing like that, *bien sûr*.

As she walked quickly along the road, she fingered the *cadeau*, the gift Brett had given her. She hoped it was a token of his love, although all he had said was, "Here, want this?" as he grabbed her hand and pressed the old shell into it. When she asked him where he got it, he just shrugged, and leaned over to brush his lips against her cheek. She could still feel the place where their flesh had met. Now she kept it in her pocket as a reminder of their romance, although something made her think it would be a good idea to put it in her secret hiding place.

Tonight she wasn't on a spying mission exactly, like the ones she had told Brett about. This time, she had to check on something she thought she had seen, and she couldn't tell anyone. Someone else was taking a walk, because she heard footsteps on the road. There was no one in sight when she turned around. It was probably the new people, the guy with the jug ears and the wife who looked like a farmer already. They took walks in the evening, she knew. Hardly anyone else in Reigny came out after dark for some reason.

The crickets were quiet at this late hour. As she ran on tiptoe up the Bellegardes' paved driveway she heard an owl hooting in the woods. There were lights on upstairs in the château. There was also a bright light over the doorway arch, which made it harder for her to poke around without being seen. She eased into the darker area under the trees to think. She wanted to look around in the high grass next to the driveway, where she and Brett had been skateboarding. Maybe the light would be turned off soon.

Ten minutes later, she sighed. This was boring. Maybe she could go out to the grass. No one was looking out the windows, after all. Suddenly, the hair at the back of her neck prickled. What was that sound off in the trees behind her? She turned her head quickly, but there was only silence and dark. A rabbit perhaps. As she turned back to the upstairs windows, wondering if the body of Monsieur was still there, laid out under the blanket like in a movie, there was more rustling behind her. This time, she thought she heard a breath too. Did rabbits make breathing noises? The time she found a baby rabbit next to the road and brought it home, it had been silent. But then, it had died soon after, so maybe that didn't count.

A moment later, a twig snapped nearby and with it came a slight grunting sound like no animal that she could think of. Perhaps the murderer had come back to check on his work? Or to get rid of anyone who might have seen him? Because

Jeannette believed Monsieur had been dispatched by someone. Everyone in Reigny said so even if they didn't agree on who did it. Did that mean she had seen the killer, maybe even knew him? She shivered at the idea.

Then, out of the darkness, something touched her shoulder. It was a human hand on the bare skin of her arm. The blood rushed to her head and her vision blurred. She screamed and, unable to think, thrashed her way out of the trees, running at full speed down the driveway, hearing someone running behind her, maybe speaking, maybe catching up.

She rounded the bend into the village, gasping and crying, and threw herself into the house. "Papa, Papa," she shouted.

Her father stirred, staggered to his feet, and started shouting too. She skidded into him and hugged him tightly, weeping. She knew he was asking her all kinds of questions, but she couldn't get enough air to answer at first. She looked over her shoulder at their courtyard, which was empty except for pacing and yapping dogs. The boys had woken up and were staring at her openmouthed from the stairs.

When she calmed down, she assured him she was all right, that she had thought a fox was in the yard and had gone out to shoo it away so it wouldn't try to grab the puppies. But it had lunged at her. It was big, bigger than a fox. She brushed her tears away.

Her father shook her gently. "Ah, 'Nette, the dogs can take care of themselves. Anyway, it was only a barn owl. They swoop in to get the mice that hide in the grassy edge of the yard, you know that."

But as she drifted into sleep an hour later, she again felt the touch on her shoulder and heard the sound. It wasn't simply an owl, it wasn't an owl at all. She shuddered and pulled the thick blanket up to her neck.

CHAPTER 7

The next day was hot and sultry, the humidity high enough to suggest rain was on the way, although the puffy clouds were white and innocent-looking. Katherine was too restless to paint. Michael had come outside to practice. "Tell me what you think, Kay. I may be too rusty at this to know if I've got something good, but I kind of like it."

It was good, a ballad with the right mix of wistfulness and spirit, a lament for an absent lover who might or might not be worth chasing. When he finished singing and the last notes of the guitar faded, Katherine said, "Bravo, Michael. I already want to hum it. Will you sing melody if you do it with Betty Lou?"

"Don't know. Her voice is stronger than mine. If we wind up doing it in a key she's comfortable with, I'm likely to let her lead and I'll stick with backup. You know, I haven't sung much in a while." He gathered the sheet music he'd made notes on and stood up. Coming over to her, he kissed her full on the mouth and looked into her eyes. "You're still the best critic I've got. You'd tell me if it was crap, right?"

She put her arms around his neck and laughed. "I would, I promise. When it's crap, you will hear it first from me."

He grinned, reached around to slap her rear end lightly, then disentangled himself from her embrace and said, "And with that, I shall go and present it to J.B. He's actually a pretty astute guy when it comes to this stuff. If you like it, and he likes it, Betty Lou will go for it."

"Hooray, and while you're working on it, I'll be trying to turn my current painting, which *is* crap at the moment, into something half as good."

After he left, the dogs settled in for naps under the lilac bushes, and Katherine realized she was feeling at loose ends. It wasn't that she expected to be treated like Adele's family and kept up to date, but, yes, she guessed privately that she did. After all, who brought Adele and Albert jars of home-made pear compote from last year's meager harvest? Katherine had offered to paint a portrait of the elderly couple in a style suitable to be hung alongside Adele's ancestors somewhere in the cavernous château. Pity they hadn't at least gotten in a few sessions. She could have winged it after that, a skill she had picked up at art school on the numerous occasions when she overslept and missed a figure-drawing class.

Albert was dead. Funny how the truth of it came and went like a light flickering on and off, causing her stomach to flip uncomfortably each time. She wished she had taken the time to get past his prickliness. He had intimidated her with his frown of disapproval and air of superiority. She couldn't recall an occasion when he had been more than civil, polite in an impersonal manner, as if she were one of those tourists one put up with only because one had to. But he had occupied space in the village and in her mind, and now that space was vacant and called attention to the missing person in unsettling ways.

They couldn't see Château de Bellegarde or the road to it

from their house, so Katherine was hampered in what she could learn about events merely by watching. She might take the dogs for a walk. Katherine wasn't snooping, she told herself. She cared about Adele, and she worried about Sophie's ability to be a significant help to her mother. Sophie was not a strong person. She was pale, ate like a bird the few times the families had dined together, and hardly said a word. Katherine sometimes thought Sophie might be unstable. No, nervous was more accurate. Someone who was easily startled and perhaps moody. Definitely not someone who was going to be much help to her mother in a time of crisis, especially if she was still feeling the blow of being romantically rejected by Yves.

Thinking about the bookseller irritated her. How could she have thought him so charming when she and Michael had arrived in Reigny-sur-Canne? He had dropped in on them while they were trying to figure out how to light the strange wall heater, which was so old that the faded and peeling instruction labels were illegible. Yves brought them a nineteenth-century edition of an Émile Zola novel, which Katherine was delighted to have in order to improve her French reading skills. "So much easier to get caught up in than the daily scandals and misdeeds that *Le Monde* chronicles week after week," she said in thanking him when she returned the visit, driving the short distance to his poky little bookstore. He was charming, a great teller of amusing stories about the village and its history, and able to converse enough in English so that she didn't spend entire evenings translating for Michael. He became a regular solo dinner guest, having explained that he was a confirmed bachelor and did not believe in the institution of marriage.

That should have warned Sophie, who must have indulged in a dream of wedded life anyway. The pickings around here are pretty slim, poor girl, Katherine thought. As soon as they were able, the children of Reigny fled to larger towns or to a city, as young people everywhere do.

That made her think about Penny, who surely came to the town expecting something different. No charming restaurants, no antique shops or patisseries, and no people her age except Yves. She spent carelessly, without understanding precisely the difference between euros and dollars, which the numerous contractors and suppliers realized at once. She signaled that she was willing to show off her house if people wanted to drop by. But Katherine and Yves were the only people who took her up socially.

That Penny had not quite graduated from Cleveland's finest college after returning from a botched freshman year at Wellesley was not lost on Katherine, but not widely known among her Reigny neighbors. What was known was that Penny's indulgent parents had had the good taste and generosity to die within months of each other before Penny turned thirty, leaving her the brick mansion she grew up in, several million dollars, and, when all was said and done, no reason to stay in Cleveland. After choosing a high-rise apartment in Chicago and touring Europe's major cities, she had decided she must have a place in France. A persuasive real estate agent found a lovely country property in Burgundy, nestled in the heart of the wine country and only a few miles from the fast train to Paris. Penny had jumped at the chance to possess a seventeenth-century stone house for what had seemed like a bargain price.

Katherine smiled at the recollection of Penny's indignation when they first met. "They have to move an entire stone wall to make the bathroom big enough to turn around in, and there's one dinky little outlet in the kitchen and no place for my dough maker." Her eyes had begged Katherine for sympathy and Katherine hadn't had the heart to tell her what life was going to be like as she pushed and pulled the charmingly decayed mill house into her decorator magazine ideal. Deaf to subtle hints, Penny created small and large waves, casually disregarding the status quo, territorial lines, and delicately defined social order that kept the village functioning. Her constant references to superior American workmen may have gone over the heads of the Polish work crews who came for the summer, but probably not her local plumber's.

"She really ought to lay off the comparisons, at least when the neighbors are around," Michael had whispered one night while they were enjoying a meal cooked to perfection on Penny's gas grill, sitting on Penny's new flagstone patio. Katherine had shushed him, in part because Penny had opened a Chablis Grand Cru, which was ambrosia to someone who could only afford *vin blanc* from the nine-euro bin. Katherine did not like to bite the hand that was feeding her so well, at least not during the meal. This latest business, going after Yves when poor Sophie finally seemed to have landed him as a boyfriend, was an insult to the entire town, *une scandale*.

"Come on, animals, let's go out and see what's been happening in the neighborhood. I can't gossip all by myself." The dogs struggled to their feet, probably puzzled. Katherine liked them well enough, but they were Michael's animals and he was the walk master. Still, anything to get outside and catch the newest smells. "We'll sniff around at the old quarry, shall we?" Katherine said, snapping on their leashes as she planned a route that would lead them past the château's driveway and give her a chance to peek. "When Michael gets home from rehearsing, we'll be ready with the news of the day."

The château was quiet and there were no cars visible in

the drive when she walked past. The dogs were still engrossed in their investigation of the old quarry path fifteen minutes later when Katherine yanked on their leashes and turned them for home. As they emerged onto the narrow paved road, someone in the distance waved at Katherine, who squinted, not sure at first who it was.

"Hallooo," the voice called, loud enough to make the dogs stop and turn their heads. Pippa jogged up to Katherine and explained that she had heard about M. Bellegarde's death and wondered what had happened. She had been informed by the woman who owned the food shop, the *épicure vital,* in the nearby village that was part of the same commune, that there were a lot of policemen and maybe someone was arrested? "Was he murdered?" she asked with an eager stare.

"No, it was an accident," Katherine said, startled to hear in Pippa the same quick assumption as Jeannette's. "Albert Bellegarde fell on the old stone steps in the château, or, at least, that is what the police think at the moment. He was quite old, you know, and probably a little fragile."

Pippa's shoulders slumped and she grimaced. "I was afraid of that. There aren't many murders around here, are there?" At Katherine's look of shock, she covered her mouth with her hand. "You must think me terrible. I am sorry, of course. He was so upset at your party, wasn't he?" She rearranged her face into a socially acceptable degree of gravity. "I have to make up crime stories, but since my French isn't good enough to read the newspapers here with any hope of accuracy or detail, I'm starved for real events to get the juices flowing, don't you know?"

"I hadn't thought about where writers get their ideas, but surely you can use your imagination? If not, I would think living in London or Paris might be more inspiring, if that's the right word. And you're young," Katherine added. "I wonder what keeps you in a town that is pretty much lived in by old people."

"I wouldn't have a free home otherwise, would I?"

"You own that little house?"

"My father bought it ages ago. He and my mother were going to fix it up, rent it out in season, you know? But she died and he doesn't leave his flat in London at all. Walks the dog, watches telly, and orders Indian takeaway. If I were in London, he'd want me to come over every evening and make tea like the dutiful daughter I'm not, sorry to say."

"How sad. You must miss your mother."

"She was distressed when I got so tall in the fifth form at school. She used to tell me to scrunch down when I walked or I wouldn't find a husband." Pippa shrugged. "We weren't really close."

Katherine couldn't think of a thing to say that wouldn't sound as if she was being rude, although she longed to tell the girl to stand up straight and try wearing clothes that wouldn't make her look so frumpy.

"You said the police aren't precisely certain yet, I mean about the old man's death? What do you think?" Pippa said, her head tipped to one side like a curious, tall bird.

Katherine paused. Of course, it must have been an accident. And yet . . . "I doubt the police would miss anything obvious. But they may not know much about Reigny-sur-Canne. I wish Albert hadn't offended so many people one way or another."

Pippa got a faraway look in her eyes. Katherine hoped she hadn't stirred up the writer's creative imagination too much. On the other hand, it would be nice to be able to confide in someone. Penny was too subjective when it came to Yves. And

Betty Lou didn't really care about any of this, being only a summer visitor. "I only wonder because Albert has lived in that house for the better part of forty years, and conducts his little tours that include climbing the stone steps as often as twice a week in season."

"Hmmm . . . So he wouldn't be likely to fall, would he?" Pippa said briskly. "Yes, I see. Who do you think did it?"

Katherine blanched. Lord, but the young woman was tactless. "I'm not saying anyone did it, only that he had been up and down the stairs many times before. I'm only thinking out loud."

"Of course, I understand," Pippa said, although the look on her face signaled that Katherine's comment had gone into some corner of her brain, to be taken out and examined earnestly over tea. "I've slowed you down enough. Such lovely dogs. Thank you for inviting me to the lunch. It was rather an event, wasn't it? If I hear anything or have any ideas about Albert, I'll pop over and we can think through it together. Must get back to feed the cats and rack my brain for a way out of a locked cellar." Pippa beamed.

"Someone's in your cellar?" Katherine said, thoroughly confused.

"In my manuscript, you know."

"Come on, beasts, I have no more time for this," Katherine said ten minutes later as she opened the gate to let the dogs back into the garden. They wandered off to check out something or other, unperturbed, and she drifted into the cool of the dark living room. Katherine was still thinking about Pippa. Should she ask her to be in the fête, or would it lose its French character even further? She had felt awkward including Betty Lou, but at least this woman lived here. Everyone knew about her, if only because her Fiat was a familiar sight as it zipped past on market days. Maybe she could be pressed into selling plastic cups of wine.

She knew she should pull out her easel and work on the big painting, the centerpiece of her upcoming exhibit, the one that would stop people in their tracks to exclaim over her sly capture of rural Burgundy's past and present. Jeannette was a fine model if you didn't mind her twitching and talking, which Katherine didn't since what she needed most was the drape of her long blue dress and the tumble of her hair, which had the unsettling effect of turning into a golden halo when the sun was directly behind the girl's head. No angel, that one, Katherine silently fussed, but it was not to be borne that she should be allowed to crumble into her father's stunted lifestyle, sloppy and manipulative with no goals beyond grabbing at things, any things, for the sake of getting something for nothing. No, it wouldn't do. She would talk, discreetly of course, to Betty Lou about that son of hers. No good simply hoping Jeannette would have the good sense to avoid sex with a summer visitor if he paid even the slightest attention to her.

The phone rang. "Katherine, is that you?"

It was Adele, and Katherine was as pleased as if she'd been given a present. Adele was thinking about her friend. "Adele, dearest, how are you? Have the officials left you in peace?"

"There is no peace for me ever again." Katherine heard the pain in the new widow's voice, but also the smallest touch of something else, perhaps irritation? "Sophie is here." An image of Adele and Albert's adult daughter, passive and frowning, presented itself to Katherine.

"You know I will help any way I can."

"She did some shopping for me, and is home again, but would you come over? There is some shocking news. Sophie is having what you Americans call a nervous breakdown, I am sure, and I am simply not strong enough to take care of her and deal with the undertaker and the newspaper writer and the police. It is too much, too much." Adele choked back a sob.

"*Bien sûr*, and I'll bring some food, shall I? A dish for the oven. But I don't understand. Why is a newspaper pestering you, and why are you still having to talk with the police?"

"It is frightening and too much to relate on the phone. I shall tell you everything when I see you, yes? When might that be? I am not sure how much longer I can maintain calm in the face of all this."

Worried and curious in equal parts, Katherine bundled the duck confit she had planned to serve that night, plus some plump green beans she had cooked in garlic, mushrooms, and olive oil into her second-best tureen, a piece of milky-white *faïence* in the shape of a bird. She had found the piece a month ago under a pile of musty-smelling tablecloths at an otherwise disappointing *vide-grenier* in a town that had missed out on Gallic charm and was simply a place they went to when they needed garden stakes or new tires for the Citroën. She would have to think of an indirect way of asking Sophie to make sure the pot was returned. Things had a way of disappearing, and it was too much to think of losing such a beautiful piece, and such a bargain too. She would deal later with Michael's disappointment about a dinner of leftovers.

"They found a gun," Adele said, waving a fresh handkerchief. Katherine was so distracted by Adele's changed appearance that she didn't immediately grasp what the woman was saying. Adele, always impeccably groomed, calm, in control, had given way to an old woman hunched on the sofa in a bathrobe, her hair frizzy, no makeup, no pearls. "One of Albert's. In the shrubbery." She waved an arm vaguely in the direction of the driveway.

"He was shot? Not an accident?"

"No, no, not shot, but the gun was removed from his display case." A sob caught in her throat and she applied the handkerchief to her eyes.

"Stolen?" Katherine balked at this magnitude of change in what had been described as a simple fall by an elderly person twenty-four hours ago. "Who told you this?"

"The police were here this morning." The voice came from deep inside a tall wing chair. Sophie Bellegarde leaned forward without saying hello. She was a wisp of a thing who looked much younger than her thirtysomething years, with pale hair that seemed to be demonstrating its own sorrow by hanging listlessly on her neck. She did not appear to be breaking down, Katherine thought, but her face was white and she looked like someone who was being forced to chew and swallow her own grief. When asked by Katherine, she said Maman had been like this almost since she had arrived.

"My Albert," came a moan from the sofa, "how can I not weep?" Adele draped the cloth back over her eyes and collapsed into the sofa, clutching the neck of her robe.

"Of course, Maman," Sophie said through clenched teeth, "I don't begrudge you your grief. But I do wish you would give me some direction." Her voice was surprising, with a quality of steel that helped account for her success in her father's business.

Although, Katherine realized, the urgent need to step in and run the company on a day-to-day basis might account for the voice.

There was no response from the new widow other than a loud sigh. "I will have to arrange everything," Sophie said to Katherine, switching to impeccable English for the recital of her burdens. "You know, the undertaker, the neighbors, the papers the gendarmerie has asked for." Her brow contracted and she grabbed her lower lip with her teeth. "And the lieutenant wishes to speak to me, too, although I cannot think why. I was at the apartment in Paris when my father fell."

"The police are not satisfied?" Perhaps the French had procedures Katherine wasn't aware of, or Albert's former status in the government meant they needed to be especially vigilant in their reports. Had they found a clue upstairs?

A weak voice spoke up from the couch. "*Alors*, I am being besieged by policemen, Katherine. They are everywhere, looking into the cupboards and churning up the flower beds." Adele pulled herself to a sitting position. "I have not even had time to prepare a tisane for my poor, poor Sophie and myself, something to give us strength."

Sophie said in rapid-fire French, "That is going beyond the facts, Maman. There are no gendarmes here now and I saw no disturbance in the gardens other than what the rabbits have done. The only sign of the intruder, if there was one, was the unlocked window in this room."

"Albert always locked all the windows," Adele said in a tragic voice. "He cannot be faulted."

"The window is unlocked, Maman, and there were some small signs that someone could have entered. They have checked for fingerprints."

"And made a terrible mess of my window," Adele said, tragedy now blended with indignation.

"So there may have been an intruder. Do the police think that person pushed poor Albert?" Katherine said.

"No, I would have heard an argument," Adele said, through fresh tears. "He must have heard something and slipped when going to check on it. But the police keep poking around, disarranging everything and telling me nothing. We cannot move without being harassed." She began to wail again.

Adele had seemed clearheaded yesterday, Katherine thought, looking from one woman to the other in confusion, but perhaps she had been in shock. Not knowing what to say and looking for a chance to do something after her walk over in the midday heat, she said, "Let me put this casserole in the refrigerator, then I can fix some tea, or coffee if you would rather?"

Fifteen minutes later, the women sat at a low table in front of what Katherine was tempted to call Adele's fainting couch, porcelain cups in their laps, a small measure of normal existence restored. "I doubt the police will have many questions for you, Sophie," Katherine said, not really sure but wanting to ease the younger woman's obvious tension.

"They can't, can they? I wasn't here," Sophie repeated. "It is so frustrating that I had to catch the late train. Everything is happening too fast."

Apropos of nothing, as the rapid French was directed toward her and she nodded in what she hoped looked like sympathy rather than confusion, Katherine registered the fact that Sophie's nose was pink and shaped a little like a rodent's. A pity, Katherine thought, since, with her ashy-blond hair, red-rimmed eyes, and slight overbite, she looked like one of the rabbits her father tried to eradicate from the château's garden. It couldn't be helped, she chided herself, and was ashamed that she was so shallow as to notice it at a time like this.

The coffee was a good idea, Katherine told herself. Adele calmed down and Sophie retreated to the big chair again, but with a bit more color, as her mother filled Katherine in on the police visit. Albert had died of a broken neck, most certainly caused by falling hard and at a terrible angle on the steep stairs that wound down to the kitchen. The gun had been taken from one of the cases that were set into small alcoves along the steps, places that Albert explained were built so servants running up the stairs with hot-water bottles or breakfast trays would not collide with servants running down the stairs with laundry and chamber pots. The key for that case, kept in the lock, was missing, but the old pistol had been found, almost by accident, by a uniformed policeman looking around because he thought he heard someone moving in the overgrown shrubbery on the other side of the driveway. Katherine immediately suspected Jeannette as the source of the sound but said nothing. After all, the girl wasn't a criminal for being curious. An unwelcome thought caused Katherine to feel a sudden chill. The girl couldn't have—wouldn't have—climbed in an open window to prowl around, would she? Should Katherine try to find out, or would that simply cause Jeannette to lie if she had? Katherine was uncomfortable. "The gun was lying there in the grass? How odd. Were other guns missing? Was anything else stolen?"

"Not that we know of. Albert would not have removed it from the display case unless he felt he had to use it. I think he kept it locked, didn't he?" Adele looked over at Sophie.

Sophie looked up. "How would I know?"

"But you know everything, my darling girl."

"Well, I don't know that."

Katherine guessed that mother and daughter were so close that sniping at each other was routine, and the stress right now had to be terrible. "I'm sure there's some perfectly simple explanation for all of that," she said, working to keep her own concern out of her voice.

"I can't tell if the lieutenant thinks the explanation is a criminal one. He doesn't say," Adele said. "I wish he would be more clear."

"Has he said anything specific about someone else being involved?" Katherine asked, curiosity getting the better of her.

Adele gave her a helpless look as if to say she had no clue. When Katherine turned to see what Sophie might say, the woman was looking down at her fingernails. There was no hope of getting any closer to the facts at this point.

"The best thing might be for you to rest a bit," she said, standing up. "I need to get home and work on a painting that has to be done soon so the gallery in Vézelay that's showing it doesn't smell like turpentine and varnish on the day of the opening. Oh dear, I suppose you won't be coming, Adele. I wonder if I should postpone it out of respect to Albert." She held her breath, wishing she hadn't opened the door for Adele to shame her into changing it. The invitations had been printed and sent. It would be a disaster to cancel it now.

"Of course not, Katherine, although I doubt I will be strong enough to come. Perhaps Sophie . . . ?" She trailed off and looked pointedly at her daughter.

"*Desolée,*" Sophie said quickly, then switched back into English to explain to Katherine. "I expect I'll be back at the office. With Papa gone—" She hesitated for a second. "—there will be much business to attend to."

"Well," Katherine said, feeling relieved and guilty at the same time, "I must go, but you will call me? Enjoy the confit. I'll come around again soon." Her good-byes said, she hurried out. She was halfway down the driveway when running foot-steps and a childish shout made her turn.

"Not you again," she said, startled by the adolescent who almost ran into her on long, gangly legs.

" 'Allo, 'allo, Katherine," Jeannette said, grinning and slipping her hand around Katherine's arm, falling into step with her. "Is it true," she said in a loud whisper, "that M. Bellegarde was very, very rich and that his money has disappeared?"

"Where did you get such an idea?" Katherine said, trying ineffectually to shake off the girl's hand.

"Papa says maybe he was murdered. Papa says he was a Nazi and made his money by having people killed."

"He did no such thing, and it's not nice to pass along rumors. He became a French citizen long before you were born. Anyway, he's too young to have been in the war."

"But Papa says not. He says there were teenage SS in the Yonne and that the neighbors hid in the forest and shot at them. He says there are still Nazis around, even here."

Katherine could well believe the girl's father would say something like that. Hatred of the World War II German occupiers was alive and well in this region of Burgundy, and reminders of the brutality were everywhere, never to be forgotten. As the head of a long lineage of poor quarrymen, and acknowledged everywhere in Reigny as a petty thief, he was the lowest in Reigny's social standing and might be expected to stir neighbor against neighbor out of spite.

He had been indignant in his criticism of Penny's renovation project behind her back, making a show of being unable to fish in the stream that her rectangular lap pool had slightly infringed upon, pretending to all who would listen that his children depended on his catch to have food in their bellies. It was ridiculous. They lived on a diet of chips and canned cassoulet as far as Katherine could figure out. It was more likely that Jean hadn't gotten any work from the project and was stewing about the missed opportunity to overcharge her for moving piles of bricks, or repairing the roof in his fashion. However, if there was one person the villagers were less likely to accept than the local thief, it was the rude American who threw her money around. They had banded together in dislike of Penny. Katherine wondered if they would do that now, turning on Albert in death as they had not dared to do in life, letting their generations-old resentment against Germans emerge.

With her new suspicion nagging at her, Katherine stopped walking and looked hard at the girl. "Do you know anything you haven't told the police? If so, you must tell me now."

There was a flicker of something in the girl's eyes before she said, "No, I promise. Only what I've heard from Papa." As she spoke, she began rubbing something she'd been carrying between her fingers. Nerves? No, it was impossible to believe this innocent girl could be involved in a murder. Katherine would not give in to such fanciful ideas. Leave that sort of fiction to Pippa.

"All right then, child, understand that the poor man fell down a steep flight of stone steps in the dark. I almost fell down the same stairs when the Bellegardes gave me a tour last year, and that was in the middle of the day, when there was some light on them. That's all it was. You must not gossip, and you must be kind to Mme Bellegarde and her daughter."

"But what about that show-off, Yves? He was so angry when Monsieur broke a plate on his head—that was so funny—and maybe he sneaked back and pushed Monsieur. Or maybe someone else did."

"Nonsense, Jeannette. Stop that right now."

Jeannette fell silent, only squeezing Katherine's arm with her free hand and leaning into her side, trying to match her steps to Katherine's. Feeling hemmed in, Katherine disengaged her arm, then scolded herself. The girl had no mother, a constricted and not entirely pleasant life, and was undoubtedly bored to death in a place with no one else her age. Katherine recognized, or at least interpreted, the teenager's noisy affection as a symptom of the same longing she had felt at that age to be loved, to be noticed and valued. If she were being entirely truthful, she still felt like that, although she didn't have enough nerve to go up to Mme Pomfort on the street and take her arm as companionably as Jeannette had taken hers.

"Tell you what, *cherie*, you can go with Michael and me to the *vide-grenier* in Noyers. There will be at least forty tables set up with books, toys, china, and other wonderful things to look at, plus food stalls. If Andres, the man who sells ukuleles, is there, he and Michael may play some duets."

That was enough to set the teenager dancing around Katherine in circles, swooping in to kiss her on both cheeks before running off down the hill, probably to tease her little brothers unmercifully about what they would be missing. Katherine shook her head and wondered if she was helping Jeannette or merely indulging the child's impulsive nature.

CHAPTER 8

That evening, Katherine sat on the chaise with her arms wrapped around her knees while Michael picked out the tune of another new song he was writing. The white dog curled up at the foot of the chair, watching them both with liquid brown eyes while Gracey attempted to climb onto the battered chaise and Katherine's lap.

"Down, Gracey," Katherine said, pushing ineffectually at the mass of black fur that leaned its full weight against her shoulder. "Darling, I'm afraid. Remember when Yves and Albert came to blows? If the police hear about that, will they suspect Yves? I mean, should we not tell the police if it will only make things worse?"

Michael looked up at her, pencil poised in one hand, smiling quizzically. "You think Yves snuck up on Albert in the middle of the night because Albert broke a plate over his head? That's a little extreme. I don't think you can keep it a secret, Kay. Everyone else saw it."

"We could ask people not to mention it, couldn't we? I could call everyone and explain."

"Explain what? Adele was there, remember? And J.B., who wasn't even there, threw it out in front of a cop."

"Oh, damn, that's right. At least part of the story, not the whole thing. Do you think the policeman understood?"

"I'm not sure he paid any attention. I'm just saying you can't cover it up." He plucked a few more notes, strummed a chord, and jotted something on the score paper on the stand in front of him. "I know you have good intentions, Kay, but next thing you know, you'll be arrested as some kind of accessory. Think about it. I won't be able to bail you out because I don't know how the system works and can't speak a word of the language."

"Oh." Katherine was quiet for a minute, looking meditatively at a spot on the wall.

"I was teasing, sweetie, but I don't much like your look. I have a hunch you're considering something that will make matters worse."

"Michael," she began, drawing a deep breath, "what if—"

Her husband shook his head and smiled at her in exasperation. "This hasn't got anything to do with us and, unless you start meddling, it won't. Please, sweetheart, stay out of it."

Katherine opened her mouth to speak, but shut it again. Michael was only trying to protect her, and she loved him for it. But if he was determined to keep this tragedy at arm's length, she had her friends to think about, or at least Yves, who had brought suspicion on himself with his bratty behavior, but who was hardly a murderer. Katherine worried that if the story of his quarrel with Albert got around, he might be interesting to the police. Who should she call first? She still had the serving plate Penny had lent her for the lunch party and it was past time to return it. Yes, that would be tomorrow morning's chore. That and finding those missing silver spoons, which she was sure she had put in the armoire in the kitchen.

Katherine didn't have to call. Penny was waiting for her on the patio when she and Michael got home after their early-morning drive for baguettes and coffee.

"Darlings," Penny said. "Something is going on. Police cars and vans, every one headed up to the castle. I was trying to reason with the builders the whole time, so I missed it. I would have walked over, but they actually proposed bringing the pipes to the new bathroom right through the kitchen, under the ceiling. Can you imagine?"

Michael exited the conversation into the house, as he frequently did when Penny showed up, and Katherine waved Penny to the chairs under the pear tree to fill her in on the tragic happenings at the château. She had hardly begun when a voice called, "'Allo, *mes amis*," and a middle-aged string bean of a man in jeans so short his ankles protruded jogged the length of the driveway to join them. Emile had recently retired from his dental practice and was concentrating on his twin passions of *pétanque*, France's age-old version of bocce or lawn bowling, and playing music, in which, he said, he was inspired by Michael Goff, the famous American rock star who was now his neighbor. Nothing Michael had said could disabuse Emile of the conviction that Don Henley might show up any day for a jam session with Michael.

"Emile, do sit. I'm glad you're here," Katherine said, patting the chair next to her. "Now I can tell you both at the same time." Emile pulled the women up one at a time to kiss them properly on both cheeks, then dropped into the chair, a nascent potbelly visible under an old striped jersey.

"It is terrible, *non*?" he said in shocked tones. "Our own

Albert, shot to death by robbers in the night. And the thieves tied up poor Madame and took everything from the safe." He shook his head repeatedly as he spoke.

"What?" Penny said. "Robbers here? And they killed Albert?"

"No, no," Katherine said. "I mean, yes, he is dead, but he wasn't shot and Adele wasn't tied up."

"Yes, yes," Emile said. "Madame Durand at the *super-marché* told me, and she heard it from the man who delivers the baguettes." Emile began to explain how the bread truck driver had heard, but Penny interrupted.

"Oh my gosh, are we safe? Maybe I should go lock my front door." Penny stood up suddenly. "My car's not locked either, and my jewelry—"

"Sit down, Penny," Katherine said in a sharp voice so unlike her normal one that Penny sat as abruptly as she had stood, and both she and Emile stopped speaking. "Adele is fine, well, not fine, of course, but not injured. She told me she simply found him on the stone steps at the back of the upstairs hallway, which they use to go down to the kitchen, when she went for his morning coffee. She told me she thought it might be a heart attack." For an instant, Katherine saw Albert, his crumpled, fragile body as it must have been, and the reality of his death as something other than a test of her social standing washed over her again. She shivered and jumped up to straighten the oilcloth on the rickety table between her and her guests. "It's terrible," she said with a lump in her throat, and plopped down in her chair again.

Penny and Emile sat silently for a moment, absorbing this new information, Emile looking stricken that his unimpeachable source at the supermarket might have gotten her facts mixed up. Penny looked worried.

Penny broke the silence. "I hate to say it, darling, but while Albert may be pitiable in death, he was hardly loved even before he hit Yves over the head with a plate."

"*Quoi?*" Emile said in a shocked voice. "What? Albert and Yves were fighting? But, do you think that Yves, he perhaps—"

"No," said Katherine and Penny at the same moment.

"It wasn't—"

"You mustn't—"

"Oh dear, this is what I was worried about," Katherine said. "The police may not understand how trivial their quarrel was, and I think it would be better not to mention it at all."

"Agreed," Penny said, the anxiety in her voice making Emile look at her appraisingly.

Katherine took comfort in the realization that Emile wasn't good friends with anyone who had been at the party. He was unlikely to probe elsewhere. Unless, of course, the bread deliveryman had heard it from Marie, the young cheese maker who had recently moved to Reigny. Marie and her husband lived within sight of Emile's house, so he might well run into them on the way to the café or the *poubelle*, the only communal gathering places in Reigny.

"Even if the police didn't put much faith in the idea that someone killed him, they'd have to at least check out people's motives if there are rumors," Katherine said. "We don't want them wasting time looking at anyone in the village."

"Of course not," Penny said.

"But who would do such a terrible thing?" Emile whispered.

"Tourists are in and out all summer," Penny said, jumping on the idea of alternative suspects too quickly for Katherine's taste. "Maybe someone saw something worth stealing and . . .

Oh well, best not to speculate," she added, seeing Katherine's frown and slight shake of the head. "I guess I'll go back to Chicago without stories of dining with the landed gentry in their châteaux. Not that I thought they'd invite me. They snubbed me even before Yves flirted with their daughter." She shrugged.

"He never spoke to me." Emile's look said he was insulted by this slight in village propriety.

"Nonsense, Emile. He spent a long time talking to you at the last *pétanque* event, remember?"

"Ah, but that was to tell me that my friends were too noisy and that one of them drove into his hedge."

Katherine attempted to bring the conversation back to her point. "So, we're agreed we won't say anything about the little fuss at the lunch party?"

Emile shook himself. "I myself am inclined to believe the bread man's story, although I must keep an open mind until all the facts are known, no? Perhaps I shall stop in to visit with Henri. The sheriff and I, we need to discuss the maintenance of the *pétanque* court while I am on vacation in Spain in any case."

Katherine hid a smile. Emile relished his self-appointed role as the town's living newspaper almost as much as he enjoyed putting together the annual *pétanque* competition, where he played the accordion for three days straight and sang French café songs in an increasingly boozy voice. At the moment, she was sure he was trying to convince himself that no robbers would break into his little house, with its modest garden patch and the old Renault in the dirt driveway.

"I am not worried," he said bravely when she asked. "My accordion is hardly the thing a robber would want, is it? Of course"—and here his voice took on a serious tone—"it might be something a *mec* could sell in Paris. Perhaps in the future I should keep it in the armoire, although that would mean finding somewhere else to put my suit. My dear Katherine," he said, leaning forward, "I have the thought. It is not nice, I know, but Jean could have done this, *non*? Should we tell the police?"

"Why on earth would you think that?" Katherine said. "He's not a violent man, and anyway, Jean would hardly creep into the Bellegardes' house in the middle of the night."

"He is a thief," Emile said, his voice becoming heated. "One of these days he will wind up in the detention center in Joux-la-Ville, you will see. Last year, my new automobile tools disappeared from my shed."

"And?" Penny drawled.

"The very next week, that Jeannette was using a brand-new wrench on her bicycle. When I asked her, she denied it was mine, but she would not let me inspect it."

"That's hardly persuasive," Penny said. "You'll never convince the police that Jean murdered the old man to steal car parts. Honestly, you let your imagination run wild sometimes, Emile." She turned to Katherine. "Adele and I aren't friends, but if there's anything I can do, you'll let me know?"

"Sophie has arrived, so it may be best to wait until things have settled down," Katherine said. "The policeman in charge seems sharp. Unfortunately, he didn't share any information with us. The doctor came to verify that Albert was truly dead, which I guess they have to do legally, and there were two uniformed gendarmes there when Michael and I went over."

"You went to see what was happening?" Penny's eyebrows shot up and Emile looked envious.

"No, I mean, we went over, but only because Adele called in a panic and asked us to come. And now I'm a tiny bit worried." Penny looked her question. "They may have misunder-stood Michael and J.B., for one thing. J.B. said something about the little upset at my ladies' lunch."

"Damn him," Penny said. "What did the detective say?"

"What was this?" Emile said at the same time. "This is the fight you tell me about?"

"It wasn't a fight, really," Katherine hastened to say, real-izing she had made a tactical error. She turned to Penny. "Actually, he only made reference to the argument, didn't even say Yves was involved. And it was in front of a gendarme who didn't appear to be taking any account of our conversa-tion, and I stopped J.B. right away."

Penny's frown had reached the line between her perfectly shaped brows and she was gently chewing her lower lip. Emile was sitting on the edge of his chair, his head snapping back and forth between the two women and his expression alert.

Katherine sighed inwardly, but realized she had better finish her thought before Penny left. "I think the best thing you can do is to keep Yves away from them, and away from Sophie. Last time I saw her, I got the feeling she was still quite upset with all of us."

"Not with you, surely?" Penny said.

"Yes, I think so. You know how it is—a person who's been rejected imagines everyone is against her. Anyway, tell Yves to behave, will you? It is awkward that he and Albert had such a public falling-out right before Albert died. . . ." Her voice trailed off. She wished she knew what to do about Emile, who had a passion for gossip and was absorbing everything, as attentive as a cat with a new toy.

"That won't be hard," Penny said, getting up and pulling her cardigan around her shoulders. "He called this morning to tell me he went to an estate sale near Paris yesterday and stayed at a hotel there. He wanted me to have his assistant sit the shop today since he's not sure when he'll be back."

"But no, he was in Chablis yesterday," Emile said. "I saw him when I was driving to the new music store after lunch."

"Not him," Penny said, kissing Katherine and making her way to the steps, calling out as she went. "He went up to Paris before lunch so he could have a look at the man's library before the sale began. *Au revoir*, I'll see you later, Katherine. Let me know if I can do anything."

"I think I must tell the police about Jean," Emile said, sitting down again and running his fingers through his hair, which looked afterward as if a squirrel had used it for a nest.

Katherine, who had been hoping Emile would leave when Penny did, sat down too. "I agree with Penny, Emile. It wouldn't be right. After all, you have nothing concrete to back up your suspicion, and think of the children. What if the police took Jean in for questioning? Who would take care of them? It would be hard on Jeannette. Everything would fall on her shoulders."

Emile sniffed. "Ah, that one. She is her father's daughter. She sneaks around, you know, spying on people. I have told you, you need to watch her, dear Katherine. She takes things. Last week—"

"Jeannette's a child, for heaven's sake," Katherine said sharply, remembering her own moment of doubt and feeling obscurely guilty for it. "Please, Emile, leave the investigating to the police. Remember, there's no proof that it was anything other than an accident." She hesitated. "And, Emile, *mon ami*, I must ask you to keep our conversation about the little spat between Albert and Yves to yourself. It could so easily be misunderstood, and we don't want that. Reigny is too small to cope with people turning against each other."

" 'Spat'?" Emile said, looking confused, which might have been, Katherine realized with a stab of something like annoyance, a ploy to avoid responding to her request.

"An argument. Emile, you must give me your word. Don't discuss it with the grocery checker or the music store clerk or anyone, promise?"

Pinned down by her look, he said, *"Bien sûr*, my dear Katherine. Of course not." Eyes twinkling, he made a little zipping motion over smiling, pursed lips, a gesture that didn't entirely reassure her. He unfolded himself from his chair, waved gaily, and loped up the driveway, elbows high and out to his sides, almost as though he intended to take off flying any moment. Katherine sighed as she looked after him. She knew he was not thoroughly satisfied with the outcome of the conversation and had a hunch his mind was full of crackpot ideas to better protect his possessions from whomever was roaming his village looking for people to murder in their beds.

Katherine admitted to herself that she was uneasy also, beyond the shock of the old man's death, although she couldn't quite name what was bothering her. The possible tearing of the fabric of shared history that held the little town together, perhaps, if someone was guilty. Even the accusations were pulling at the threads that bound Reigny-sur-Canne into a community. They might not have accepted her yet, but Katherine was determined that she would find her place here. It would be too awful if Reigny was torn apart before it had become her community too. As she put out a plate of scraps from yesterday's lunch for the yellow cat and snipped some parsley from the patch next to the kitchen door, she worried that the sudden death would affect everything until the mayor and sheriff told everyone all was *normale*. Meanwhile, she told the cat, "The best thing is to focus on Reigny's fête, agreed?" It would be good for the village and show everyone, once and for all, that she was one of them. "Truth is, little one," she muttered, looking down at the oblivious animal, "we really don't have anywhere else to call home. You're stuck with us, *mon petit*." Thinking about their lack of financial options made her momentarily breathless. When her American friends e-mailed her—because no one ever wrote real letters anymore, "And don't get me started on that," she said to the cat—they told her how envious they were of her life in close proximity to Paris, eating at two-star restaurants, immersing herself in the sophisticated lives of the French.

"We make what we can of it, don't we?" she said. "And right now, I must prove my worthiness to this sophisticated crossroads in the middle of nowhere by shining at my job for the fête." It made her nervous to realize the weekend was only a month away. The townspeople would have absorbed the news of Albert's death by then, milked it for all its gossip value, and moved on, as people do. "The first battle is down the hill in Mme Pomfort's garden." She frowned at the cat. "You must wish me luck."

Katherine had looked everywhere for her shoe, half of her favorite red pair, and now she was late. She pulled on her black boots, humming tunelessly in irritation under her breath. If one of Jean's offspring had taken it . . . but why would they? Who wants one shoe? None of Jean's brood was one-legged, at least that she had noticed. Don't be unkind, she scolded herself. You sound like Emile. Their mother is dead, their father's no help. What you should do is invite the children

90

over for American-style ice-cream sundaes. She added it to her mental list of small gestures that might help civilize the feral creatures, even though reason suggested hot fudge was a dubious antidote to total parental neglect.

Snatching up her straw basket, she eased past Fideaux, napping in his usual spot in front of the door, and down the slate steps. It was only a few minutes' walk downhill to Mme Pomfort's, but the woman was a stickler about promptness, and Katherine didn't want to give her something else to complain about. Mme Pomfort wasn't crazy about Americans. Mme Pomfort wasn't crazy about anyone who wasn't French. She was even suspicious of Parisians. But she must be courted and placated because she had the highest hereditary standing in the village. If Mme Pomfort decided you were not *comme il faut*, you might not get your firewood delivered until after the first cold rain, or a good seat at the *pétanque* dinner, or her help with decorations for the fête, which was why Katherine was rushing, not even pausing to admire the clusters of tiny purple flowers that had sprung up to decorate the edge of the road.

"Here I am, Madame," Katherine called out as she reached the iron gate that guarded a neat rectangle of stuccoed house with its ground-floor shutters closed against the daylight. The door opened and the solid shape of Mme Pomfort stood framed in it, almost filling the low doorway. Madame was a widow, with nieces who came bearing covered dishes once a year. She had no pets, because, she had told Katherine sternly one day when Katherine was being dragged down the road by her two shaggy beasts, "Animals are unhealthy."

"*Bonjour*, Mme Goff, you are only a few minutes late," the old lady said with a pinched smile.

"Ah, I'm sorry, but I brought you a little something from

my garden." Katherine pulled a plastic container from the basket and held it out. "Strawberries, the first of the season."

"*Merci*, Madame. How lovely," Mme Pomfort said, pulling up a corner to peer at them. "But they do not look quite ripe."

Katherine smiled energetically, all the while thinking that's because they are the first and probably the only strawberries the little patch will produce, and we had cold days last week, and it breaks my heart to give them to someone who doesn't even want them. "It's been a cold summer."

"Indeed." The hostess parked the container on a table outside the door but didn't invite Katherine in, instead leading the way across the narrow road to a wood-fenced patch of land next to the ancient, crumbling church that sat at the center of Reigny. The building, made of undistinguished local stone, was pockmarked from centuries of exposure and neglect. The local commune opened the locked doors a few times a year for subdued christenings, weddings, funerals, and special Masses, presided over since Katherine had arrived in Reigny by a distracted African priest who had the air of someone running badly behind schedule. Mme Pomfort made a great show of producing a key to unlock the low gate into the side yard and closing it with a clatter behind them. "We'll take the sun in my garden."

Yves had explained that the Pomforts laid claim to this spot, about sixty by sixty feet, through Mme Pomfort's extended family. "Trouble is, the Robiliers insist they have a stronger claim. Mme Robilier, the woman who works in my shop, says this piece of land was granted to a great-great-great-someone-or-other when it was taken from the Church during the Revolution." Apparently, Mme Pomfort's parents erected the fence and the gate one week forty years ago during an upheaval in the Robiliers's lives, and Mme Pomfort now tended the space for at least a few minutes almost every day of the year to protect her family's position.

Yves said that this feud had been going on for generations, with the occupancy seesawing back and forth. The current resident Robiliers, whose grown children had fled for livelier places, had not been able to figure out how to strike back. There had been a spectacular move made right before World War II by M. Robilier's father, something involving a large number of pigs and chickens, that had temporarily, at least, turned the land over to them. The war, the damage done by the hated Nazi occupiers—who had taken all the livestock— and the senior Robiliers's deaths of old age had given the current Pomforts an opening; hence the fence, the gate, and the lock.

On one side, a tidy herb garden laid out in medieval fashion, its sections separated by small stones, sent out a spicy fragrance. Scraggly tomato plants leaned against the church wall behind them. On the other side of the raked path, two rows of roses, the ground under them almost scrubbed clean. Circling the perimeter on three sides, tall hollyhocks, red geraniums, and espaliered jasmine. Not a leaf out of place, Katherine thought, wondering what Madame would make of her own wild space.

"You'll have lots of flowers by the time of the fête, I expect," Katherine said, to steer the conversation toward the point as quickly as possible. "Your gladiolas are budding and your roses are blooming so much more than my own."

"One never knows. The weather, the soil. I wouldn't want to say prematurely."

"Yes, well, you see, I'm hoping that I can count on you to contribute some of your bounty to decorate the front of the stage for our little show. Your flowers are the most beautiful in the village. I could ask Mme Robilier, I guess. . . ." Katherine thought the silence might stretch to ten seconds, but Madame couldn't resist that long.

"Oh, I am sure I shall have enough to do the decor. One wishes to do one's part. Indeed, Mme Goff, I am not entirely sure I understand how you came to have such a role as you do this year. The mayor appointed you, I believe?"

Katherine was on touchy ground here. The mayor had indeed appointed her, but only after Katherine spent several months during the winter flattering him to excess, painting a portrait of his ten-year-old daughter for free, and promising Michael and Betty Lou as entertainment. Mme Pomfort would never approve of an American taking such an important role as entertainment producer, so Katherine had had to lobby for it away from the widow's hawklike attention.

"*Oui*, Madame, I am so honored, but I think it was most likely because of my husband's talent and the famous singer with whom he is recording a new album, you know." She dared to lock eyes with the old woman for a moment.

"A commune festival with a foreign entertainment. The next thing we know it will be Gypsies. What is to become of poor little Reigny, once the home of great families?" Madame cocked her head to one side and sighed like a true tragedienne.

"Not at all, Madame, *je vous assure*. After all, Michael and I live in Reigny, don't we?" Katherine bit her tongue to stop from mentioning Penny, who might be called a resident but who was surely on Madame's list of alien invaders. On the spot, Katherine decided the inclusion of another foreigner would have to wait. Pippa would not be asked to sell wine.

"Yes, well," was all Mme Pomfort said before moving as swiftly as politeness allowed to the real reason she deigned to speak to Katherine this morning. "I have already delivered some potted jasmine to poor Adele. You have seen her? She was resting when I called on her."

"She's terribly upset," Katherine said. "She's not seeing anyone. Sophie is with her."

"Ah, Sophie, yes," Madame said, making it sound like a problem, which, Katherine supposed, it probably was, Sophie being so dramatic and so delicate.

"Poor Albert, it was a horrible way to die." Katherine waited for the village's unofficial social leader to press discreetly for details so she could emphasize the accidental nature of the tragedy.

There was a silence while Madame examined her hands. Her left hand, Katherine noticed, held the thinnest of gold bands. Then she said in a murmur, "One does not like to speak ill, one wishes to be polite. He was, however, a German."

Katherine squeezed her jaws together, willing herself not to leap into this and further threaten her relationship with Reigny's arbiter of social life. She had to remember the plaques she saw everywhere, nailed over doorways and on posts at the intersections of the smallest roads, memorials to French patriots. Maquisards, they were called, locals organized into de Gaulle's French National Resistance, who had been summarily shot on this or that spot by the Nazis during the occupation. The people here, living on the edge of the Morvan's forested hillsides, had paid dearly for their support of the Resistance fighters and were, Katherine understood, still sensitive, especially the ones whose fathers, aunts and uncles, or grandparents had not survived. Who was she to criticize them?

"Albert would have been awfully young to have been a

soldier even if he had still been in Germany," she said in hopes of softening any implied guilt without ruffling Madame's feathers. "His family was living in Switzerland, Mme Bellegarde told me."

A sniff, and then, "The Nazis sent very young officers into the occupied zone near the end. There is no proof of where Monsieur was living. Read your history, Mme Goff, read your history. But of course a naturalized citizen is not the same thing as a French person in any case." Madame said this dismissively and with another audible sniff. "I would not be surprised if his death was traced back to his business. You have heard about it?"

"The police haven't told Adele anything different from what she believes, that he fell on those uneven stone steps in the back quarter of the château, perhaps even had a heart attack which caused him to collapse."

"He was a merchant," Madame continued as if Katherine had not spoken, "of German-made guns and ammunition. Young Yves told me last year that he is known as a man whose riches came directly from supporting police states. A man like that must have many enemies." Mme Pomfort spoke with triumph, as if she had parsed a secret reason for Albert's death while sitting among her rosemary and roses.

"I wouldn't know anything about that," Katherine managed. "He lives—lived—here so quietly."

"Monsieur Robilier, that is, the Robilier who died before you arrived, not the current one, was a German sympathizer. I believe his mother was German."

Katherine waited for some explanation of why this was relevant, but Madame merely looked at her with an expression that seemed to say this explained everything, or at least something. Katherine fiddled with the fraying brim of her straw hat, wondering how to get back to a neutral topic before she offended Madame. Michael would be furious if the firewood was late again this year, so soon after Katherine had figured out what to do to ensure delivery by early October, when the nights got chilly.

There was nothing to do but plunge in. "Well, thank you so much for offering to do the stage flowers. I am sure everyone who comes will notice how elegant they are."

"Will the gendarmes be interviewing anyone in town, do you think?" Madame said, not ready to let go of her conviction that an enemy of a war profiteer, or perhaps another German—her theory was a bit fuzzy—had snuck into Albert's castle in the middle of the night and dispatched him.

"I really don't know. There is an officer from the gendarmerie assigned to investigate, so perhaps he will ask Henri to check with everyone about their whereabouts." Maybe that was it. Mme Pomfort wanted an excuse to grill the sheriff, and the suggestion of foul play might be her strategy to get Henri's attention.

"My whereabouts are hardly the issue." Madame's veined hand flew to the scarf neatly tied at her throat.

Katherine's shoulders slumped. Really, she could not seem to avoid insulting her neighbor. It was bad enough being American, having a French accent that sounded more like Paris than Burgundy when it didn't sound like California. But to also have a husband whose guitar playing, gentle as it was, managed to trickle in Madame's open windows on warm summer nights was too much. Mme Pomfort had instructed Henri the sheriff to demand that Michael be silent by dinnertime, Madame's five-o'clock dinnertime. Henri had been unwilling to go that far, but he had hesitantly asked the celebrity musician living among them if he could choose only *"les ballades tranquilles"* in the evenings. She wondered if Pippa, hidden away in her cottage at the opposite end of town, annoyed Madame as much as she, Katherine, seemed to, or if the young woman cared half as much as Katherine did.

"Of course not. I only meant that they will ask all of us whatever they think will help explain what happened. Adele is miserable, and Sophie is struggling with what needs to be done."

"C'est tragique," Madame said, more in judgment than pity, rising to walk Katherine to the gate, which she opened with a flourish. "It may well prove to be a criminal associate come to get revenge for a double cross. Or something like that," she finished, less certain of the specific motive than of the truth that a stranger had invaded Reigny-sur-Canne's peaceful existence. "In any case, he will have fled long ago."

CHAPTER 9

Katherine promised herself every day that she would not have a glass of wine until five o'clock, and then only one. There were times, many of them, when circumstances beyond her control almost required that she break her rule. Mme Pomfort's company might have tempted her by itself, but when the kitchen door slapped shut behind her, she heard voices and realized they had company. J. B. Holliday's voice would make a decibel measure tremble anywhere, but it was particularly difficult to deal with in a small, enclosed space like their living room, never mind what he was saying. And what he was saying made Katherine reach without conscious thought for a tumbler and fill it to the brim. She took a big gulp and ruined her entrance into the conversation by having some of it go down her throat the wrong way so that she coughed and sputtered for a full minute.

"Hey, Kathy," J.B. said over her distress. "I'd get up but I'm too damned comfortable. Tell this husband of yours I can make him a rich man, indeed I can." The record producer had settled into the only large, upholstered seat in the room, the chaise usually shared by Katherine and one of the dogs, and she doubted very much if J.B. could get up at all, much less bobbing up to be polite.

She glanced at Michael. Being married to someone a long time was helpful at moments like this. He hated talking about money because, she had long realized, it underscored his embarrassment at having none. It was his style to carry a roll of bills and to peel them off easily when she asked him to pay for the beef roast or the incredibly cheap silver tongs she found at a flea market table, but that was small stuff. He couldn't afford, say, a new car if the Citroën had engine problems. Right now, with J.B. talking like a big shot who had plenty of money and large investment ideas, Michael needed rescuing.

"J.B., I've been meaning to ask you about that handsome son of yours. He's a sweet boy, but I wonder if he should be a little more careful when he's on that board thing and flying down the hill? What if a van is coming around the corner, or an unwary tourist who's already lost and confused, since any tourist who winds up here surely is lost?"

Michael's shoulders relaxed a bit. J.B. chuckled from some deep place, a little like a motor turning over. "Brett? That boy'll be the death of me yet, but I sincerely doubt he'll die in the process. I live for the day he's old enough to set loose on the world, I tell you. These days, if he's not raising hell somewhere else, he's hanging around that girl who lives in the house with the junk-filled yard. She's something else, that one. All tease and no mistake." He laughed, slapped one hand on his thigh, and winked at Katherine.

Was Brett making some kind of play for Jeannette? The thought made Katherine uneasy. Brett was seventeen and American, raised on hip-hop, sexy movies, and God knows what else, which made him seem older. His parents may have tried to counter the popular trends, but his mother confessed to Katherine that he'd been caught with some pot back in the States when he was only sixteen. Meanwhile, Jeannette was motherless and naive. It was too much to expect her father would care. He'd probably see Brett's attentions as an opportunity, although Katherine refused to define to herself what she meant by that. Katherine moved a talk with Jeannette to the top of her growing list of projects for the next couple of weeks.

"She's young," was all she said. "I think it would be a good idea to mention the possibility of oncoming traffic to the boy, though. Michael, we're due at Adele's in fifteen minutes, sorry as I am to break up your visit."

Michael opened his mouth, no doubt to protest having to go into that gloomy house again so soon, but Katherine caught his eye and he shut his mouth abruptly and stood.

"Don't want to keep you from the widow's side, for sure." J.B. started the process of rising from the chaise, windmilling one arm while the other clamped onto the seat. Michael went to the door to whistle the dogs in as J.B. patted a file folder on the chaise. "I'll leave this with you, Mike, and we can talk about it when you come over for rehearsal. I'm telling you, this will be a gold mine. You'll leave those Crazy Leopards in the dust."

Michael mumbled something Katherine couldn't hear as the two men walked out to the SUV with her trailing behind them.

J.B. turned around. "Say, Kathy, any developments over there, at the castle, I mean? I'm guessing the cops must be finished by now."

"Still investigating, although Adele has been assured it's really a formality."

"Good, good. I'm chewing on what I should do about that deal we had going. Maybe I should meet the widow."

"I think Sophie Bellegarde, her daughter, is pretty much running the business right now."

"That right? Well, we'll see. No big rush, right, Mike? We're good to go on our deal." He slapped Michael's shoulder and lifted himself into the driver's seat, tapping his horn several times as he backed out of the driveway. She started to drag out a long hose for watering before she remembered her white lie that they were supposed to be leaving for Adele's in a few minutes. Instead, she ducked back into the kitchen and topped off her wineglass. It was five minutes after five, so she was on solid ground with her conscience.

As she rooted around in the refrigerator for something to go into a casserole other than celery root or cabbage for the third or fourth time this week, she wondered if she would enjoy having lots of money. On days when rainwater dripped into the corner of her studio or when she didn't have the train fare to go to Paris to catch an exhibition, yes, she admitted to herself, she wished they had more money. But there was always enough for the small finds she uncovered at the flea markets, which were her main entertainment until the cold of autumn shut them down, and for paints and canvases, which occupied her the rest of the year.

Michael, on the other hand, had never let go entirely of the bitterness of betrayal that began when the four musicians he had counted as his best friends went on to form the Crazy Leopards all those years ago, leaving him behind but taking with them the two songs that he had written, which would make them famous. He never talked about it now, but when the washing machine needed parts, or Jean wanted too much for repairing the low wall along the edge of their property, she knew some festering heat rose in him for what might have been. Probably it wasn't the money, but the public insult that made him hard to live with at times. "The past is never over, is it?" she said to the cat, which had nosed open the door and was checking the dogs' dishes for leftovers.

"Man, he drives me crazy at times," Michael said, shooing the cat out gently with one boot a few minutes later as he joined Katherine in the kitchen and reached around her to open the battered old refrigerator. Opening a bottle of beer, he headed out to the patio.

"What's the deal he's talking about? An album with you?" she called, rinsing a knife and setting a pot of onions and beef on the stove. When they had browned a bit, she would sacrifice a half bottle of the heady Burgundy she'd picked up the other day at the little cave in Noyers, a small miracle of Pinot grapes aged and bottled thirty kilometers from her kitchen stove.

"No, a new digital studio in Memphis, which he claims would be completely booked with big musicians for their next albums."

"He came to you for money? Why in the world would he think we had any to spare?"

"No, not quite. He wants introductions."

"Introductions? To whom?"

"Who do you think?"

"Eric? The Leopards? You told him no, of course?"

"Told him I didn't have any pull. He mentioned the business with 'Raging Love.' Not sure how he heard about that." Michael looked at his wife, who had stopped what she was doing and come to stand in the doorway.

"I'm sure I didn't. I mean, I don't think I've ever had a conversation with him . . . oh, damn. Maybe I did, but it was under the influence of too much good wine the first time we had dinner at the house they rented, and I'm not even sure what I said, only that you had proven your point with Eric."

"I thought we agreed that's over and done with. I got the hundred thousand in the settlement, and there's no more to be had. Now you've gone and opened up a can of worms."

"Darling, I am sorry if I said anything I shouldn't," Katherine said, coming out and kissing the top of his head. "It couldn't have been much. I was probably name-dropping. You know me, I want everyone to know how talented you are and that you were in the music business at such an interesting time."

"You could just as easily say I was in the construction business, since that's what I did for ten years after the Leopards dropped me. Moved lumber and nailed studs, more the true story of my career. If I hadn't hurt my back, that's what I'd be doing right now." He moved his head away, took a long drink from the bottle, and looked up at her hovering over him. "I wasn't in the music business, not in any way that means something today."

"You were, and you still are. You're writing songs and I know you'll sell some soon."

"Kay, it pisses me off when you do something like this, you know that. I don't want to talk about the Leopards, about Eric, about those songs. It's history. Now, what if J.B. makes my begging Eric for a favor part of any deal to record new material? Your bringing the old stuff up could kill any new chance I have."

Ever since they settled in Reigny, Katherine had fought occasional moments of panic where she saw vividly that she would be lost without Michael. Her instinct since childhood was to run from anything even remotely uncomfortable, and, thousands of miles from their past life, he was the only one she could run to. When they argued, which they rarely did, the ground shifted ominously underneath her.

She retreated into the house, leaned down, and petted the cat, which had taken over the chaise vacated by J.B. It jumped up at the violent nature of her strokes and stalked away. It wasn't her fault if that annoying man had pumped her for information to the point where she couldn't help mentioning the Crazy Leopards and Michael's brilliant songwriting. Damn that J.B. anyway. She wanted to like him, if only for what he was doing for her husband, but he had a big mouth.

CHAPTER 10

Penny laughed. "You'll be blamed for everything that goes wrong. The wine, the tablecloths, the wind, Emile's singing. It'll all be that American woman's fault. That's what I always feel when I come down here, as though everyone's gloating over my mistakes."

Katherine had taken advantage of a glorious day to drag out her easel and continue working on the painting that was giving her fits. The sheets were flapping on the clothesline, the ripe cherries that hadn't been claimed by the birds were in a bowl on the kitchen counter, and a chance meeting with a farmer's wife at the *poubelle*, where big plastic recycling and garbage bins were lined up for community use, had netted her a volunteer assistant for the set-painting job at the fête. But Penny's dire predictions about the possible outcome of her big play for becoming a successful event producer made her stomach flutter.

There was no word yet on the cause of Albert's death, no one was gossiping, at least not to her, about the gun, Michael was still in a touchy mood, and her work for the painting show wasn't going well. She had almost decided to call the difficult painting *Poor Little Lambs*, although that might not explain the tractor. She could have done without Penny and Yves showing up for a chat.

Penny obviously didn't have enough to do, and Yves? He needed to feel he was being admired, and so trailed along with Penny while he enjoyed his long midday break from the shop. He had come over at Penny's insistence to apologize for the drama he'd caused, he explained, and having said that much, said nothing more, certainly not that he was sorry. Now they were talking of happier things, like the fête.

"Mistakes?" Katherine knew what the villagers thought of her friend but was surprised that Penny had absorbed any of the muttered insults uttered in slangy French that trailed behind her as she walked through her renovation-in-progress.

"Oh, you know. The lap pool went over some invisible line in the creek, the sound system on the patio kept an old lady from her beauty sleep at nine P.M. Whatever I do to improve the property, it always seems to offend somebody, and people around here gossip all day long."

"They were worried they would lose their access to the fishing spot below the mill, and this is such a quiet village, tucked into a little valley of sorts, that any amplified music can seem too loud. Henri even spoke to Michael about his guitar playing."

Penny rolled her eyes. "Such a dull place, not at all what I expected. If it weren't for you and Michael, I would move in a heartbeat."

"But wait, not because of me, *cherie*? I am heartbroken." Yves, parked in the rattan chair, placed one hand over his heart, or where it would be, Katherine thought, if he actually had one.

Penny chose to ignore his comment, but said to him instead,

"I'm not sure I'm up for a duet with you, so what will you sing? Not that ridiculous number about yourself, I hope."

"Why do you call it ridiculous?" Yves said, his voice rising. "It is a classic troubadour's storytelling. I add to it for every performance so that it is the ongoing saga of my adventures. It is a song tradition. All cultures have it."

"Maybe." Penny shrugged. "But it's usually not about the singer." She made a small shape of irritation with her mouth. "I mean, how egotistical is that?"

"I won't let you criticize my project," Yves said, pointing a long finger at her. "I said something insignificant about . . ." His voice trailed off and his finger moved hesitantly toward the treetops.

"Precisely," Penny snapped. "Insignificant. A casual insult shared with the whole world, and through a microphone, no less."

Yves shrugged. "You take things too personally. It was not the whole world but a little party, and it was not about you, it was about life in general. All I said—"

"—was that you were not interested in old women."

"*Non, non*, my dear Penny. I have explained to you that I was talking about—how do you say it, Katherine—the girls from one's past, *les vieilles copines*?"

"Bad enough either way, but don't let's quarrel," Katherine said, her face close to the canvas as she frowned at her version of a tractor, which seemed more baroque on the canvas than when she had sketched it in the pasture. She guessed that her friends were in the prickly stage of making up from a quarrel in which Penny had undoubtedly told Yves they were finished, and Yves had agreed and now they were faced with finding a way to justify getting together again before Penny left her Americanized French house in October for her French-themed apartment in Chicago. It was their way, Katherine thought with an inward sigh. With few suitably aged, unattached people in the neighborhood and no desire to expend the effort of finding a mate farther abroad, Penny and Yves would keep circling each other, at least until their physical passion was consummated. She wondered if they were having an affair. They behaved more like people in the flirtation stage of a relationship. In her and Michael's day, no one questioned the idea that sex was as much a part of beginning a relationship as was sharing one's drugs or food. It led to problems, that free-for-all approach, but on balance she thought it was preferable to this pouting. As it was, Katherine understood her role was to be the audience for their posturing. Right now, she was impatient.

"Penny, what do you think? Does this look like the mayor's tractor from where you sit?"

"It's lovely, Katherine. Don't worry," said Penny, who hadn't bothered to glance at the painting. "You worry far too much about these things. It's a new gallery and they're not particular at all. Oh, I didn't mean that the way it came out," she said as Katherine straightened up and turned toward her.

Katherine felt a flush of something like anger warm her face, and forced herself to take a deep, slow breath. Children, she reminded herself. Penny and Yves were emotionally the equivalent of ten-year-olds, charming but thoughtless, likable but unable to see that the world didn't absolutely revolve around themselves. She needed to be patient. She was, after all, a professional artist with an advanced degree, preparing for a solo show in a good gallery in a region of la belle France that prized art, for heaven's sake.

"Voilà. You see?" Yves said, his voice rising. "These little meanings, they are not what they seem. So, darling Penny, you must remember that and make up." He jumped up, pinned Penny in her chair, kissed her noisily on the lips, and stood straight, brushing his fallen locks off his face. She glared at him for an instant, then softened.

"I'm sorry, *cherie*," she said to Katherine, who was standing still, a brush suspended in her hand. "I meant to be encouraging, but obviously went quite wrong. It's a lovely sky, the painting is sweet and quite pastoral in its theme, and we are going to drown you in compliments and Crémant de Bourgogne at the opening. And now, if there is no more news about the Bellegarde scandal, I must go."

"Scandal? Don't be ridiculous, Penny. You sound like Pippa Hathaway, trolling for mystery and mayhem in all of this."

"What does she know about it?" Penny said.

"Nothing. She is apparently interested in finding something that might make a good story, and stopped me, practically drooling with curiosity."

"Did she run you down with her little car?" Yves said. "She drives through town like the demon, you know?"

"No, she said she was out for a walk, but I think she was really looking for news. She'd seen the police cars."

"I hadn't met her before your party. Does she live here all year?" Penny said.

"I'm not sure. She says her father lives in London."

"She plans to go to London for one month every year," Yves said, and the women turned to him, the same question in their eyes. "She paid Mme Robilier to feed the cats and hold her mail in April. Madame says the cats are too shy to be petted and only peek from under the lilac hedge when she puts their food out."

Penny shrugged impatiently, and kissed Katherine and

Yves. "Unless Adele was having an affair with my plumber and pushed her bossy husband down the stairs to get rid of him, I really don't think Albert's death qualifies as a mystery. Although," she added as she started down the flagstone steps, "I can see why someone might be tempted to give the old man a shove."

"Quit it, Penny," Katherine said in protest, but there was no answer, and in a second, the iron gate screeched in a protest of its own as Penny closed it.

CHAPTER 11

The rain that flattened her hollyhocks during the night drifted off with the sunrise. Steam rose from the garden and snails glided across the stone steps in glistening lines. Katherine's shoes were wet from an hour spent tying up the tall flower stalks before breakfast. "I don't know why I bother," she said to Michael. "I suppose one might say it was vanity. Everyone else's hollyhocks will be a mess."

"Do we have to go to Serein today?" Michael said, putting his treasured Gibson acoustic guitar back on its stand. "We got enough cheese to last a week at the market yesterday and I know you'll want me to drive you over to some other flea market next weekend. I want to work on a new song."

"Between the lunch guests and the dogs, the cheese is pretty well gone, which is a tragedy given that it was so expensive. Anyway. L'Isle-sur-Serein's *vide-grenier* is huge, one of the biggest flea markets all summer, and I read that they're having a carnival *'avec géants du Nord.'* You know, giant puppets? I told your friends we would show them a bit of the local color."

"They're not friends, Kay, so much as they're possible

business partners. And they haven't shown any interest in rustic ceremonies as far as I can tell."

"Well, yes, but that's the point, darling. They should be interested. Ancient village customs and all that. We agreed we'd meet at the river, near the statue of Saint Somebody-or-Other at noon."

"I could live without the parade. Last year's was more than enough."

Katherine laughed as she pulled on dry shoes, stood up, and executed a quick tap step. "I know, really silly. Reigny's fête will be more sophisticated and we won't have a parade, thank heavens."

Michael grunted. "You'd have to dig bodies up from the graveyard to get enough people for a parade here."

"Don't be ghoulish, darling. It makes my skin crawl. After all the recent drama here, I don't have the appetite for anything other than some mindless fun."

Two hours later, Katherine had walked purposefully, if slowly, down one long street in the medieval town that backed up to a river shallow in the summer. Along the way, she had accumulated a black-fringed shawl warm enough for the coming winter days, two old books with illustrations worth studying, and a pincushion studded with round-headed pins. "Perfect," she said, holding it up in triumph. "Only one euro."

Michael wandered over to a table piled with what looked to Katherine like rusty junk, but which turned out to be the hiding place of a small table vise and a hammer. "But Michael, you have at least four hammers in the shed already," Katherine said, puzzled.

"You can never have too many hammers."

"Well, it looks as though this man did," she said, waving her arm toward the piles on the table. She reminded herself that she already had several black shawls and that perhaps it would be best not to make an issue about hammers. It's the fun of finding treasures, after all, she thought as she hurried to keep up with his long strides.

At noon, they were sitting under chestnut trees on the stone wall overlooking the river, looking for the Hollidays. At twelve fifteen, Michael got up. "Can we go now? If they're here, we'll bump into them, but I'm hungry."

The little café across from the river was busy, but they squeezed into a corner table under the awning and had the *plat du jour*, nine euros' worth of salad and a bit of chicken under sauce, decorated by a small boiled potato. Still no sign of the Americans, and the sound of a loudspeaker and raucous singing was coming closer. Katherine gathered up her purchases and they picked their way down the steps and into a large crowd moving sluggishly along the street next to the river.

Two crude, ten-foot-tall puppets led the villagers, their papier-mâché faces and sloppy costumes causing laughter and applause. "What are they supposed to be?" Michael said.

"Women, maybe saints? Although they don't look very holy to me," Katherine said.

Behind the figures was a rudimentary float, a truck with an open back on which two old men dressed as women sat holding on to the equipment that was providing the sound. They held up wineglasses as they sang, or, rather, yelled, along with the music.

"Can you make out what they're singing?" Katherine said, as much to herself as to Michael. The quality of the speakers was so bad—loud and fuzzy—that Katherine couldn't catch the words of the song. The live chorus belting out the words on the street in back of the truck wasn't much better. But it was a parade, and parades always made her want to rush into the crowd and become part of the moment. She straightened her back, tilted her head to one side, and began a jaunty shuffle and riff step in her hard-soled boots, hampered by the flea market finds she was holding. Grinning at the passing crowd, she was feeling part of the fun until a pinch-faced woman standing nearby looked sharply at her, and the moment was spoiled. She stilled her feet and felt, as she was wont to do when faced with seeming disapproval, foolish and old. The feeling didn't go away when the woman took off down the street in the opposite direction from the raggedy rows of cross-dressing men.

The dancers were exclusively men dressed as bizarre parodies of females. The large group danced in formation, having rehearsed some vague choreography that called for periodically waving one leg in the air in unison and throwing their arms high above wigged heads. Most of the heavily made-up men carried old-fashioned pocketbooks, which were either slipped into their armpits or swung wildly around their heads when they raised their arms, causing bystanders to duck and howl with laughter. Wine had been drunk and inhibitions set aside, and the result, Katherine decided, was not what she looked for in a summer fête.

Suddenly, a hand grabbed her arm and she almost lost the pincushion.

"Mme Goff," roared a six-foot-tall character in a red wig, a tentlike dress, and a frightening smear of brilliant orange lipstick.

Squinting, Katherine looked up at the clownish figure. Could it be—yes, it was—the nice mechanic who had brought their Citroën back to life at least twice last year. "Is that you, Nick? Look, Michael," she said, determined not to be stuck with a drunken car repairman on her own. But Nick-the-Female had already broken contact and was prancing across the road, joining hands with another fellow and shouting out the refrain of the song with glee.

Looking at the goods being offered from people's closets and attics was impossible in the chaos and she was about to suggest to Michael that they give up and go home. But at that moment a particularly loud uproar from the bystanders made her turn. A young man, swarthy and muscular behind his platinum tresses and five-o'clock shadow, had begun a flirtatious dance with someone on the sidelines. The dancer grinned, tossed back his mane of ill-fitting hair, and stroked his huge false breasts, which were set, Katherine noted, so high on his chest as to be a joke in themselves. He shimmied over to his target on high-heeled shoes, mincing as the tight skirt hobbled his normal movements.

Whomever he was pretending to romance reached out and grabbed at the breasts. The dancer mugged in pretend horror, holding his handbag up as if to hit the lecher.

"Michael, look. Isn't that Brett fooling around with the guy in drag?" At this moment, in the heat of the afternoon and with the adrenaline of the crowd feeding him, the teenager's cheeks were flushed, his lips were rosy, and his hair flopped over his forehead. He reminded Katherine of the surly models that decorated perfume ads for scents with names like Perversion and Trouble. The bystanders clapped and the dancer skittered back, still smiling and waggling a finger to admonish his would-be seducer as he melted back into the line of dancers moving down the street in a loose rhythm, shouting out their song. "Betty Lou and J.B. must be around. We should say hi." But Michael was half a block away, moving in the other direction.

"Too crowded," was all he said over his shoulder. Katherine didn't protest. He was right, and, anyway, once her husband made up his mind, he was unlikely to budge. The route away from the parade was quieter, and Katherine had time to consider buying a hat (too loose on her head), a pair of gloves (too tight on her hands), and a pair of garden boots (so large she couldn't take a step in them) before the tables set up against the stone houses tapered off and then disappeared.

Later, as they wove their way among the cars parked in someone's field, Katherine saw a knot of teenagers clustered near the far corner, screeching with laughter. "It's the Hollidays' boy again. What's he doing?" she said, reaching out to tap Michael's arm. The boy had taken off his shirt, his hair had fallen onto his face, and while she watched, he upended a beer bottle and drank deeply. Someone in the group whooped and tried to grab the bottle, but the boy lifted it out of reach with one hand while lowering his other shoulder and butting the other kid. All of a sudden, the chatter turned into something more urgent.

"Michael," Katherine began.

"No, Kay." Obviously, he had seen it too. "They're old enough to deal with it themselves. From what J.B. and Betty Lou say, he's due for a lesson. J.B. will be around somewhere." He unlocked their car, slid into the driver's seat, and started the engine. She had no choice but to duck into her seat.

As they pulled away and bounced down the makeshift lane between the cars, she twisted her head to watch the group. A shoving match had broken out and she got a glimpse of the bare-chested American boy glaring at someone. Then she saw J.B., immediately recognizable by his Hawaiian shirt, heading over to the group. A few other people in the vicinity had turned to watch.

"Poor Betty Lou," Katherine said as they left the town behind them and zoomed along a narrow back road between plowed fields. "I don't envy her.

"I meant to ask you. You said Betty Lou's music isn't popular anymore. Then why is she making another album?"

"It's the style that's gone out of fashion—country music without rock. Still, she's the best of her kind still recording, and she has a core of fans who'll buy anything she puts out. She's an icon, like Tammy Wynette or Dolly Parton. J.B. and I are trying to persuade her to move a little toward country rock. She's a pro and she still has a great sound."

Katherine heard the warmth in her husband's response and a little voice inside her wondered if it was too late to take singing lessons. Michael respected her for her commitment to painting, but it was hard to tell if he liked the work or was merely being supportive of her for trying. She picked at the fringe of her new shawl. "Then I guess we'll be spending more time with them?"

"I wouldn't mind getting a shot at recording something with her," Michael said, "but I have to wait and see. We need more time before J.B. says we're ready, if he ever does."

Katherine opened her mouth but couldn't figure out what to say. She was afraid of sounding too eager and making him feel worse later if it came to nothing. Again. Still, her husband and the singer were spending a lot of time together, in the intimate way musicians do when they're making music. Fortunately, Betty Lou was not as pretty as her voice. Michael had always liked pretty women, and the fact that he was five years his wife's junior, which hadn't mattered a thing when they fell in love, had begun to make her a little self-conscious at odd moments. She reached up and smoothed her hair away from her forehead, lifted her chin, and sat up straighter. Yes, she wanted Michael to have another chance. He had suffered more than he would admit. But she had an uneasy feeling about these summer visitors who seemed destined to be part of their lives, at least for a few months. She would be careful not to ally herself too closely with them. Mme Pomfort would be watching.

CHAPTER 12

Jeannette wiped the dirt from Mme Pomfort's vegetable bed off the stolen tomato before biting into it. Juice squirted onto her T-shirt, but no matter. She would rinse the shirt in the morning. It was quiet tonight. The stars were visible when you turned away from the cluster of houses with lights on and looked instead over the fields. Late night was her favorite time in the summer. It was warm, her brothers were in bed, and her father was usually at the café or home sleeping off the wine he'd drunk. People had their inside lights on and their windows open, which made spying easier. No one suspected she was entertaining herself this way.

She grinned. She was probably the only one in Reigny who knew that the husband and wife who moved into his family's old farmhouse and were trying to start a cheese business had just found out they were going to have a baby. She had had to stuff her hand into her mouth, hidden behind the oleander bush outside their parlor window, to keep from laughing out loud when the husband put his big ear against his wife's belly and cried when she told him the news.

Mme Pomfort had been watching *Danse avec les Stars* and eating strawberries, holding each berry up to the light of her

120

table lamp to inspect it with a deep frown before popping it in her mouth.

Yves's house was dark, but there wasn't anything to see in any case since he lived upstairs, above what had been the parlor and dining room but was now his bookstore. When she had started dropping in for lack of anything better to do, he had explained that he didn't have children's books or magazines, or anything she might like to read. She had stolen a book anyway. It wasn't so bad, old-fashioned, but a good story about a mysterious masked man who was in prison for years and who turned out to be the twin brother of the king of France. It had been handy to know about because she could tell it to the little ones before bedtime and get them to quiet down. She had memorized the author's name so that if she had the chance, she could pinch another story by him.

She avoided spying on the witch's house at the far end of the village. It sat at the bottom of a long, wooded driveway and the back end of the house seemed to disappear into the forest of the Morvan. The forest was a bad place to go, filled with ghosts of the fighters killed there by the Boche in the war, her father once told her. The witch was really only a strange lady who spoke English with a funny accent and who had a hundred cats—well, maybe not a hundred, but a lot. One night, though, when Jeannette had gotten up her courage and tiptoed down to look in a window from across the grass, the woman had looked out, right into Jeannette's eyes. Then she smiled and waved as if to say, "Come here." Jeannette had run all the way up the driveway, up the street, and home without stopping, frightened by what she couldn't say. She hadn't been down there at night since, and though the woman drove past her at top speed often in her red car, she never seemed to see Jeannette and never waved at her again.

She hadn't seemed so scary at Katherine's lunch party. Maybe her evil side came out only at night.

Thinking about that scary night, she shivered as she walked up the street toward the sharp curve in the road, taking care to step only on the grass so she wouldn't make noise.

One of her favorite stops on her nighttime prowls was Mme and M. Goff's house. They usually sat on their patio with a light on, and if Katherine wasn't talking or reading aloud, he was playing the guitar softly and singing. Her mood lightened as she walked. Jeannette knew who he really was, of course. Like the man in the mask, he was in a kind of disguise, pretending to be nobody when he was really a famous rock-and-roll singer. Her suspicions were confirmed when Brett's father arrived to start recording an album in secret. Why else would they be here?

Brett had not told her much except that his mother was a professional singer who used to be famous before he was born. He told her that at their home in America, there were big posters of his mother on the walls. She was thin then, Brett said, and had dark hair down to her waist. There were pictures of her with famous people; at least Brett said they were famous. Most of the names meant nothing to Jeannette although she'd never admit it. But Mick Jagger, yes, she knew about him, of course. Mick Jagger, the Rolling Stones. Think of it, Brett's mother was friends with the Stones, and now she was Brett's girlfriend and Michael's friend, also, and Michael was Brett's mother's friend, which proved Michael was famous. Maybe Reigny was not such a bad place to live.

She melted into the overgrown lilacs that bordered Katherine's fenced garden. The lilacs were finished blooming, but roses spilled over the fence and scented the air. Before the

Goffs planted them, Jeannette and the older of her brothers used to climb the fence. Now, the roses had too many sharp thorns and the gate creaked, which made the dogs bark, so if she couldn't climb into the pear tree unobserved, like she did sometimes at night, she couldn't get closer to the house.

The dogs must be sleeping, she thought, as she sat on the stone step below the gate to listen. The words of the song he was singing softly were in English and his odd accent made it hard for her to understand what they were. But the music was so cool, like something you'd hear on a CD or watch a band perform on TV. Katherine's voice cut into the song, and she sounded upset. "J.B. must have gotten to you. You've been singing that for the last hour."

He said something that Jeannette couldn't hear, then Katherine spoke again. "Have you thought about how we'll fund a trip back? Will J B. pay for it as part of the promotion?"

"He'll have to even if he takes it out of profits from the tour. But I'm not sure I can do it. What about the dogs?"

There was silence for a minute and then Jeannette heard Katherine's laugh, which sounded like a pony she once rode at a traveling fair. "You're joking. You are joking, aren't you? Turn down a chance to poke a stick in Eric's eye because of the dogs?"

Jeannette wasn't sure she'd heard right about hitting someone with a stick, but then she heard her own name.

"Jeannette can feed and walk the dogs. The girl could use a little spending money of her own. God knows her father's not giving her any." And after something else Michael said that Jeannette couldn't hear even though she had crept up so close a rose thorn was poking into her hair, "She's plenty capable. She looks after those boys on her own, and she's almost fifteen. Anyway, we'll worry about that when we come to it. The important thing is this is your chance, darling, and you have to take it."

The guitar playing had stopped and Jeannette heard a chair scraping back on the patio stones and then the kitchen door banging shut. The Goffs had retreated to their house and from here it was impossible to follow what they were saying. To make it worse, the door squeaked open again and she heard the snuffling sounds of the dogs headed down the path to the garden gate. Silently, Jeannette slipped away, back down the street. Take care of those dogs? She wasn't sure she liked the idea, but the money, yes. It would be nice to have money of her own. Maybe she'd buy a new dress or save for a bus ticket to the Riviera, if buses went there.

That reminded her of Brett. She wondered if Brett knew that his father had gone to see the German man in the château the night he died. It had been so late that the living room lights in all the houses in the center of Reigny were out. But Brett's family were staying in a big house farther out, one she never spied on because it would have been too long a walk in the dark to get there and back. She had ducked off the road and into the trees opposite the Bellegardes' driveway when she saw the car lights approaching. But Brett had said nothing about his father having been there, so Jeannette decided not to mention it for now. She didn't want to upset Brett, and he had already made a sarcastic remark about her creeping around.

She yawned. Nothing more to see tonight, and the little ones would be jumping on her bed early in the morning, always wanting to eat and to be entertained. Time to go home.

CHAPTER 13

Katherine was preparing a salad of new potatoes, red and white rocket-shaped radishes, and the fat white asparagus she had splurged on at the outdoor market in Avallon. She had also indulged her taste buds with two delicious, lumpy "sausage of the Morvan" at the charcuterie, seduced by the twinkling owner, whose brisk, smiling wife had wrapped them up in white paper before Katherine could think about the damage to her shopping budget. There was a knock on the door. She finished unwrapping a little pillow of goat cheese, a tangy *crottin de chevre,* and looked up. It was still early enough that the morning sun was shining behind the visitor. It took Katherine a moment to recognize Sophie Bellegarde.

"*Bonjour,* Sophie," she said, wiping her hands on her apron and steering the young woman to the wicker chairs under the pear tree since there was not enough room to invite her into the tiny kitchen. She was curious. Sophie had never been very social and, since her disappointment with Yves, wasn't friendly because, Katherine surmised, she believed the Americans were sure to be on Penny's side in the romantic tug-of-war over Yves's affection.

"I had to talk to someone who knows what's going on.

I hope you don't mind," Sophie said. "My mother has decided we will both be murdered in our beds, the woman who owns the boulangerie in the next village was muttering about Gypsies when I went in for a baguette, and Father's office has called to say they need someone to sign for a shipment of wheel bearings coming in from Frankfurt. I'm not sure I can cope with anything more."

"You poor dear," Katherine said, mostly because Sophie's manner made it clear that was what she was supposed to say. Sophie's sense of the unfairness of the world must have been boosted immeasurably by the events of the last few days. She looked as though she had fallen down some stairs herself. Her shoulder-length hair was straggly, her beige cardigan hung off one shoulder, and there were mascara streaks under her eyes. Katherine wondered if she had deliberately avoided refreshing her lipstick. There was something a bit stagey about her condition of dishabille, the sort of half-dressed look a suffering ingenue would aspire to in an off-Broadway play, only Sophie was hardly an ingenue.

"The police told Maman they found the gun under some bushes next to the driveway. They also saw signs that someone had been hiding there."

"Was anything stolen?"

"We're not sure. There are so many little things lying around, you know? Nothing from her room or Papa's. Some of the guns were worth money, so if someone came to steal, they might have known."

"Why does anyone think Gypsies were involved?"

"Oh, you know. There are *gitans* in the area at this time of year. I'm sure the village will have a dozen other candidates to suggest if the investigation drags on longer." She paused and seemed to be debating with herself before she added,

"I fear someone will suggest it was Yves." She looked into Katherine's face anxiously.

"Ah, the plate-breaking incident. You heard about that?"

"*Bien sûr!* Maman told me as soon as I arrived."

"You don't seriously think Yves would have broken into the château to get back at him, somehow?" For one thing, Katherine added to herself, breaking in under cover of darkness and secrecy wouldn't be public enough for a man who liked to sing of his prowess with women whenever he could get a microphone. No, if Yves were bent on revenge, he would opt for a showdown on Main Street.

"Of course not. But I worry that Maman will say something to the lieutenant that makes them suspect him."

"Did you ask her not to mention it?"

"I didn't right away because I knew she would think it means I am still interested in him. Which I am not," Sophie hastily said, but not before a short silence made Katherine wonder. "I thought perhaps you could."

"You mean suggest she withhold that episode and Yves's name?" Katherine could hear Michael's voice, hear his warning about getting in trouble with the local *flics*. "I'm afraid it's too late for that. There were so many other people present, you know. But I don't think the police will see that as sufficient motive for murder, truly."

Sophie looked at Katherine, her eyes measuring Katherine's reaction, her lower lip in a pout to show her unhappiness that the answer was no. Katherine had heard that one can see in adults the children they once were, and this seemed obvious with Sophie. I wonder, she thought, if that's why I am so interested in Jeannette and her welfare? Or, perhaps, why I avoided the issue of children until it was not an issue. So many possible problems.

She left that observation for later examination, but before she could assure Sophie that she had no intention of talking about Yves's and Albert's adolescent behavior, the dogs leapt up and began barking furiously. It was a charade they performed happily as long as there was no possible danger to themselves. They raced down the path to the gate, hurled themselves ineffectually toward it, then wagged their tails and rolled around in her precious peonies. Katherine stormed down, yelling at them to no avail, pulling the little dog out by his matted hair and kicking ineffectually at Gracey while saying, "Dammit, get out."

Having had their excitement and realizing that it was a lot cooler on the slate slabs under the living room window than out here in the sun, the dogs retreated, still wearing bits of leaves and flower petals, leaving Katherine breathless and staring through the iron bars at the gendarme who had been in charge at Adele's house. "Well, you might as well come in," she said in English before thinking how rude she sounded. She started again, this time in French. "*Desolée*, Monsieur. You have no idea how hard I work to make this garden into something nice." She half turned, then gestured for him to open the gate. "It's hot today. Come up and have some iced tea."

He smiled ever so slightly, nodded, and followed her up the steps. "Lieutenant Decoste, Madame. Your garden is charming." In English, which undoubtedly meant he'd understood her first comment. She mentally apologized to him and to the entire population of France for her rudeness as she darted up the steps.

Waving him to a seat on the patio, she ducked into the kitchen to pour another glass of tea. Katherine started to call through the kitchen door what a coincidence it was that he and Sophie should both be there when she realized Sophie wasn't. The young woman wasn't on the first floor, not even in the bathroom, and Katherine doubted she would be upstairs. That would be too intimate a trespass for a French person. The young woman must have slipped out the side gate.

She didn't have time to think about the oddness of that because within a few minutes Katherine realized she was being, if not grilled, at least questioned.

"Did you happen to be on the street and see anyone out of doors that night?" Decoste said.

"No and no. But you said Albert died of natural causes. Are you suggesting someone broke into the house that night?" She was concentrating so that she wouldn't reveal that she knew what he had said to Sophie, but it was hard to keep all these little conversations separate. "Are there Gypsies around, have you heard?"

"They do not normally shoot their victims," he said with a slight smile and a shrug. "They much prefer empty houses and silver teapots."

"But Albert wasn't shot, I thought?"

"No, I was referring only to the gun, which I'm sure you know by now was found on the grounds. I am sure, Madame, that you know all that happens in this little town, *non*?"

"Hardly," Katherine said with a small snort. "I am frequently the last person to know anything." His smile was slightly ironic, Katherine thought, and he wasn't pleased. Did he think she was nosy? If he had met Mme Pomfort, or Pippa, he would know who the real snoopers were.

"In any case, Mme Bellegarde says nothing seems to be missing, no spoons, no teapots. We will speak with her daughter to see if she noticed anything. The château does seem to have a great many objects that a thief might put in his pockets. Did Monsieur have any enemies in the neighborhood that you know of?"

Katherine shook her head slowly and sipped her tea.

"Do you know an Yves Saverin, by any chance?"

"Yves?" She cleared her throat. "Lieutenant, you know every little group has its quarrels. But Yves would never harm anyone. My goodness, he's simply a local bookseller who has strong opinions."

"And about what does he have these strong opinions?"

"Well, about things, you know, nothing important . . ." Her voice trailed off. What was she going to say with the cast-off Sophie in town and the girl's mother still incensed by Yves's behavior at the party?

"I understand he became violent toward the deceased recently."

"Violent? I'd hardly say that. He and Albert exchanged angry words, but it was Albert—" She stopped abruptly. Dammit, she had wandered into this and wasn't sure how to disentangle herself. Would it be better to tell him the whole story so he could see how minor it all was, or should she say as little as possible? She took a long sip of iced tea and tried to think. It was too much like chess, which had always eluded her.

"M. Bellegarde became violent?"

"In a way. Nothing serious." He was looking at her as if to prompt more. "He broke a plate." The lieutenant was still watching, waiting.

"Over Yves's head. But," she added quickly, "it was a little plate and it did no damage, except to the plate, of course, which I have to admit annoyed me. It was one of a set, you see." Best to stop there, she realized, not liking the expression

130

of keen interest on the lieutenant's face before he lowered his head to write in his notebook.

Katherine smiled as if to say that was the end of the story. She wished Michael were here. He would know how to get out of this. She kept one ear tuned for the sound of his car, or anything that would end this awkward moment. She looked around as if distracted by the scenery, and noticed Sophie's glass of iced tea, still dotted with beads of condensation, sitting on the table next to the policeman's. Would he ask her who had been here, and where that person might be now? If he did, what should she say? It would be awkward to admit her other guest, the victim's daughter, had vanished at the sound of his voice.

She was saved by the squealing of the gate and a voice that called out to her from the bottom of the garden. Penny came into view, fetching in snug jeans and a gauzy peasant blouse, a string basket hanging from her wrist and a piece of paper clutched in her hand.

"Darling, I have an idea. Oh." She stopped on the last step. "I didn't realize." She smiled winningly at the strange man on Katherine's lawn, switched to French, and held out her hand. "Penelope Masterson. I own the mill house down the road. I dropped by to bring Katherine a treat from the market. I hope I'm not interrupting."

Katherine wondered what might be behind Penny's behavior, which seemed a little over the top. However, it was a distraction, and she had been praying for one. She whisked away Sophie's glass, which the lieutenant didn't appear to notice, and darted back out with a new one. Penny extracted a tawny Époisses cheese from the carry bag, so perfectly ripe that Katherine's mouth began to water at the aroma. If Katherine thought the policeman would give up and leave at this domestic moment, however, she was disappointed. He sat there calmly, looking from one woman to the other, sipping his tea, his expression blank.

"You must be here because of Albert Bellegarde's accident," Penny said, retreating to English to be sure of making her point accurately. "Such a shame, but he was old, you know, a bit shaky on his feet, didn't you notice, Katherine? For all we know, he might have had a touch of vertigo." She smiled brightly at the policeman and touched her temple to illustrate her medical diagnosis in case his English didn't run to technical terms.

"I was asking Madame to tell me about an argument that happened here a few days ago," he replied, also in English.

"Argument? I don't recall anything. Do you, Katherine? Perhaps a little debate after Katherine's delicious lunch, is that what you mean? A difference of opinion?"

"A plate broken over someone's head," Decoste said flatly.

Penny darted a look at Katherine as if to accuse her of some treachery. Katherine thought that was unfair, especially since she had been the one to urge everyone to be silent about something so easily inflated in importance. "Adele may have mentioned it," she said to warn her friend.

"Oh, Adele, poor thing. She is understandably rattled. It was nothing at all, hardly noticeable."

"It was, I believe, M. Saverin who argued with the deceased?"

Penny shot another look at Katherine. "Yves? I guess it was, although I cannot for the life of me remember what they had words about. Can you?"

Penny was pushing her into an untruth, Katherine thought, and a sudden flush of anger made her neck warm. It was one thing to hold back something irrelevant, but another thing to lie openly. She wasn't good at lying. She took a slow sip of her tea, wondering how to escape the bind Penny had put her in to protect Yves.

Before she could answer, the policeman spoke, reading from his notes. She noticed that his English seemed to be improving rapidly. "The deceased's wife said they were arguing about an insult this M. Saverin had made publicly toward their daughter."

Penny was silent for a moment, her smile frozen in place, her glass stopped midway to her mouth. Katherine wondered if Penny only now realized that her name might get dragged into this mess. Seeming to come to a decision, Penny shook her head and laughed. "I don't even recall what they had words about, honestly, so I'm no help. Yves was away the night Albert fell, in any case. In Paris for a book show."

The lieutenant appeared to consider her comment seriously, then made some kind of decision, got up, and put his notebook in his jacket pocket. Saying he hoped he wouldn't have to bother them again, he bowed slightly and made his way down through the garden and out the gate. When the rusty gate had stopped squealing and his car engine started, Penny looked at Katherine, the smile gone. "What on earth have you and that Adele woman been telling the police, for heaven's sake?"

"He's with the gendarmerie, Penny, and you don't want to be lying to them," Katherine began, feeling more defensive than she had any business being. "I didn't say anything he didn't already know. I explained that Albert hit Yves with a plate, not the other way around."

Penny wasn't mollified. "Everyone's pointing fingers at Yves, and it's not fair. The poor man is being scapegoated for Albert Bellegarde's death, which I'm sure was an accident."

"You didn't help by rushing in with an alibi for Yves." Katherine got up, shook out the folds of her full black skirt, festooned with embroidered pink flowers, Spanish from the 1950s, she was sure, and one of the best finds of last year's summer shopping. She was impatient with this invented intrigue, wanted to put it out of her mind and focus on her painting. But here was Penny, pouting, and there was Sophie doing the same, and all because silly Yves insisted on being the center of attention, and Albert got flustered and fell down the steps. "You made it sound as though it was a crime, that someone else must have been involved. And no one's trying to suggest Yves killed Albert. In fact, I've heard Gypsies, gun dealers, neighbors, and Nazis suggested already. One would think we were overrun with outlaws in our backward little village. And you yourself suggested someone pushed him last time you came by."

"I was joking, for heaven's sake. This stupid town has such an active rumor mill. That Englishwoman is probably stirring things up. She would see assassins everywhere, since she writes murder mysteries."

"I doubt that, darling. She's practically a hermit, and I can't see Mme Pomfort striking up a conversation with her over a morning coffee, especially since they couldn't speak in French."

"Please don't give the police any more ammunition to persecute poor Yves." Penny rose. "I hope you like the cheese. Yves and I drove over there this morning. Such a pretty château, with its own dry moat and a team of gardeners hard at work. I wouldn't mind living there, although if it weren't for the fast train to Paris, I think I'd be going a little nuts by now, never mind the Roman ruins and old churches you drag me to all over the place."

Live in the Château d'Époisses? Was Penny that rich? While Katherine tried to imagine Penny strolling into the courtyard or reviewing the gardens with the staff, Penny leaned over to give her a perfunctory kiss, and then she was off, leaving Katherine struggling for a suitable retort.

CHAPTER 14

Until the Hollidays had come up with their scheme to record with Michael, he had been a creature of daily habits, perhaps as a way of exerting some control over a life led among people with whom he couldn't hold a decent conversation. The dogs got a long walk every evening at twilight, uphill to the *pétanque* court, which was a sandy rectangle laid out under a canopy of old trees and protected by a wire fence, nothing fancy, but kept raked and level by Emile so no one could claim a bad roll of the ball. Then, down past the dirt road entrance to the quarry. After a little sniffing in the overgrown and weedy land there, the threesome continued to the river with its pebbled shore, more like a stream since Penny's retaining wall and pool had been built. Once in a while, there was a man or a boy slouched on a plastic chair or squatting on the gravel, tending a fishing pole. The dogs would check out abandoned plastic bottles and candy wrappers for a couple of minutes before turning away in disinterest, humans being so predictably messy. Then, Michael would follow them, their leashes no longer straining, past the dun-colored café building perched right up against the pavement, its handful of parking spots mostly empty at dinnertime, before heading back up the hill to their garden gate.

Katherine usually took the time to clean up the kitchen, but this evening, she told her husband she would join him. She wanted his reaction to the visits of the day and his advice on what she should do. She might not take his advice, which tended to be lacking in nuance, but she needed to think about the effect Albert's death was having on the people she knew in Reigny-sur-Canne before she could decide what her role was in bringing peace to the community.

"I never heard so much stupid talk," Michael said when she finished telling him about Sophie's aborted visit, Penny's aggressive defense of Yves, and the policeman's opaqueness. "What's gotten into everyone? The man fell down the steps and had a heart attack or broke his neck, whatever the coroner decides, period. Why you all have to turn it into something mysterious, I don't understand."

"That's not fair. I'm not doing that. You should say that to Penny, or Emile, or particularly Pippa, who's probably busy writing an entire fiction about it without knowing a single thing. I'm only trying to calm everyone down."

"Why do you have to do anything?" He picked up a fallen branch and tossed it down the path to the delight of the dogs, who galloped ahead of them, snuffling.

"But what if he didn't fall? What about the gun?"

"What about it? You said he wasn't shot with it. Maybe Adele's right, and someone was going to steal it, but old Albert heard him, came out to investigate, and fell while chasing the thief."

Katherine thought about this for a minute. "Yes, that could be what happened. But then, who was he chasing? The women think Gypsies, all except Mme Pomfort, who has decided it was a Nazi enemy of Albert's, or maybe she meant someone who hated Nazis. I'm not quite clear. Anyway, the policeman obviously doesn't agree with the Gypsy theory."

"Albert was at least twenty years too young to be a Nazi, much less have Nazi enemies."

"I've been thinking. He was close to ninety, Adele told me. He sold guns once, remember."

"To anyone who'd buy them, with the approval of the French government, if I understood him, and he told me he got out of that business a long time ago. Unless you think he was goose-stepping around with a gun and live ammunition when he was Brett's age, he's too young to be blamed for all the shit that happened around here."

"Mme Pomfort says some teenagers were. But not him, I'm sure. What if it was a Gypsy and you're right that Albert was chasing him when he fell? If they find the Gypsy, is that murder?"

"You just told me the police don't believe that's likely. Everyone piles on about Gypsies whenever there's trouble," he said, rolling a cigarillo around in his mouth with enough force to make Katherine wonder if it would end up in tatters, "but I've never even seen Roma or Spanish Gypsies here, have you? And the French ones, what do you call them—*gens de voyages*?—you'd know if they were camping nearby. Jeannette's father is the sticky-fingered one around here."

They were at the riverbank by the time Michael had finished his rant. Not that he was wrong, but some topics agitated him so much that Katherine tried to avoid them. Injustice for Gypsies was one of them. She picked up a small rock and tossed it in, a habit from childhood. As the ripples spread, she was distracted by how she would paint them glistening in the sluggishly moving water, and by the urge to do a painting set right on this bank at the end of the day, perhaps with golden sunlight slanting in among the trees. And a girl sitting at the water's edge in a long skirt, dabbling her fingers in it. Jeannette would model, of course. She'd catch up with the girl in the morning and set a time for a modeling session.

"I think Penny suspects Yves. Listen, Michael. When Penny told Emile and me that Yves was in Paris, Emile said that couldn't be true because he'd seen him in Chablis. What if Emile was right?"

"Emile is hardly the most observant guy in the world. But even if Yves wasn't in Paris, it doesn't mean he was at the castle. He might have another girlfriend."

Katherine gasped. "Does he?"

"I don't know, but the man's always looking to be the center of attention. Maybe he found someone who gives him more than Penny or that sad-looking daughter of Albert's."

"Penny doesn't give him much more than attention," Katherine said with a small laugh. "I think she's still dangling the promise of sex."

Michael snorted. "That only works for young kids. If she really is holding out, that makes my idea even more likely. Let's let the cops figure this out, if it's anything other than the most likely reason for Albert's death. You'll only get burned if you try to influence the investigation." To soften his words, he put an arm around her shoulder and pulled her in for a kiss on the cheek. "Maybe you and that writer should get together and solve a pretend mystery."

She laughed. "Poor girl, she doesn't get any respect around here, does she? I think I will invite her over for tea. No," she said when Michael raised an eyebrow, "not to figure out whodunit about Albert, but to talk with another Reigny outcast and see how she handles it. Although, I think she doesn't handle it at all, simply doesn't care as much as I do."

"There's a lesson for you, Kay. Sometimes you care too much."

"Michael, darling," she said, staring at the water and changing the topic to one that was pressing on her even more than the drama in Reigny. "If J.B. is able to get a tour set up for the new album, you will go, won't you? I mean, you really wouldn't let the opportunity slip past?"

"First off, he's a big talker. So far, we don't have ten songs I think anyone would pay to hear us sing. And let's be real. Betty Lou might have a fan base of old hippies who'd come out for her, but me? I'm an unknown, I sing ballads, I'm no Mick Jagger, ready to prance around in tight pants."

She grinned lasciviously, but said, "No one would expect that. James Taylor's no Jagger either, and you're as good as he is."

"Maybe, but people have been listening to Taylor for a few decades. It would be 'Michael who?' and I don't relish sitting in front of a bunch of empty chairs." He called the dogs abruptly and started walking. Katherine had to trot to keep up with him.

"J.B. says a lot of people will remember the early days of the Crazy Leopards, and he said he found some old photos you're in. Plus, the songs you wrote are famous."

"Kay, you're forgetting that part of the deal that gave us the stake to move here was my signing a paper saying I wouldn't perform either song."

"But J.B. says he'll get a lawyer to fix that. Didn't he say something about it being easy to challenge?"

"J.B. is a wheeler-dealer. He'd say anything to get what he wants."

"He wants you to make some money, for heaven's sake. And you know we need it. I'm afraid to think about what happens to us when the settlement money is gone. This is our chance—your chance, Michael."

"I know we could use the money. I agreed to work on an album, didn't I? J.B. can promote it any way he wants." His voice tightened. "Maybe if there's some interest, well, we'll see about a trip to the States. Wait 'til we have something worth putting out there, though."

Katherine had to be content with that. He hadn't said no. She was daydreaming of repairs to her little studio as she climbed into bed.

CHAPTER 15

Jeannette was late, of course. Katherine had told her specifically that she wanted to catch the late-afternoon light for the first couple of drawings, the color sketches that would help her decide the composition of the new painting. Doing one at the quiet riverbank, with its deep green grasses and the rich bark of the horse chestnut trees was an inspired idea, and she itched to get started. She had dug out a skirt of some stiff old cotton that Jeannette could slip on over her habitual shorts as she sat. The billowing fabric and Jeannette's flyaway curls would make such a lovely contrast to the stillness of the setting. But it was already a half hour later and the light wasn't coming into the glade at the perfect angle.

She turned as she heard footsteps. "Ah, there you are, child," she began, then stopped as the stern face of Mme Pomfort came into view. "You startled me," she said with a short laugh. "I have asked Jeannette to model for me and I thought I heard her."

"Model?" The way she said it made Katherine nervous. Surely the old woman didn't think Katherine was going to ask Jeannette to take off her clothes?

She jumped up from her stool to explain, holding out the

skirt. "As an eighteenth-century shepherdess, you see. Isn't this pretty? I found it at a *brocante* last year. I love the old rose color."

"Why you encourage that child, I cannot understand," Mme Pomfort said, standing with her feet apart and her hands clasped in front of her torso. "She is a thief. She will come to no good. No one in that family ever does."

"She's only a child," Katherine said, smiling to soften the fact that she wasn't agreeing with the town's arbiter of acceptance. "She needs some good examples, people like you, for example, to show her how to behave."

"Nonsense. She is already throwing herself at that nasty American boy, and only the other day trampled my geranium plants with her bicycle and rode away when I called out to her. She is of bad stock. Those boys are ruffians already. I know they steal my beans and tomatoes. And her father, well, no one speaks to him unless it is to try and recover something he has stolen. You should not encourage her," she said again.

Katherine fiddled with her pastels. She had already set out a handful of the colors she wanted to use. What should she say? It appeared Mme Pomfort was waiting, would wait as long as it took, perhaps for Katherine to pack up and retreat back to America, leaving the village to itself. At that moment, sounds of raised voices reached into the concavity of the river's edge, followed immediately by a sprinting Jeannette, two of her youngest brothers and, bringing up the rear, Jean, the father, dressed in dusty pants and a sleeveless undershirt, a cigarette hanging from his lips.

"*Bonjour*, Madame," Jeannette called out as she skidded to a halt next to Katherine and quickly kissed her cheeks. She looked sideways at Mme Pomfort but made no other move to acknowledge her.

"Hey, Madame," Jean said in a rough voice, taking the cigarette out and waving it, *"je jeux vous parler."* He took a few sliding steps down the side of the gully as he spoke, and jabbed his finger in her direction.

"You want to talk to me?" Katherine said, confused, thrusting the costume skirt at the teenager, and instinctively gathering the expensive pastels as the little boys crowded up to her, chattering to each other and reaching for her large pad of paper.

"What you want with my girl, eh? You want her to pose for you, you must pay." He swaggered close enough that Katherine could smell his sweat and the wine on his breath. "What kind of posing? No clothes? I don't like that for my girl."

"No," Katherine said, as much to the little boys who were trying to pull out sheets of her expensive paper as to the father. Jeannette was grinning at everything and nothing and pulling the skirt up over her hips. Mme Pomfort was standing like a stone. "No, I mean, yes, certainly with clothes on, like she did for the last painting. She was a shepherdess in that one too." She realized Jean had probably not seen the painting, which was still on an easel in the studio while she decided if it was finished. "Boys, here," she said, snapping a precious pastel crayon in two and handing a piece to each along with half a sheet of the precious paper, not sure how else to quiet their manic attack on her art supplies. "Go over there and draw the tall yellow flowers."

Mme Pomfort now stirred. "You see, Mme Goff? To get along here, you must not ally yourself with these . . . these people." She glared at Jean, who seemed to see her for the first time. Because she was speaking in rapid French, Jean could not miss the insult.

"Ah, it's you, Madame. I heard that you told Emile I stole his garden tools. You are a troublemaker, you know?" He advanced on her, shaking the fist in which he held the cigarette, as he denounced her as a busybody. "You would do well not to slander me that way, if you get my meaning."

The old woman drew herself up as tall as she could, standing her ground as solidly as a boulder, staring him straight in the eye. Even though Katherine couldn't be completely sure because the two were speaking so fast, she was confident insults were being traded at machine-gun speed. When she noticed that the corners of Mme Pomfort's closed mouth had turned so far down they made the shape of a crescent moon, Katherine decided the doyenne of Reigny society was winning, and she wasn't surprised that it was Jean who backed off marginally.

"You are a disgrace, you and your family," Mme Pomfort hissed, "and no one around here will have anything to do with you, you understand?" She turned to glare at Katherine. "*Prennez-garde*, Madame." Then, having warned Katherine to watch out for her disreputable neighbor, she spun on her heel and marched up the slope, leaving silence behind.

Jeannette peered at the departing woman with watchful eyes and a thoughtful expression, then shrugged the rest of the way into the skirt, which covered her down to the ankle. The little boys paid no attention, being thoroughly engaged in trying to fold their drawing paper into boats. Even Jean was silent for a beat before turning back to Katherine.

The gist of his demand seemed to be that Jeannette was missed at home and that he, Jean, couldn't work if she wasn't there to take care of the boys. Since the boys in question were more likely to be nosing around the *mairie*, the village's business office, or trying to steal candy from the café's meager display than to be sitting at home, Katherine wasn't moved. She had a hunch any money he managed to wrest from her would get spent on wine the same day. When Jean saw that she wasn't going to cave easily, he called his brood and demanded they all go home. The boys went easily, laughing and knocking into each other, waving their pastels like the spoils of war. Jeannette said something fast to her father, who shouted at her but left without repeating his order.

"Well, *cherie*," said Katherine in the quiet that followed. "I don't know about you, but my bucolic mood is gone for today. I'll take the skirt back—yes, I'll bring it next time we try this—but today's not a day for painting, *desolée*. Tell you what, though," she said as she folded the travel easel and slipped the pad of paper and box of pastels into it, "I would be glad to pay you a model's hourly rate. It's quite small, the trouble for models through the ages, but if I give you euros, can you keep them for your schoolbooks or clothing?"

The girl's assurances burst out and she danced ahead of Katherine up to the road, her face alight with excitement. It saddened Katherine to know that the girl's future was laid out for her in such a negative way by the tiny society of Reigny-sur-Canne. It bothered her even more to know she, Katherine, was already bending to Mme Pomfort's will in thinking to herself that she would arrange her small support for the girl so no one else knew about it.

As she trudged up the garden path and toward her little studio building, a leaky nineteenth-century add-on to the main house that had been a shed before she claimed it for her work, Katherine heard a woman's voice coming from her living room. Adele, perhaps come to find sympathetic company? No, she heard a throaty chuckle. Betty Lou, then, which made

146

sense since locals never paid an impromptu call on her. Still outsiders after three years, and now Mme Pomfort would be watching to make sure she cut her ties with Jeannette.

As she dumped her art supplies and made her way back to the house, she realized Adele hadn't called with updates about Albert's death, or even news of a funeral date. Adele wasn't much of a friend, in all honesty. Why had she called, then, when she was so upset?

Michael was sitting in the wooden chair he always occupied in the crowded living room, where he played for hours on end. Sometimes Katherine thought he was singing to pacify the universe, an endless lullaby to keep it from crashing down on their heads in case the money ran out or one of them became too homesick to continue in a foreign land where everything except lying low cost too much money. They had agreed that as long as they owned their little house outright and didn't eat at restaurants they could make do here a lot better than in California. So they had persevered, stretching his settlement money as far as they could, short of making the dogs give up their bones. She wondered if that accounted for the sad, fretful tune he was playing and that Betty Lou was humming.

"Kathy." Betty Lou stopped when Katherine came into the room, and boomed at her. "This insanely talented husband of yours was telling me you're having a show at a gallery next week in that place with the steep hill and the drop-dead gorgeous church at the top. We were over there the other day looking for some vineyard that was written up in J.B.'s wine magazine, but got lost, I swear for the third time in a week. All these little back roads are pretty as can be, but they do look the same, don't they? Anyway, that's fantastic. Two stars in one family. We'll come to the opening, wouldn't miss it."

She beamed up at Katherine from the chaise into which Katherine had intended to collapse.

"Thanks," Katherine said. "Vézelay has a fascinating religious history, with lots of church politics mixed in. But the gallery is way up the cobblestone street and I live in fear no one will trudge up the hill, and I'll be forced to consume an entire case of wine and all the pâté we're bringing." She laughed to cover up the truth of her words.

"You're both amazing," Betty Lou said, shaking her head.

"I don't know about that," Katherine said, bending to give Betty Lou the traditional French greeting before realizing the singer didn't understand what she was doing. "May I get you something?" she said.

"No, I have to go. I thought I'd say hi while J.B. went to get a newspaper at your café. I want to tell Mike that J.B. thinks we're ready to record the first couple of songs. We'll lay down some tracks and let my genius husband tinker with them to see how they come out. I'm feeling real good about how it's coming along. This new song of Michael's is dynamite. I'm thinking we should postpone our little trip to the Riviera long enough to capture the good stuff while the energy's still there, you know?"

Michael hadn't said anything about energy, or the Hollidays leaving, so she only smiled and wheeled back to the kitchen. Yes, five ten, cocktail time. The small glasses were dirty so she took a larger one and filled it, hoping it wouldn't attract Michael's attention. Hell with that. She'd had run-ins with two of Reigny's nastier people in a short time while he was up here singing away with his new musical partner.

Thirty minutes later, Betty Lou waved as she pulled out of the driveway and Michael sat on the patio rather than go back into the stuffy room, where vintage damask drapes made it snug in winter but sweltering in July. Katherine reclaimed her upholstered chaise and tried to let the day's frustrations slip out of her tense body. No painting done, run-ins with the neighbors she had seen, and no contact with the few who did include her. Of course Penny wasn't really a resident, and would fly off when the nights got longer and the need for company was greater. When Penny wasn't here, Yves didn't visit or include them in any social activities, assuming he had any in Reigny.

Emile, bless his pointy little head, dropped by now and then, usually in a state of upset over something. The mail truck had run over his rock garden, the mayor had threatened to shut down the *pétanque* court if the players couldn't control their noisy arguments. Reminded of Emile, she pulled herself up and went outside, where Michael was strumming softly and chewing on his cigarillo.

"Darling, all this distraction about Albert made me forget about Emile's intention of playing rock music with you at the Reigny fête. Has he talked with you yet?"

"Not going to happen."

"Well, that's easy to say, but have you said it to him? He's going to be massively disappointed, you know. Maybe one number, to be neighborly?"

"If he asks, I'll tell him. He'll be wanting to sing, too, and you know he can't hold a note."

"I do know," she said, remembering Emile's voice ringing out at the Christmas program in the little church, not merely off-key but always too slow or too fast, or both. "Poor Emile, he must have a role, and he does have his heart set on sharing the stage with the famous Michael Goff."

"I'll talk with him if he comes to me about it. I promise to be nice. Doesn't he play the accordion? Maybe he can do some French cabaret songs."

"Oh, he hates that idea. Says he's too young to sing those old-fashioned pieces. Believe me, I tried that already. I wonder if there are any rock songs that feature accordions?"

"Spare me," Michael said, laughing. "The problem isn't the instrument, I guess. It's Emile; he's not a musician. He's a retired dentist."

Katherine paced. "That's not the point. It's not like you're going to record with him. It's for a day—no, not even that, an afternoon—and he's been a good neighbor to us."

"He has?" Michael laid down his guitar, placed his hands on his knees, and squinted up at his wife. "I seem to recall him delivering a long lecture on how not to exit the driveway in a way that would leave tire tracks near his yard. And I distinctly remember the time he and his buddies got drunk and threw beer cans at our roof. You didn't think he was such a great neighbor then."

"Poor Emile. You know he's lonely, he's never been married, and he wants to be liked. We all want to be liked, don't we?" A picture of Mme Pomfort, her mouth turned downward in the mother of all frowns, flashed into Katherine's head, and she sat down abruptly. "Oh dear, I think I'm doomed around here, Michael, I really do." She took a long sip of her wine and proceeded to tell him about Jean and Mme Pomfort and the ultimatum.

When she finished, Michael picked up his guitar again and started playing some chords quietly while he talked. "The old lady has a point. Get anywhere near that guy and it winds up being trouble. I know you like the girl, although I'm positive she took your iPod last fall. She's in and out of the house all the time and never announces herself or asks if it's convenient."

"I don't think many teenagers would, my love."

"And she lies. J.B. said she told Brett her father used to be a policeman, which is a joke."

Now Katherine laughed. "It's a stretch, I'd agree, but there's no one else to talk to. I try, but all people do is look sideways at us in the café or the market. We've been here three years, Michael, and I miss having a friend."

"What about Penny and that idiot Yves? They hang around here all the time. And this summer there's Betty Lou and J.B. No one's gossiping about us, especially now that Albert's dead."

"How would you know what they're saying? You don't speak a word of French. For all you know, they could be saying we murdered him."

"Maybe you should make friends with that English writer. At least she speaks the language, and she doesn't have any friends either, as far as I can figure out. If you really don't like it here, come up with another plan and I'll make it happen—as long as it's not L.A. again. But if you complain too much about Reigny, you sound like Penny."

Stung by his words, she gulped her wine and looked up into the pear tree. "I'm going to heat up the ratatouille and sausage," was all she said, and she jumped up and took off for the kitchen.

CHAPTER 16

The next morning, still feeling bruised by her encounters with the neighbors and Michael's lack of sympathy, Katherine walked to Yves's bookstore. She rarely bought any of his stock, it was so expensive. She couldn't afford a rare copy of anything, and looked only for secondhand copies of French novels, poetry, and translations of her favorite American authors. Yves carried a lackluster selection of these, usually leftovers from a purchase of better books. But she was restless today and, if she were to take Madame's advice, she had better curry favor with Reigny's acceptable citizens, starting with Mme Robilier, who worked part-time for Yves.

The little bell tinkled as she pushed the door open—an affectation of Yves's since he could see anyone who came in from his desk near the door. His chair was empty, however, and a worn cardigan was draped over the back. She heard voices and saw Yves and another man in the far corner chuckling together over something. He glanced at her and waved but didn't come to meet her. A small woman with steel-gray hair in a matching gray dress with a blue scarf wound around and knotted at her throat appeared at the end of a tall bookcase, flapping her thin hands.

"Bonjour, Madame," she said, turning bright, black eyes on Katherine. "May I help you?" she said in English.

We might be strangers, Katherine thought, instead of neighbors who see each other once a week while walking through the village. *"Bonjour, Madame Robilier. Comment ça va?"*

"Not so good, Madame, not so good." She was still speaking in English, which Katherine took as a put-down of sorts since her own French was surely passable for casual chat. "My rheumatics plague me every day, you understand? My husband tells me I must not complain, but, then, he is healthy always." She said it like an accusation and did not refer to the fact that her husband was suffering from dementia and would be an unlikely source of informed comfort. "Are you looking for something special?"

Katherine remembered that the American habit of asking how one felt was understood to be insincere at home, to be answered with something simple, like "Fine." Not always so in France. Maybe it was the same most of the time, she thought, but if you ask an older person, at least, you had better be prepared to hear the answer. "Do you have any Balzac that isn't too rare for my purse?" She smiled.

"Balzac, you say? M. Saverin is quite a collector of Balzac. Let me fetch a few for you to examine." She trotted off, still unsmiling, while Katherine sat obediently in one of the chairs that faced the desk, wondering what she needed to do to make Mme Robilier like her. Yves made no further move to greet her, still caught up with his other customer, a stranger to Katherine.

Fifteen minutes and a shocking twenty-five euros later, she still had no idea how to get the prim woman with the perpetually fretful expression to smile in a neighborly way. The bookseller's assistant had remained formal as she pressed a shabby copy of *Lost Illusions* on Katherine. Fitting, Katherine thought, and wondered if this was another veiled comment on her status in Reigny.

The only clue came when Madame commented, seemingly out of nowhere, that she understood Mme Goff recently paid a call on Mme Pomfort. "One of my neighbors happened to notice—not me. I do not peer out at the comings and goings of the people who live here." The unnamed neighbor had apparently reported that Katherine had been seen in the church garden on the church bench. Katherine thought she understood the implications. Mme Robilier was being upstaged by Mme Pomfort in some way that Mme Robilier was unclear about, but about which she was intensely curious.

"Yes, I need flowers for the stage at the fête. You know I am in charge of this year's entertainment, which I'm happy to help with."

Mme Robilier sniffed and muttered something about the general taste for ordinary flowers. Katherine left, feeling quite sure that she had to pay a call on the bookseller's assistant right away and offer her a prime spot onstage for her blooms. How to do that without further incurring Mme Pomfort's wrath she could not imagine.

She got no enlightenment until Yves bounded up the garden steps an hour later, singing out his usual *"Bonjour, Katherine,"* as he came. He was, Katherine decided as she abandoned her fight with the cranky washing machine, which was refusing to spin with more than one towel in its basket, irrepressible, not unlike a toy she remembered from childhood, a scary-looking inflated clown doll that you were supposed to knock down. The damn thing was weighted so it popped back up immediately no matter how hard you hit it. At age nine, she had begged for the toy, but soon lost interest when she realized you couldn't win against it. Her mother berated her for wasting such an expensive gift. Given that her mother was running through her husband's disposable income faster than he could replace it, spending more on Johnnie Walker Black Label than on inflatable clowns and matching socks for her children, it struck Katherine as ironic later on when she was old enough to buy her own scotch.

Childhood was overrated, she had often thought, and maybe her jaundiced view was the reason she had shied away from inflicting one on a child of her own. Lucky for her, Michael didn't much care. Music was—or had been—his life. Funny if he should find his way back to his dream at this time, after such a crushing blow to his ego.

"Thank you for visiting my humble shop," Yves said, pulling her attention back from her private thoughts. "I hope you will enjoy the Balzac. See, I have brought you another, which you will adore, as a gift." He held out a small cloth-covered volume.

"Buy one, get one free?" She laughed. Really, he was hard to resist.

"Yes, well, I cannot help myself when someone as charming as dear Katherine comes calling." He plopped into a wicker chair, shooing away the dogs who rushed over to be petted or played with. "Go, depart," he said sternly, but in French, so that they merely grinned at him with open mouths and settled near his feet. "I wanted to tell you something," he said, the smile disappearing, as she slipped into the other chair, "something about Mme Robilier. She was not warm to you, yes?"

"Yes," Katherine said, "I did notice. I assume it was because of the flowers for the fête. I felt I had to invite Mme Pomfort to supply them since I have been given the responsibility for the stage. I was told she always does the flowers and expects to be asked."

"Yes, well, she certainly does, and I think Mme Robilier had hoped you might upset that tradition. But that's only a bit of it. Mme Pomfort tells anyone who will listen that the Robiliers are Nazi sympathizers from the war days. You may not believe it after all the years, but that is still a huge insult to a Frenchman."

Katherine nodded. "Mme Pomfort managed to hint about that to me. Surely if it isn't true, everyone knows."

"It is not so simple. Mme Robilier's dead father-in-law was of German extraction. His mother was German, and when they came to Reigny long ago it was to take possession of a parcel that had been in the French side of the Robilier family for many generations. So this German woman and her son were here when the Vichy government was in power. This area was Vichy-controlled, but the forests were where the patriots hid out, you know?"

"Yes, I went to the Musée de la Résistance en Morvan to see the historical exhibits earlier this year. Such brave people."

"It's not history around here. It's as though it happened last week, you know? Nazi troops came through during the occupation, although they didn't take over the town, stealing everything to eat, and shooting suspected spies, who were usually local farmers driven to join the Resistance, if they were even involved."

"If they were Vichy sympathizers, wouldn't the Robiliers have been dealt with harshly? I've read terrible stories."

"There was no proof. The Nazis took everyone's livestock and everyone's milk. My great-aunt told me when I was a child that Reigny was so disrupted by the war that no one had the stomach to continue the violence a moment more. Better to forget and move on, although, in truth, no one has forgotten, only accepted that what's past cannot be repaired.

And I do not think the Robiliers were actively sympathetic, anyway."

"It sounds as though at least some of Reigny's residents didn't move on, not completely. I know about the fight over the church garden. I thought that was why Madame made such a point of saying it was the church's garden where I sat with Mme Pomfort last week. The Catholic Church doesn't own it, right?"

"Precisely. The churches and lands were seized centuries ago. The Catholics use the church building but the state owns it. But there was some documentation long ago that awarded the land next to it, they say, to the ancestors of the Robiliers."

"An old wound. Are there papers somewhere?"

"Yes and no. Papers, but not as clear as the Robiliers profess them to be." Yves leaned forward. "My assistant says Mme Pomfort told the police lieutenant the other day that the Robiliers had some kind of Nazi connection to old Albert. It sent him to call on them, fishing for a possible motive for her husband to have broken into the Bellegardes' château with the intention of doing harm to him."

"But that's absurd. Madame's husband is ill, everyone knows that. He can hardly get out of the house. I've seen her leading him to the church for the Christmas festival. How ridiculous, and how mean of Mme Pomfort."

"Yes, well, you can see how it might upset my poor assistant to be lumped together with the German in the château."

"You too? Poor Albert. He must have felt as though he had a target on his back half the time."

"*Pauvre* Albert, as you call him, says he was out of Germany by the time he was eight years old, but how do we know, eh? The elders here are a scarred and bitter bunch. You know Mme Pomfort has never invited any of the Bellegardes to her garden party the week after the fête. It bothers Sophie greatly."

"Oh, damn Mme Pomfort. I'm sick of hearing about her. Who said she gets to make up the rules?"

Yves paused and raised an eyebrow. "But you do not know? She is related by birth, yes, by birth, not marriage, to a grandnephew of a Bonaparte. It is a distant connection, but quite correct."

"So? I'm related distantly to a lieutenant governor of Colorado, but I assure you my family never tried to run my hometown." Not that being related to poor Horace Tabor would have counted for a lot, she added to herself.

"Ah, but you are not French," Yves said with a tight smile. "Here, these things matter. We are not as democratic as we would have you believe."

"Obviously." Katherine sighed. "In any case, I don't understand why your Mme Robilier should be so unfriendly to me. I have no part in all this social one-upsmanship."

"What is that word? Ah," he said, waving Katherine's attempt to explain it away, "Katherine, *cherie*, the lieutenant came to see you, too, and people are talking about your sudden friendship with the Bellegardes." He shrugged.

"Sudden? That is so unfair. No one else will have anything to do with me, as if I were an Ugly American, which I am not. If the Bellegardes extend a hand of friendship, I'm supposed to reject them, the only people who do? Other than you, of course."

"It is only that we—they, I mean—have to wonder why the Bellegardes bring you into their *affaire*."

"What can you mean?" Katherine cried out. "I'm beginning to think all of Reigny has nothing better to do than make trouble. Or, that you all hate Americans no matter how much we try to fit in. Maybe the police have other reasons to think Albert didn't fall."

Yves stared at her. "But, you mean me? Penny said you mentioned me to the police. She is very upset with you."

"The police already knew you and he quarreled at my house," Katherine said, wondering if this was why he was touchy. "The lieutenant asked me about it when he came here. I told him it was nothing. Surely Penny reported that to you while she was at it?"

"But, dear Katherine, how would they know in the first place?"

"Half the town was here, or at least half the women." She didn't say that it had been J.B. who first mentioned it in front of the gendarme. If the French had to stick together, she was beginning to think the Americans did also. J.B. was too important to Michael's and her future to throw to the mob. "Our young English neighbor would probably love to conjure up a murder, but she doesn't speak French, and anyway she hardly knows anyone in Reigny."

"Philippa knows me. She comes to my shop regularly to see if I have picked up any Maigret in English translation. Sometimes, if I see a cheap French edition of an Agatha Christie, I pick it up for her. She told me she practices her French skills on them because she knows all of the books in English. Are you telling me she believes someone killed the old man?"

"Not really. Pippa is fantasizing, you know, making up a story. No one really thinks Albert was murdered." Her words sat there, surrounded by silence. "Do they?"

"What about the gun?" He looked at her from under his bushy eyebrows and she wondered briefly how he knew about the gun unless he had spoken with Adele. Then she recalled

Sophie's look of desperate, badly concealed concern. Of course. Sophie had told him.

"From what I heard, it wasn't fired. It was thrown in the bushes."

"Were there fingerprints?"

"How would I know, Yves? You can ask the gendarmes."

"Once the captain took on the case the Auxerre gendarmes became silent, which is too bad for me because a few of them are buddies from school." He looked glum.

"Have you been questioned? Are they treating you like a suspect?" She looked at him with new interest. Was Yves more than the local bad-boy flirt?

"I was in Paris that night for a book event."

So Penny had said. But Emile thought he saw Yves fifty kilometers from Reigny. Yves was capable of flying off the handle, of childish behavior, and of a frequently expressed glee in getting even. That being so, Katherine chided herself, it hardly equated with trying to kill someone. "I'm sure you're not a suspect, then, as long as your alibi is good."

"Alibi? Suspect? *Merde*, I feel I am in a police station at this very moment."

"I didn't mean you are a suspect, Yves. Calm down. I was only saying that from the detective's perspective, you're in the clear."

But she saw the bookseller's propensity for self-drama had been fired up. Yves disentangled himself from the dogs and prepared to leave. "I'm sorry you feel that way," he said in an aggrieved voice. "I hope you enjoy the book." And before she could protest further, he had retreated down the steps and out the gate.

"Damn and blast," she said, wondering how many residents of her new hometown she could insult in one day. She would call Adele, the only friendly face left, unless, of course, Adele had turned on her too. She picked up the book and headed in to the telephone, sorry that her disagreement with Michael the evening before meant she would not have as sympathetic an ear when he returned. He was, as always these days, deep in the studio work, twenty kilometers away. If this music project didn't pay off, he would be disappointed, even if he'd never admit it. He was so armored against the hurt of the Crazy Leopards days. It had better work. She had seen and then promptly turned away from the bank statement last month. She wasn't sure where the money had gone, but it was becoming obvious their nest egg wasn't going to stretch far enough. A lot was riding on the album and the tour to promote it, more than either of them had admitted to each other.

The dogs roused themselves to stand in front of the refrigerator, tails slowly waving, faces turned up expectantly. "No, dammit. Nothing 'til dinner. You're bankrupting us," she said, and nudged them out of the way. Where would it end? she thought. Will we all be eating dog food five years from now? With that image foremost in her mind, she dialed Adele's number. It still nagged at her, that Adele had called her when Albert died. Was it because there was no one else in Reigny whom the aristocrat with the German-born husband could lean on? Or no one else who would accept her explanation of events? She wasn't sure she liked this town she and Michael had chosen to live in. Maybe they should rethink the notion of retiring to a quiet place in the Yonne. Was all Burgundy like this? Was it France? Was Michael right, was she beginning to sound like Penny? Would they all end up in Cleveland?

Sophie answered the phone and explained in a low voice that her mother was feeling calmer and was napping. No, they didn't need any help, and the lady who cleaned for them had brought in some provisions. She thought a visit by Katherine might be better tomorrow or the next day. No, they had not set a date for a memorial service. It might not even be in Reigny-sur-Canne but in the old city of Nemours, where the Bellegardes had family.

"I wondered what happened to you when the policeman came by my house," Katherine said. She half hoped it would rattle Sophie's composure. At the very least, she didn't appreciate what felt like a brush-off from her friend's daughter. She also wondered why Sophie would go to such lengths to avoid the man investigating the circumstances of her father's death.

"I had a headache," Sophie replied in an expressionless voice. "I knew he would be too tiresome and I did not wish to hear more speculation about my father's death."

"You can't mean me, my dear. I have no basis for any guesses."

"No, of course not. I meant that policeman." Her voice took on a little color as she added, "Did he, I mean, was Yves mentioned?"

Katherine was tempted to say Sophie should have stayed to find out, but she only assured her that while Decoste had brought it up, she had insisted to him that it was nothing.

"Maman thinks Papa was disturbed by a sound and that my father might have taken the gun out of the case, intending to scare off a burglar, only whoever it was grabbed it from him and ran."

"Wouldn't Adele have heard something?" Katherine said, finally finding an opening to ask one question that had been bothering her.

"*Jamais*. Never. She won't admit it, but Maman takes a big sleeping pill every night and sleeps like someone unconscious. It has become a kind of family joke, the sound of her snoring."

"It's too bad it was so late at night that no one saw a strange car or someone running away," Katherine said. Again, something pushed at the edge of her memory, but it was vague, and slipped away in an instant. "But the police will figure it out soon. All of Reigny is worried, you know." She didn't add that half of them were worried it was a Nazi plot and the other half were worried they'd be tarred with the anti-German mood that seemed to be rising. To her surprise, Sophie appeared to have read a different meaning into Katherine's remark.

"Yes, well, if everyone had enough faith in Yves, it would be a good thing for him. It is sad when one aligns oneself with someone who does not believe in one with all their being."

It took Katherine a moment to untangle the meaning from the thicket of words, and then she couldn't think of a thing to say about Penny and her supposed lack of faith in Sophie's former suitor, or Emile's conviction that the Lothario was not in Paris when he said he was, so she asked to be remembered to Adele and ended the call. Sophie clearly was not over Yves.

CHAPTER 17

The wind had picked up, and the undersides of the clouds sweeping across the sky were darkening when she gathered the sheets from the clothesline. The Citroën putted into the driveway, pulling forward so the Hollidays' big SUV could rumble in behind it. She stopped with an armful of linen to look at the men getting out of their cars. Michael looked grim and J.B. unhappy. Briefly, she wondered if the choice of his shirt today had affected his mood. It was another Hawaiian number, a particularly bilious shade of green, festooned with what she thought were neon pink hibiscuses that would make a gardener cringe. Her husband didn't acknowledge her as he walked past her and into the house, but the music producer halted as he reached Katherine and turned on a smile.

"Hey, Kathy, how ya doing?" Being an American, he didn't wait for an answer. "I can't tell you how great this recording is going to be. It'll knock 'em dead, guaranteed. Now all we have to do"—he leaned his bulk in close to her, grabbed her arm with a soft, warm paw, and spoke in a stage whisper—"is convince that hubby of yours to give it the best shot possible."

Michael came back out the kitchen door with a bottle of water. "The music can stand for itself, I told you. Touring is for kids and superstars who can pull in audiences that will pay good money for a known thing or a new thing."

"Betty Lou's a known thing, and once we get the PR machine rolling, you will be too." J.B. planted his feet wide, raised his arms as if seeing a large billboard, and said in a loud voice, "The genius behind the stars! The mystery singer-songwriter steps into the limelight!"

"More like the man who couldn't cut it, the musician they left behind. You think the press won't jump on that? You think they won't ask Eric and the rest of the Leopards to rehash the whole history? I'm not setting myself up for that, J.B., and that's it."

"No tour?" Katherine said. "Is it that important for the CD to sell, J.B.?"

J.B. dropped her arm and made his way to the patio, where he sank into a wicker chair that threatened to come apart at the seams with his weight. "It's essential, as I explained to your husband. These days, you have to be out there where people can see you and you can get their attention. People find ways to download music for free, you know, or buy singles as MP3 files. Event tickets are hard cash and big money."

"Does that really mean having to talk about the bad blood between him and Eric?" She paused in her folding of sheets to glance at Michael, who had pushed his Stetson far back on his head and was silently fingering his guitar.

"That's old stuff, Kathy. No one gives a hoot. Hell, no one even remembers it. Fans love the tunes he wrote. They're classics, no matter who's singing them. If anything, it will spice up media interest."

"J.B.'s talking about having me sing them on tour, which is not going to happen," Michael said from his seat.

SUSAN C. SHEA

Katherine darted inside to drop the laundry on the chaise, then came back out. "Wait, you know he's not supposed to do that, right? How can he without bringing on a lawsuit or at least some embarrassing confrontation?" And having it cost money to defend, money we don't have, she added silently.

J.B. made a rude noise and waved one hand over his head. "Bring 'em on, I say. I know lawyers who'll demolish any move like that in a heartbeat. It's been twenty years, Kathy, and Mike is listed as the cowriter on the copyright for both songs. There's even some old amateur footage on YouTube of them playing at a concert when Mike was with the band, and he's singing the damn song. He's a legend, a mystery man. Looks like a hell-buster in those black leather pants too, I can tell you. Will go over big with the ladies. We can plaster YouTube with new video weeks before a tour gets underway. It will jack up sales, guaranteed.

"Look," he said, putting his meaty hands on the arms of the chair and pulling himself forward to make sure he had their attention, "the tour is an absolute must if we want to make money on the deal."

"You haven't told Katherine the rest of it," Michael said, looking up at her. "Tell her about the expenses."

"Well, hell, it costs money to make money. We all know that. So you up-front a little cash, you'll earn it back easy once the music starts selling on the Internet and at concert venues." He chuckled.

"How much money?" Katherine said cautiously. She supposed they could afford a couple thousand dollars if the return would be as much of a sure thing as the record producer said. It would mean no more *vide-greniers* for a while, and Michael's favorite veal roasts would be out. She would still need her paints, but maybe Michael could help her stretch her own canvases.

J.B. rotated his hands from the wrist in a gesture that admitted he wasn't sure. "A few thousand, maybe a bit more, but the best investment you can make."

"How much, exactly?" Katherine persisted.

"Twenty thousand," said Michael.

"Twenty?" Katherine managed to say. "But that's . . ." She stopped. No need for J.B., who obviously had plenty, to know how close to the bone she and Michael operated. "Impossible," she finished.

"Maybe ten," J.B. said, looking from one to the other. "Last thing I want is for my star musician to feel pushed into anything. We could start with that, and see how things go. But PR isn't cheap, and even with a tight touring operation, we're talking about having to book the spaces and guarantee sales. It's a tough business going in, but, man, the rewards are there for those who put their minds to it."

Katherine looked at Michael with a sinking heart. Should they gamble with such a big chunk of their nest egg? It wasn't that she didn't believe in his talent. And there was the question of leaving Reigny, leaving the dogs and the house. Was it even thinkable to leave them in Jeannette's care?

She sank into the wooden chair where she usually set her palette, remembering only afterward that her skirt might pick up the sticky remnants of the oil fingerprints that transferred themselves to surfaces all over the studio and the patio. "How much money do you think we—Michael—will make if he does this?"

"Big bucks, honey, that much I know. Look at how much money Betty Lou makes each time we put out a new CD. And

SUSAN C. SHEA

if I get that new studio going back home, I'll be able to produce a second CD for less, so we can follow up on the buzz
from the first."

"If you really think—" she began.

"No," Michael said in a harsh voice. "I know what really
happens most of the time. Half-empty auditoriums, poor
ticket sales that mean canceled venues, playing for goddamn
tips by the time you're done. And sales? A few CDs at inter-
mission, no slick video to jack up interest and buzz online. I
may be sitting it out here in France, but I watch what goes
on, I check the music sites, I read the blogs. It's fucking de-
pressing and I won't do it. That's final. The album, yes. The
tour, no. And I don't appreciate your ganging up with J.B.
against me, Kay." He put the guitar down gently but wasn't
so easy on the kitchen door, which slammed behind him as
he went inside.

J.B. chuckled. "He'll come around, you'll see. He's invested too much to let it go to waste, and he knows the music
is going great. He's written a couple of sure winners already.
Come on over to the next rehearsal and see why I'm so sure
about this. They sound mighty fine together, enough of Betty
Lou's great country style to please her loyal fans—and they
are loyal, believe me—and the magic of Michael's songwriting and rock genius to bring in that crowd."

"Thanks, I'd like that, but what do you mean, Michael's
invested already? You mean his talent, right?"

"Well, yeah, although he had to put up a few bucks to
help pay for the postproduction work that has to be done." J.B.
slid over this as if it was too minor for her to think about,
as if he wished it hadn't come up at all.

A few bucks. Michael hadn't mentioned paying J.B. to her.
"We really appreciate all you're doing, J.B. Betty Lou's so en-

couraging, and you obviously know the business." Maybe her job was to be Michael's agent, keeping the producer happy and running interference for the artist. "You have to understand, Michael was shocked when the band took his songs and then went behind his back to get their record deal and the first big tour. And then he had to fight to get any royalties for 'Raging Love' and the other song he wrote for them before they split."

"Darlin', I do understand. But you have to get back on the horse, know what I mean? Mike's been nursing that hurt for way too long. I'm going to show him he can make it. He's not too old and he still looks and sounds good. We're going to grab what we want, and what we want is a major hit for Mike and Betty Lou. You're with me on that, right?" He hoisted himself from the chair with a grunt. "Well, I got to get on back. Duty calls and all that. Talk to him, will you? He'll do what you say." With a wink, the producer got into his car and backed out of the driveway.

Dinner was quiet, with both of them picking at the roast chicken and leaving the cheese course untouched. Neither was ready to grapple with J.B.'s ultimatum. Finally, as she gathered the plates and put them in the sink, Katherine ventured a comment. "Is it the money, Michael? I'm wondering if we could find it somehow. My cousin in L.A., maybe . . ."

"It wouldn't work. You know we can't leave the dogs, for one thing."

"The dogs? Oh, for heaven's sake, I can find someone for the dogs. That can't be what's holding you back from the chance of a lifetime."

"That girl Jeannette? Hell, no. For one thing, her father would rob the place blind. Like leaving the cat with the canary." This, she felt, was a barbed analogy. Katherine had purchased a pair of songbirds when they first came to Reigny. The yellow cat, who came with the house, had dispatched them within the month, tracking them around the house. Katherine, who had never owned caged birds before, had let them fly around inside as a kind gesture while she cleaned out their cages. How was one to know they would decide to sit on the edges of low chairs rather than on top of the armoire?

"We could find a way. What about the money? Do you think you'll make it back?"

"No, I do not. J.B.'s been smoking something if he thinks we'd clear that much. Remember, I'd get only one share of the profit."

"Oh, of course." She hadn't thought that through. And yet. "What if you knew you could at least make the money back even if you didn't make a profit? And it might set you up, like he said, for another CD."

"J.B.'s been looking for someone to underwrite that studio for a while. Look how he went after Albert, who had zero background in the music business and didn't even know where Memphis is. I have a feeling my twenty thousand would find its way into his studio back in the States, and I'd still be singing for tips when he was done with his claims of big PR."

"Aren't there contracts for these things? I mean, it's a business. Don't put any money up until you have it in writing."

"You heard the man. Contracts are there to be broken, just like he'd have me do with the songs I wrote for the Leopards."

Katherine felt an undefined anger welling up inside. "Dammit, Michael. No matter what the plan is, you have a reason why it won't work." She came back and stood at the table, soapy hands on her hips. "You know what J.B. said? He said you have to get back on the horse, and I think that's right. Yes, Eric was a bastard, and yes, you didn't get to be part of the band. Who knows if it was the right decision or not? But I think you're afraid to find out, afraid you aren't good enough." Her voice had risen and she realized she was close to shouting, something she never did. She made light of things, danced away from awkwardness, never confronted problems head-on at full speed. What was wrong with her tonight?

Michael stood and pushed his chair back so hard that it fell over with a clatter. "That's a vote of confidence. Thank you for appreciating how I guard our pittance of a savings so you can continue to buy junk we don't need and more food than we can eat." He was yelling now. "Thank you for your belief in me—you think it was the right decision to cut me out of the band the moment it went big? You know nothing about music, nothing at all, but you're ready to send me back to the States to be J.B.'s bait while you dance around here like the lady of the manor and suck up to a bunch of sour old ladies."

He slammed out of the door, and a moment later Katherine heard the car screech out onto the road and grumble away. Part of her wondered where he could be going. Reigny's café was a five-minute walk downhill from the house, and they'd never in all their time here taken in any nightlife in the nearby towns. Was he going to commiserate with J.B.'s long-suffering wife, who probably had lots to complain about with a husband who saw her as his ticket to the good life? The larger part of her brain was playing back Michael's accusations, trying to avoid seeing them as stored-up grievances. She sat heavily, determined not to give in to tears. She had thought Michael was happy here, with her. This was, quite possibly, the worst day of her life.

CHAPTER 18

The girl sat hidden, like a statue, the way Katherine had told her to when she was trying to paint some little detail. She was shaken. Her father shouted all the time, and the kids all knew it was nothing, *pas important*. M. Robilier shouted at his wife every day, although he never made sense now that his brain was, her father explained, rotting away. Brett's parents, on the few occasions recently when she had been invited to their house for lunch, fought all the time. Brett said that was how they were and it didn't mean anything since they wanted the same thing, to make lots of money. But Katherine and Michael never fought. She wished her English were better so she could understand what they were saying when they talked so fast. The dogs, Brett's father, something about CDs, and a horse named Eric? It was a jumble, but no mistake, they were mad at each other. She had been forced to hunch down in the roses when Michael burst out of the kitchen door and drove off. Now she had to stay still in case Katherine came out. It would not do for her friend to see her spying.

Was there some way she could help fix it? Katherine was the only person who looked out for her, and Jeannette didn't like to see her unhappy. Would it help if she returned the spoons and the pretty cup and saucer she had taken for a lark? Maybe she could leave them at the kitchen door some night if that would cheer Katherine up.

Tentatively, she pulled the vines of the rose out of her hair where they were tangled, and picked at a spot on her shoulder that had been stabbed by a thorn. Only when she saw the light from the bedroom go off did she slip away, upset for some reason she couldn't say by what she had overheard.

CHAPTER 19

Michael eased into bed after she dozed off into a light sleep but, even though she half woke, she didn't speak to him as the bedsprings squeaked and he curled away from her. She drifted off sometime later, and in the morning he was up before her and the car was gone. Rehearsing, probably. Not for the first time, Katherine admitted to herself she was glad Betty Lou was no longer the ethereal young woman on her old album covers. In her current state, Katherine would have contrived to feel jealous.

As she tended to her garden halfheartedly, she replayed J.B.'s case for the tour. What if she stayed here? It would cut travel costs, and the argument about the dogs (and the yellow cat, of which she was fonder than Michael was) would be settled. She would miss the excitement. Reigny was not likely to take her to its collective breast no matter how hard she worked to make the fête's entertainment the best they'd ever had. But if it was successful, and it had to be, the tour might set Michael's past hurts to rest. She resolved to talk to J.B. and Betty Lou and help them convince her husband to give this a shot.

Screw Eric for all the misery he had caused, she said to

herself, and then took it back. Part of the history between the leader of the Crazy Leopards and Michael was, after all, that she had done just that. Only once, and before she and Michael were married, but still. She yanked hard at a weed, which turned out to be a delphinium stalk. "Oh, rats," she said.

"Talking to your plants again?" said a voice behind her. Penny stood, waving a hand in front of her face. "These flies are a pain. Sometimes I wish I'd never bought that house." She parked herself in the same wicker chair J.B. had sat in, looking down in surprise as it gave a little. "I was at the market in Auxerre and you'll never guess what I heard."

Katherine figured it wasn't her job to guess. She straightened up, feeling a dull ache in her lower back that could be from her weeding or from a bad night's sleep. She sat on a bench in the shade and looked inquiringly at the younger woman in front of her, whose smile was almost coquettish.

The gate rattled and both women looked down the steps to see Pippa, taking the steps as though they were an exercise challenge. "My goodness," she said, panting and looking at Penny with an eager expression, "I tried to catch up with you, but the hill is so steep and you do walk extremely fast. I'm sure it's why you're so slim. Do you mind if I sit with you for a minute?"

Wishing she could say no, Katherine smiled and pulled a chair out from the table. "Penny was filling me in on the investigation into poor Albert's death." She knew it was wicked, but at the very least it might get Penny off the topic sooner if she thought Pippa ought not to be thinking of Yves as a suspect in a nonexistent murder.

Pippa's face lit up, her eyes widened, and she nodded rapidly, her curls bouncing in a shaft of sunlight that caught her hair. "Brilliant," she said to both of them, "absolutely brilliant."

Penny, after a hesitating moment, continued. "The police are checking out a stranger who came into Yves's shop twice right before Albert died, buying everything he could about the château. And guess what?" She was looking at Katherine and, not waiting for an answer, added, "He was German."

Pippa raised her eyebrows and looked back and forth at the two women. "Is that a clue or something? I mean, it sounds rather important in a vague sort of way."

"Oh, Penny," Katherine said. "This is significant how? I mean, at this time every year visitors do come from all over Europe and the States to visit the château. Monsieur in the café said people have been coming in complaining since the CLOSED sign went up on the driveway the day Albert's body was found. Parts of Château de Bellegarde date from the twelfth century."

"Thirteenth, actually," Pippa said, sitting up straight and nodding. "Later, King Charles the Fifth had something to do with the place, although I can't remember exactly what."

"Thank you," Katherine said. "The point is, Penny, it's important in Burgundy's history, so of course lots of people want the guidebooks."

Penny's impatience showed. "No, that's not it. Don't you see, it's the timing, the fact that he was so focused on only this château, and that he was another German? He was even asking questions about the owners. For all we know, he might have had something on Albert, like blackmail, some kind of illegal gun dealings or something. He might have tracked Albert down to Reigny."

"My, that's awfully sharp," Pippa said. "Gun running, do you think? I started a story once about smugglers. Of course," she added thoughtfully, "it was set in the Caribbean, so there were ships. I may have to dig it out and finish it."

Katherine ignored the writer. "Michael told me Albert's gun-dealing days are long since over. He runs—or rather, ran—an investment company, or import-export or something. The police are taking this seriously? It sounds terribly thin, especially if you're saying Albert's fall might be murder, Penny. Are you?"

"It's a definite possibility. Yves says he was treated as a suspect before this clue was discovered, and a suspect for what if not murder? Why else would they have questioned him so long?"

"I didn't realize they had. Is it possible Yves exaggerated a bit? How did they find out about this stranger?"

"Yves told them." Penny was triumphant. "He remembered it while they were questioning him. The woman who works for him noticed the man too. She hated to admit it since she's part German too, which only makes it more credible."

"Your beau is a suspect?" Pippa clasped her hands and held them close to her chest. "Good heavens, how interesting. I wonder if I might speak with him?"

The rapt look on Pippa's face and the feeling that this conversation was getting away from her like a large kite in a high wind made Katherine uneasy. "For heaven's sake," she said, blowing out a loud sigh at the speculations of both of her guests. "What a lot of half-truths you've picked up. I'm sure Yves is not a serious suspect for anything. Mme Robilier is not German. Her husband's mother was German, or maybe it was his grandmother."

Penny lifted her chin and glared at Katherine. She sat up straighter. "You don't want Yves to be arrested, do you? The police are looking everywhere for the man. It's a shame Yves didn't think to write down his license plate."

"There's a nice image—the bookstore owner keeping

track of his customers' license plates on the off chance they turn out to be murderers."

Pippa was not to be denied her role as an armchair sleuth. "I say, if he bought books from the store, there will be credit card slips, won't there?"

"He paid in cash," Penny said in triumph. "He obviously didn't want to be traced."

"That is a complication," Pippa said, rubbing her hands together. "How old was he, approximately? Because Mr. Bellegarde was an old man, and if this chap was a former business associate, one would assume they were at least marginally in the same generation. Did Yves mention that, I wonder?"

"He'd have to be ancient," Katherine said, but neither of her companions paid any attention.

Penny told Pippa she didn't know, but Yves had said he was suspiciously chatty about the château.

"Pumping him, I think you say in America? Yes, he might well be worth checking on."

Katherine was too worn down by her fight with Michael to continue arguing with them. If the policeman wasn't smart enough to see through this ridiculous German assassination theory, then that was his problem. Admittedly, finding Albert's gun in the bushes was a puzzle, but she agreed with Michael. Someone might have gotten into the château, either kids or someone thinking to steal a few portable items, was discovered by Albert, who attempted to scare him off but fell down the stairs in the process. The would-be thief could have picked up the gun almost reflexively, then decided against stealing it and thrown it away as he ran down the driveway.

She did wonder, briefly, if Emile was right. Would Jean be stupid enough to try that? Her hunch was that breaking into a house at night when he might accidentally confront the owners and be recognized was beyond Jean's degree of bravado or scope of vision. He had lived in Reigny all his life and this was the first serious crime she'd heard about. With all those mouths to feed and very little call for Reigny's quarry stones, however, perhaps she shouldn't completely absolve Jean yet. She wondered how she might find out what he had been doing that night, maybe ask Jean a question or two and see how he responded. If there was anything suspicious in what he said, she could report it right away to that policeman, although, come to think of it, she wasn't sure how to reach him. Some detective she was. But she'd be damned if she'd mention the idea to Penny, who would pass along an idle comment as fact by tomorrow morning, or to Pippa, who would probably start skulking around the family's courtyard.

"You look particularly well put together today, Penny," she said to change the subject. "Are you going somewhere?"

"To Paris, with Yves. We need to shake off the stress from all this. I found a sweet little hotel near the Place des Vosges."

"One of my favorite neighborhoods, lucky you. There's a store off the square that sells the most charming ceramic roosters. Much too expensive, of course, but tourists will pay anything."

"I never stop in Paris," Pippa said, shaking her head emphatically. "Even a pot of tea costs the earth. I bring my own sandwiches and go right through to the Chunnel, you know."

Penny gave Pippa a horrified look that Pippa didn't see, being in the process of struggling out of the chair, which was losing its shape and its backbone from all the visitors who had been dropping in lately. She turned her attention back to Katherine. "There's a new show at the Pompidou Center I want to see, feminist art, and Yves wants to try this new bistro that serves only raw food."

Katherine didn't know which she'd dislike more, not that she dismissed art by women who had been left out of the museums and art history books for hundreds of years and were determined to be seen in the twenty-first century. She didn't like the branding of their work, or her own for that matter, as a special class, the same way defining "ethnic" art consigned it to a curiosity corner, leaving the main stage once again for white men. She opened her mouth to say something of this, but decided it wasn't worth the trouble. In the two years she had known her American neighbor, she had figured out that anything other than skimming the surface of ideas bored Penny. This was more properly dinner conversation with other art school graduates, conversations she hadn't had since her own days as a student. In Los Angeles, where she had moved after art school and met Michael, party talk had centered on real estate and yoga classes. Nevertheless, all of a sudden, she missed that time fiercely, missed California, missed days full of speaking in English, paying with dollars, picking up a newspaper at the corner drugstore.

"How sweet of Yves to treat you to a trendy dinner," she said, shutting that door to regret sharply and giving in to the impulse to poke a metaphoric stick at a friend who could afford to jet back and forth, keep a poor boyfriend, and spend two hundred euros on a plate of raw vegetables cut, no doubt, into strange postmodern shapes.

Penny colored and stuck her chin out. "It's hard to make a living at something so esoteric and important. Rare books are like jewels, but appreciated by a select few." She turned to the steps, Pippa right behind her with an eager look on her face that Katherine suspected meant Penny was going to have inquisitive company for her walk home. "I have to get going if we're going to make the train. I thought you'd be happy for Yves to hear the news."

"Have a wonderful time, take a few minutes to visit the Victor Hugo museum in the same neighborhood, and of course I'm thrilled for anything that eases Yves's and your mind. Good-bye, Pippa, thank you for dropping by," she said with all the sincerity she could summon. She waved at their backs as they descended from view, and when the gate creaked closed, she returned to the border she'd been working on, realizing she still held the delphinium stalk in a stranglehold.

When the phone rang, she was tempted to let it go, given the mood she was in, but thought it might be Michael. Pulling off her gardening gloves, she hurried in and grabbed the receiver. It was Adele, and she sounded much calmer than when Katherine had last seen her. She offered lunch, wanted company, and said she needed to ask Katherine's opinion. Glad for something to do other than replay her quarrel with Michael in her head or vent her frustration at Penny's ridiculous assassination proposal, Katherine accepted. She left a note on the kitchen table for Michael, shut the dogs inside, and walked through the village and up the other side of the little valley.

Sophie had gone back to Paris for a few days to take care of matters in her father's firm, which, Adele said, would come to her, so she might as well groom herself for the role. "It certainly does not interest me, and I have quite enough to live on, although not to continue the historical renovations on my own. I will have to speak with Sophie about that later. She will inherit this too someday, after all."

She poured them each a glass of the region's glorious red

wine, holding up the bottle so her guest could see the Premier Cru on the label. "Really too good to drink so casually, but what am I saving it for? I had not realized how well stocked Albert's cellar was. I must consider putting a lock on it and taking up some of the small things we chose to have around us. If there is a cat burglar in the area, I must not ignore him, *n'est-ce pas*?"

"Is that the policeman's current thinking?" Katherine said after exclaiming over the wine, which was indeed extraordinary, deserving of serious attention. She wondered if word of the mysterious German assassin had reached the widow.

"One hardly knows. They say nothing, only ask questions and permission to look around again and again. I gather they think something else was removed from the gun display. There's some kind of depression in the velvet material."

"Do you know what's missing?"

"No. Guns were Albert's passion, not mine. Honestly, I feel as though my privacy were completely taken from me."

"But you always had tourists."

"That was different. They were here to admire. And they were only allowed in certain areas, and twice a week, if that. It will be such a relief when my sister arrives. She was away when all this happened, and has only been able to arrange her schedule now."

"That's good news. I worried about you here by yourself. Of course, I imagine the neighbors have been dropping by to pay their respects."

"*Mais non*, not at all. Only that annoying, pretentious Mme Pomfort, who came to grill me, and who thinks she can give instructions to me. Imagine suggesting that a Bellegarde owes it to Reigny-sur-Canne to have a memorial service in that sad excuse of a church."

"Mightn't one think it was suggested as a sign of respect, that the people who knew him and who know you, want the chance to honor him?"

"You have not lived here long enough if you believe that," Adele said, biting hard into a piece of baguette slathered with butter. "Château de Bellegarde is the only reason anyone visits Reigny. Albert and I devoted so many years together to research its history, replace its broken walls, and preserve the valuables in it. Why, the tapestries alone are significant to France's history. But in all the years, we have never received any thanks or special regard from our neighbors."

"Surely that's not so. Everyone tells me how wonderful it is that you come to the fête each summer and contribute something delicious to the food tent." It was perhaps a bit of an exaggeration. The café owner did say that the Bellegardes normally sent over a large tray of only slightly stale baguettes and a generous bowl of olives for the big outside tables. He was alerting Katherine that someone had to be sure to bring the tray and the empty bowl back to the château. One year, they had disappeared and, he said, the village didn't hear the end of it for six months even though most people were convinced it was a dealer from L'Isle-sur-Serein who had snatched them.

Adele had begun to describe the valuable tapestries that the villagers didn't appreciate, and before she could go off into rhapsodies about the threadbare and moldy wall coverings, Katherine interrupted. "So what will you do in Albert's honor?"

"The Bellegardes will gather at our private chapel in Nemours later this year. Albert's ashes will be installed there. It's what our family has done for generations." She took a long swallow from her glass before continuing. "That is not why I have asked you here. I can deal with that ridiculous woman and her airs. Imagine thinking she is descended from Napoleon."

Adele got up and walked over to a table in the corner. To Katherine's untrained eye it was quite plain and dark, but she remembered Albert's explanation that it was untouched from its thirteenth-century origins. It was the kind of historical artifact Albert had been so proud to talk about when he conducted tours.

"What do you make of this?" Adele said, coming to stand over Katherine and holding out a piece of lined paper.

"Ask what the American was doing at your house in the night-time," it said in French. The sentence was written in pencil and it was obvious the writer had attempted to disguise his or her handwriting by alternating between crudely printed capital letters and typical French script. Katherine knew who had written it, but wasn't about to say. The child had no impulse control. Who knew why she had thought to send this to the widow, but the reason was sure to be one that would elude an adult's understanding.

"Where did you find this?" she asked instead. "Have you shown it to the police?" She hoped not. If she could figure out who had written it, so could they, and Jeannette would find herself in a heap of trouble. She had probably been hanging around here all week, looking for a way to create some mischief.

"It was under a stone outside the door early this morning when I went out to look at the garden, which is in desperate need of work. I cannot think where the gardeners are. Do they think because Albert is dead that the bushes have stopped growing?"

Good, thought Katherine with an internal smile, Adele

was recovering. She was glad. The shock of her husband's death and her relative isolation here might have crushed her elderly neighbor. It was good to hear at least a portion of her normal personality reemerging.

"I am reluctant to show it to anyone until I know who the American it speaks of is. I wanted to check with you first." Adele spread soft cheese on a cracker while giving Katherine a bright glance. The ammonia vapor from the cheese's rind caught in Katherine's throat and Adele's implied meaning had a similar effect.

"I can't imagine why you think I would know. There are only me, Michael, and Penny in Reigny. You can't think one of us snuck into your house."

"I hardly know what to think. I do not know if it is serious, or who wrote it. But it bothers me, as you must understand."

"Adele, you've been too wrapped up in the personal nature of this tragedy to be aware of it, but there are as many rumors flying around Reigny as there are residents. Believe me, you don't want to hear them. But the theme, with a few imaginative exceptions, is that it couldn't be someone who lives here who disturbed Albert. It must be an outsider. That leaves almost everyone in Burgundy, France, Europe and—yes—us few Americans too. I wouldn't pay much attention to this, really I wouldn't."

Adele gave a distinctively Gallic shrug, turning her palms up and spreading long, bony fingers, and let the subject go as she allowed the paper to drift out of her hands and back onto the table. However, her good-byes were cool and there was no talk of a next visit when Katherine took her leave.

Katherine wasn't interested in a leisurely farewell chat either. She was appalled that Adele could entertain the notion that she was somehow implicated merely because she was

American. She was determined to find the girl and give her a severe scolding. The note had succeeded in creating distance between Katherine and Adele, which left Katherine with exactly no one in Reigny-sur-Canne she could count as a friendly acquaintance.

Sure enough, the teenager appeared out of nowhere as she left the Bellegardes' driveway. Jeannette searched Katherine's face uncertainly as she came up to her. With more shyness than she usually demonstrated, Jeannette entwined her arm with Katherine's. But Katherine shook her off and said, "Jeannette, you have some explaining to do. Walk back to the house with me," and didn't respond to the girl's attempts to make her smile as they walked.

"Now," Katherine said, shutting the garden gate behind them with a bang and pointing Jeannette to a wicker chair, "why did you worry Mme Bellegarde with that note, and why did you pretend you saw one of us at their house the night Albert fell?"

Jeannette looked up at Katherine from under her eyebrows but said nothing. She chewed her lip and rubbed the little metal thing she'd been carrying around lately.

"Don't pretend it wasn't you who wrote that note. You've created an embarrassment for me and Michael, not to mention our friend Penny. *Tu comprends?* What were you trying to do? Answer me, child."

"No," Jeannette said, startled. "I didn't mean *you*. I saw a car—" She stopped abruptly, a look Katherine couldn't define sweeping over her face for a second before it was replaced with one of shame. "*Desolée.* I only wanted to help, and I could never talk to a *flic*. Papa would kill me."

"Talk to a policeman about what? What car? I don't know

what you're talking about." But even as she said it, Katherine remembered the girl skipping out of the wild growth next to the Bellegardes' driveway the morning after the tragedy. "You saw something? It certainly wasn't Michael or me. What is it you thought you saw?"

"I know what I saw," Jeannette said in a sulky voice. "It was Brett's papa's car. I saw it, but I don't want Brett to know, you understand?"

"For heaven's sake, he had business there. He told the gendarmes. He called on M. Albert long before anything happened."

"No," said Jeannette stubbornly. "I saw him late in the night. He was there. Then, later, I found something outside."

"Found what?"

"Nothing," the girl said.

"Nonsense. Either you did or you didn't."

"*Rien*, nothing. Never mind," Jeannette said, her voice rising. "I wanted to tell Brett his papa was there, but I was afraid. He will be angry at me if I say what I saw to the *flics*." She looked up at Katherine, worry furrowing her brow.

"I don't believe it. This is one of your pranks, a way to stir up trouble," Katherine said. "You probably think it's funny. Really, you let your imagination get the best of you."

Katherine was angry, angry at Jeannette's fibbing, but also at Adele's chilly behavior, Mme Pomfort's snobbery, and most of all at Michael for saying so many hurtful things last night and for leaving then and again this morning without a chance to talk it out.

Jeannette started to protest, but Katherine cut her off. "Enough. I don't want to hear any more excuses for your behavior. Honestly, you're no better than—" She stopped abruptly. Instantly she wished she could take back what she had been about to say about Jean. It was cruel and unfair. "You will go to Mme Bellegarde's and apologize for upsetting her, and when she tells me you have, we will talk again."

Jeannette jumped up, knocking the chair over. *"Merde,"* she yelled, "you have no right to tell me what to do. You're not my mother. You're like the rest." A small sob escaped her. "You do whatever that old witch Pomfort says. You're afraid of her, like the others." And she ran down the steps and out the gate, bawling as she went.

"Now I've done it," Katherine muttered. "But the girl turns everything into high drama." Not unlike me at her age, she thought. Maybe that's why I have a soft spot for her. Katherine didn't believe the girl's fantastic tale for a minute. J.B. was a respectable businessman who was going to make Michael a star—well perhaps not a star, but finally a respected singer-songwriter with royalty checks coming in. They needed J.B., and it was ridiculous to think he could be involved in Albert's death. Maybe Brett had rejected Jeannette's romantic overtures and this was her attempt at payback.

Groaning at the messiness of people's emotional lives, she opened the door so the dogs, who had been whining ever since they heard her voice, could burst out, looking around them to see who else was occupying their leafy yard. The big black dog looked up at her through shaggy bangs as if to ask what was going on. "Nothing out of the ordinary," she said out loud. "Rejection as usual."

CHAPTER 20

Of course, Michael came back. He wasn't a schoolboy running away from home. He drove up in the early afternoon, mumbling something about a tiring rehearsal. At first, they were wary of each other, talking about the need for a trip to the butcher's for more beef bones for the dogs, and getting Emile to mow the grass, and if either had checked the mailbox at the far end of the driveway. When Katherine couldn't stand it anymore, she filled his coffee cup and gestured him to his customary chair before pushing the yellow cat off her beloved chaise. "Let's not fight, Michael. I'm no good at it. I'm sorry for anything I said that upset you. You do whatever you want and I'll support it." She took a deep breath, then held it to see how he'd respond, if at all.

He looked down at his cup for a moment. She didn't expect a real apology. That was beyond his stubborn self. So, she was surprised almost into tears when he said, "You're the wisest person in the world, Kay, and I'm a fool not to listen when you tell me what to do. I told Betty Lou and J.B. this morning that I'm in. All the way. We'll do this tour even if it means standing on street corners playing for quarters. Which I sure as hell hope it won't," he added, looking up with a tentative grin.

"I love you," she said.

"Love you too," Michael said as he grabbed his guitar from the stand and picked out a chord. "Always have, always will."

Katherine was speechless. Other than when he proposed and on their wedding day, she wasn't sure he'd told her that outright. She knew he would lie down in the road and get run over for her, but an old rocker cowboy didn't talk about love. She tucked it into her heart to replay at the times that would surely come when he was grouchy or distracted. It was enough.

The rest of the afternoon was spent talking about the investment. He didn't like it, but Michael admitted he saw the point in having Katherine skip the traveling. He was worried about the money, but J.B. had assured him they could do it for less than a twenty-thousand-dollar share, and that J.B. himself would put up more than that, so they'd have a kitty going into the booking period. They ought to see some early profits from sales of the CD even before the tour was complete, thanks to the social media consultant J.B. worked with and the favorable contract he was ready to sign. Betty Lou had agreed to postpone taking her share of the CD profits until Michael had recovered half of his investment. It all sounded good, and Michael was more enthusiastic by the hour. He said J.B. was already submitting the paperwork to protect the new songs Michael and Betty Lou had written. The best thing, Michael said, now smiling broadly at Katherine, was that J.B. was serving as Michael's manager without charging him a percentage, at least not in the first year.

"It's a win-win," he explained. "J.B.'s been looking for a new talent, Betty Lou for a fresh take on her repertoire, and I've been sitting on my ass waiting for something to come to me."

Katherine was happy to see Michael so energized, relieved that their horrible falling-out was repaired. She put-tered in the kitchen and the garden as Michael expanded on the partnership with the Hollidays, his doubts gone and his faith in the venture expanding. But Jeannette's story, as far-fetched as it was, kept replaying in her head. *"It was Brett's papa's car. He was there."*

It made no sense. J.B. had no reason to sneak around the château late at night. He'd been shocked to hear about Albert's fall the next morning, and had been quick to volunteer the information about his business with the old man. If the po-lice had found even a shred of evidence linking him to Al-bert's death, they would have pounced on it, given that the alternatives were Nazi assassins, tourists, or Gypsies, most of the latter having been chased out of the country recently by politicians.

She was about to suggest they treat themselves to an early dinner at the simple *auberge* they passed each time they drove the back road to Vézelay, when the familiar sound of the Hollidays' big SUV, followed by slamming doors, alerted them that the new business partners had arrived.

"Mike, Kathy, we come bearing gifts." Two hearty laughs preceded them and then the Hollidays were opening the back door and wedging themselves into the little kitchen, their arms filled. "Foie gras, bubbly, and some of the smell-iest damn cheese these Frenchies can make." J.B.'s voice filled up the house and sent the dogs dodging past them into the garden. "We're goin' to celebrate the right way, partners."

When she glanced at the dogs, she noticed Brett for the first time, hanging around the door, picking at a finger, a sul-len look on his face. It was the same look he always wore, and she wondered, not for the first time, if it was a special burden to be the son of such dominating personalities. For their part, the parents ignored him as they descended on Michael and Katherine. Their good cheer and the volume of their enthusiasm left no room for other conversation until glasses had been procured, plates set out on the patio, and the feast arranged on a small table pulled out from the living room.

Katherine turned again to Brett, slumped deeply in the wicker chair his father had reshaped with his bulk. Katherine thought he looked worried about something under that attempt at a stone face. Darting back and forth from the house to set up the impromptu meal, she rummaged in the refrigerator for a soft drink, Michael's weakness on hot days. She opened the kitchen door and called out, "Thirsty? Hungry? There's plenty of food."

Brett looked up and opened his mouth, but his father beat him to it. "Hell, he's always hungry, aren't you, boy? Now, you take that soda," he called, not moving from the table, "and do what I asked, you hear?"

Brett's face flushed but he didn't say a word other than a mumbled thanks to Katherine as he grabbed the bottle and slunk off down the steps and out the gate.

"I hope you weren't sending him on a shopping errand to the café. Their supply of groceries and hardware is pitifully thin," Katherine said as she came back to the table. "I once needed some milk and they didn't even have that. Not 'til the next day's delivery."

"I sure do miss the Winn-Dixie," Betty Lou said, sighing dramatically. "And the prices. Lord help me, who would pay what they charge for a simple bag of grapes?"

The conversation drifted on like this while Katherine reveled in foie gras on chewy bits of baguette and inhaled the Crémant's bubbles, which tickled the roof of her mouth. Maybe when the album won a Grammy Award, she would buy real Champagne again and life would be more like this and less about *cassoulets* and leftover veal stew. Maybe they could get screens for the windows and have the slates on the studio roof replaced so her canvases didn't get damp in the rain.

She was drifting off into a happy vision of a future garden with proper retaining walls when J.B.'s voice brought her back to the present. "That little brat is sneaking around somewhere, you can count on it."

"Who?" she said, catching some real venom in his tone. "Brett?"

"Brett's bad enough, but it's that little—pardon me, Kay—cock tease, the one with the frizzy hair, I want to catch up with."

Katherine's hand froze on the way to the cheese plate. "Do you mean Jeannette?"

"Yes, I do. I assume that's her name."

"What's she done?" Katherine asked after clearing her throat and washing down a moment of anxiety with some wine.

"Someone plastered my car with eggs last week when I drove through town, and I know it was her. She's been tryin' to get Brett's attention for weeks now, but this is the last straw."

"Now, J.B., don't get so upset. You don't know it was her, and she's company for Brett. He has nothing to do around here." Betty Lou's soothing voice did nothing to calm her husband. "She loves riding over for lunch when she has a bike at her disposal. I think she's practicing her English on Brett."

"She's practicing something, all right. I just want a few words with her, that's all. She needs to stop pestering us. As far as I'm concerned, we can't get out of this place soon enough. Finding a house with a recording studio was great, but we're going to have to get back to the States to get this CD done, right, Mike?"

"Not until I swan around on the Riviera first," said Betty Lou with a warning chuckle. "I swore I wouldn't do another damn CD unless I got my week on the gold-plated Riviera, and I mean to do it. Heading right to the casinos in Monte," she said, winking at Katherine. "You ought to come with us."

To Katherine's ears, this was an alarming statement. With whose money did Betty Lou plan to gamble? She glanced at Michael, but he appeared not to be taking any special message from it. She also wondered about the "another damned CD" comment. This was hardly that. It was everything to Michael, and to her. The bread tasted dry in her mouth, and she found she had no more appetite.

"J.B.," she said, looking into her glass, "aren't you looking to build a studio in the States? I kind of remember that's why you were talking with Albert."

"Hell, I'll talk to anybody, Kay. Mike knows that." He guffawed and reached out with his knife to touch Michael on the hand. "You knew the guy was loaded, right? Saw his name on one of those lists of the richest people. It sure was a surprise to find out he lived right here."

"You knew that before we booked the house," Betty Lou said. "Don't you remember, you showed me on a map—"

"That's backward, darlin'. Coincidence, but could have been big for us. What do you know about the widow?" he said, leaning toward Katherine. "I mean, assuming she inherits, do you think she's much of an investor? Maybe I should call on her. Old Albert was ready to sign up, make some money with us. Damn shame if some Gypsy thief got to him first."

Katherine shook her head as she looked at J.B., keeping

her expression bland. His mouth smiled but his eyes were digging into her, probing for something. Did he think she doubted his business acumen? Was he worried that she had cold feet about his contract with Michael? He surely didn't know about Jeannette's note or her accusation. She wanted—no, needed—to have confidence in this man who was about to take a big part of their savings, and whose promises to Michael had raised his hopes and exposed him to more potential hurt than anything in the years since his break with Eric and the Leopards.

"I wouldn't know. Adele and I are merely neighbors."

"But she called you when she found the body, right?"

"After she called the sheriff and her daughter."

"What about the daughter? She interested in music? I'll bet she thinks Mike's pretty cool." He winked at her, a habit that had begun to grate on Katherine. Who winks at people, anyway, and what is it supposed to mean?

"I read online that the French love American country music," Michael said, mostly to Betty Lou.

"The Japanese, too," the singer said, "although I think they mean cowboy music more likely. But J.B. will get the word out everywhere, won't you? If there's an audience anywhere in this wide world, you leave it to J.B., he'll find it."

At that, the producer and the singer started laughing, and Michael looked happily at Katherine, raising his glass to her in a silent toast. All Katherine could do was smile.

CHAPTER 21

If anything, Brett was handsomer when he frowned than when he smiled. Not that he smiled a lot. His smiles were reserved for particularly good runs on the skateboard or when he crouched down to play with the puppies. Today, when he found her in her special spot under the bridge near the bank of the river at its shallowest place as the daylight faded, he was frowning. He didn't speak at first, picking up and skimming rocks over the water.

"This place is not so deep for that," Jeannette said, struggling with her English. He still said nothing and didn't look directly at her. She did a quick mental inventory of her clothing choices. The green T-shirt with something written in exotic gold Chinese characters. The green was good with her hair, Katherine had told her once. Tan shorts, a little tight because they were from last year, but that was all right because she was trying to look sexy anyway. Hair freshly washed and curly around her face, like a model in the magazine her father had brought home last week. She hoped Brett would notice. He seemed to be busy with his thoughts. He didn't have his skateboard either.

"I have keeped—kept?—the present you gave me," she

said to get his attention. She held a brass cylinder up to the light, then put it back in her pocket. She had been careful not to let her brothers or her father see it. The little ones would have pestered her for it, and her father would have demanded to know what she and Brett were doing when they spent time together.

He gave it and her a sharp glance, then looked away. "You going to the café tonight? My dad says there's a talent show, kind of a tryout for some festival they're putting on later this summer."

"The fête. I don't know. My father will probably go and he will expect me to take care of the little ones." She made a face. "Are you going?"

Brett nodded, peeling the bark off a green twig and stabbing it into the wet dirt.

"So why don't you get someone else to take care of them, and come?"

It was his style, the girl knew, to be super cool, and she did her best to mimic it as she answered. "Maybe François to do it. He is almost twelve. The house is close by, so he can come and get me if the little ones start fighting." She giggled. "You will try out for something?"

"No way," he burst out, finally looking at her and grinning. "It's old-people stuff. I'm saving my energy for the Rivi-era." He said it triumphantly in a kind of singsong, without seeming to notice her disappointment. She would be sorry when Brett was gone. That part was *tragique*. But she would be glad when his father, with his secrets and his loud voice and his staring at her when he drove through town, was gone from Reigny. It was M. Holliday who had turned Katherine against her. Katherine had been the only adult in all of Reigny who treated Jeannette nicely, who invited her to lunch and listened to her and advised her on life. Katherine had used her as a model for her paintings, the biggest compliment Jeannette had ever received. Now that was spoiled, and all because Brett's father was a liar and a thief, even if he must have thrown away what he stole. Maybe even a murderer. She shivered.

"Come with me," she said, dancing over to the American boy and daring to take his hand. "I'll show you someplace secret and fun."

Brett looked at her curiously but didn't pull his hand back. In fact, he wrapped it around hers more tightly and nodded. She had nothing to lose. Brett would be gone soon and she would have an empty summer ahead of her, with no friends and no distractions. She would make the most of the time she had left. She was determined that she would have some romantic stories to share with her girlfriends when she started school again.

She led him back to the road, then up the hill and onto the dirt road that led to the quarry. The old stone site had two parts: one that was still in use, that her father used when someone wanted stones to line their driveway, or to shore up a riverbank, or put under a pavement, and the other part, which had been left alone for as long as Jeannette knew, a huge hole dug out of a hillside where the stone was harder, too hard for her father to work without better equipment and other men.

Jeannette tugged Brett in this direction, where the road was so overgrown with high shrubbery it was hard to know it had been there, except for two ruts that led into the woods. The best part of this section was the pool made by the digging. Jeannette and her older siblings, before they left for jobs in Lyon, had constructed a rope ladder on a strong old tree.

The thick hemp hung into the water so they could walk up the sloping sides of the stone and onto the grass. The little ones were never permitted to come into the quarry. Their father threatened to beat them if they set one foot on the dirt road that led there, and the children knew he was a man of his word where beating was concerned. It wasn't until they were teenagers that any of them dared to defy their father's rule.

"The pool isn't deep, but sliding in is fun," she said, smiling up at Brett.

"Awesome," he said, walking up to the edge and looking into its shadows. "Is it cold?"

"Not so much now," she said, and then was suddenly silent. She hadn't figured this part out. She could not take off her top, which would be too revealing even though she was wearing a sports bra she had purchased the last time she went to Vézelay with her school group. Brett had already peeled off his T-shirt and, without waiting for her, had grabbed the rope and was shimmying down.

He let out a whoop as he met the water. "Not cold?" he yelled, laughing. "It's friggin' ice water." But he didn't come out, and she laughed, sitting on her bottom and slipping down cautiously into the water, which looked darker in the growing twilight.

Brett dove under, and came up whipping his hair to one side and swimming easily across the pool. Jeannette was shy again. She couldn't swim. The water wasn't too deep, only up to her neck, and she could paddle and float her way over to the rope. Now, she wished she could really swim, to look as rhythmic and controlled as Brett did. Brett swam around her, talking and laughing, splashing water at her, and offering to tow her around the perimeter of their private pond. This was a happy moment, and tonight would be a happy one also since Brett had invited her to the café. She floated and smiled up at the treetops. Brett was her boyfriend, *n'est-ce pas?* Her first real boyfriend.

When they had hoisted themselves back onto the rocks and spread their limbs on the still-warm stones to dry, Brett surprised her by moving closer until his hip was touching hers. He hoisted himself up on one elbow and looked down at her. His free hand touched her stomach lightly and she sucked in her breath. While he watched her closely, his hand played with the hem of her T-shirt, lifting and twisting it gently. She didn't take her eyes away from his when his fingers slid under the T-shirt and moved slowly up her rib cage. His smile had faded and the smoldering look he habitually wore was back, freezing her with its sexy appeal. When his hand cupped her breast through her bra, she felt odd, almost as though she had no will of her own. Her breast tingled as it had when he had brushed against it in the woods outside the château.

The boy leaned forward then and kissed her at the same time he squeezed her breast. He turned and she felt him pressing against her shorts, warm and hard. Suddenly, Brett was pushing his tongue between her lips, a big, wet thing poking inside her mouth, making it hard to breathe, and it broke the spell. Why was he doing that? She closed her lips and tried to wiggle away. Brett paid no attention and now he was squeezing her breast harder. She pulled at his hand and jerked her face sideways, managing to say, *"Non, non."*

He froze for a moment, then rolled off her, and she sat up, pulling her T-shirt down and scooting her body sideways.

"What?" Brett said in a lazy voice. "You don't like that?" He reached for her, but she had had enough. If this was romance, she didn't like it one bit.

"I have to make dinner ahead of time since I am going to the café." Her face was burning and she felt like a failure. Was Brett angry at her?

"Up to you," he said, although his tone of voice clearly said he was disappointed. He grabbed his shirt and walked ahead of her back the way they had come. She tagged along behind, miserable and guilty. She was supposed to like that thing with the tongue? Did everyone but her like it? Was she a baby for thinking it was gross?

They retraced their steps silently, and at the road he turned toward the café. "My dad's picking me up," he said. "He's hoping you'll be there tonight," he added, a sudden gleam in his eyes. "You won't disappoint us, will you?"

Confused and unhappy, Jeannette mumbled something to assure Brett she would be, then ran downhill to her house, wanting only to get home, where she could replay the business by the pool and figure out if she still had a boyfriend.

CHAPTER 22

The café, which scratched out a partial living for the wheat farmer and his wife, who owned it, was located in what would have been a good spot had there been a reasonable amount of traffic coming through Reigny-sur-Canne and if the proprietors had a sign that stuck out into the street. At the junction of two narrow roads that came together in a Y, the building stood almost in the intersection, its pockmarked stucco facade free of any modern marketing gimmicks. A flower box with some brave geraniums stood on one side of the door. The problem was if visitors didn't know that it was there, they were likely to sweep past the store and then have to look for a relatively safe place to turn around. Strangers passing through town probably said, "To hell with it," and kept on driving until they came to the next little hamlet in the commune, twelve kilometers down the road, which had its own little shop for Badoit water and yogurt.

The only sign, painted directly onto the stucco over the store window in red letters, which the owner touched up every couple of years, was economical and to the point: *CAFÉ*VIN*EPICERIE*. It didn't say "live music" because, in spite of the sound wafting from its interior as Katherine and

Michael entered this evening, there wasn't entertainment on a regular basis other than the exchange of gossip and heated complaints about whichever national government was in power. And the sign, Katherine had discovered after they bought their house, was not entirely accurate. While espresso and local wines were always available, bread, milk, eggs, and cheese were not. This was not the place to come if you ran out of *sucre* or dry beans for tomorrow's *cassoulet* unless one or the other of the owners had thought to order them for the weekly delivery or, on a whim, had gone directly to the wholesale supplier while doing other chores in the larger cities of Autun or Dijon. Everyone in Reigny knew this, of course, and did their basic shopping at the *supermarchés* in the big towns, which lessened their reliance on the Reigny café, which, in turn, lessened the urgency on the part of the owners to stock the shelves.

The coffee and wine business was booming tonight because locals who dreamed of an audience for their talent all year round were here to try out for a place on the stage of the annual Feast of the Assumption fête.

Katherine had explained to Michael that they weren't auditions because she would make sure everyone who wanted to perform got at least a little time onstage, even if it was early in the day or while the food was being served in another tent. The trick was to keep the most enthusiastic performers, who were often the least talented, from taking and holding the small stage pretty much at will. That's what had happened the prior year to everyone's annoyance except Emile's, who was fond of telling Katherine and Michael how exceptionally well received his encores had been.

Emile's only concern this year, he had explained to Katherine more than once, was that she would not invite him to perform twice—something French on his beloved accordion, and a "true rock and roll" classic on his electric guitar with the renowned American performer living incognito among them. He wanted Katherine to understand that he and his fellow *pétanque* players, a drummer and a bassist, were crowd-pleasers in both styles.

Yves, who held the door open for Katherine and Michael, rolled his eyes and murmured in her ear that he hoped Michael would not join Emile's motley crew of amateurs on the stage.

"Not tonight anyway," Katherine said. "He and Betty Lou are hoping to get some response to their new arrangements before they decide if they should record them."

Yves was twitchy with energy and soon abandoned them, and Michael headed off to get them drinks while she claimed a table. Katherine didn't like crowds or big parties. In Los Angeles, she had always felt like an outsider, which she knew made her react snobbishly, fuming silently at what she called "these pod people" while drinking too much overly oaky chardonnay. "But if I had their money," she admitted to Michael after a party she'd wanted to flee the moment they entered the house, "I would only spend it on vintage clothes and better paintbrushes and tap-dancing shoes, and I'd still look like this, and they'd still look down their noses at me and call me quaint or worse behind my back."

This party scene was as far from the modernist canyon lifestyle of L.A. as it could be. She reminded herself this was what she had wanted. She looked around at the high-ceilinged fluorescent-lit space littered with small tables and rickety chairs, the scuffed linoleum floors, a faded poster for Kronenbourg beer on one wall, and a line of decorative plates high on another. Yes, this suited her better.

A burst of laughter from the next table caught her attention. She didn't recognize a single face among the party of unshaven men upending bottles of beer and shouting merrily. After a confused moment she realized they were Polish workmen, a group of summer migrants hired to rebuild a stone bridge at the far end of Reigny, beyond Pippa's house, that had been undermined by a flood last winter. Jean had assumed he would get the job, but the district's bureaucrats had apparently not even considered the idea that a local—or maybe Jean in particular—could do it. As a result, the quarryman was looking daggers at the party from his position at the end of the zinc bar.

His glance met hers and he gave her the same belligerent glare, and when she looked away quickly, it was to see Mme Pomfort peering at her from the opposite direction, mouth turned down in its habitual moue of disapproval. The widow bent toward the other woman at her table, hand covering her mouth, and said something. That lady, hawk-nosed, buttoned tightly into a black trench coat, and looking much like a large crow, cut her eyes in Katherine's direction, then ducked her head to hear what else Mme Pomfort had to tell. Katherine began to feel as though she had a target painted on her back.

To her surprise, Pippa Hathaway was sitting in a far corner of the room, looking at no one in particular and sipping a glass of red wine, her face slightly flushed. When their eyes met, she gave Katherine a look designed to carry meaning and lifted a small notebook surreptitiously. Katherine understood she was here doing research, probably looking for clues to a murder, and was debating whether or not to signal her to join them when suddenly everyone in the café jumped as if they'd received simultaneous electrical shocks. Emile had tested the amplifier volume with a shrieking chord that vibrated in Katherine's teeth.

Before the patrons had recovered, the door opened and Penny came in wearing a floaty dress that shouted "Paris" and was wrong for the occasion. Her eyes darted around, rested briefly on Katherine, then kept moving, with only a dip of her head in greeting. Okay, Katherine thought, she's still pissed at me.

Penny saw Yves and made for him, touching his arm possessively when she got to where he was standing, talking to the young cheese makers. He tossed his hair back and moved a millimeter away, enough to make her hold on his arm tenuous, a bit of drama that made Katherine wince in sympathy.

Looking around for Michael, Katherine noticed Mme Robilier, whose flowers would have to be accommodated somewhere on or near the stage. She was sitting with her elderly husband, who looked confused by the activity. A middle-aged couple, their son and his wife, Katherine guessed by the young man's strong resemblance to the older one, shared their table. The three Robiliers who did not suffer from dementia were facing the stage with rigid backs, turned as far away from Mme Pomfort's table as possible. The speculation about German-born Albert's intruder and gossip about Nazi sympathizers in Reigny had raised the temperature of dislike between the two women, a pity, thought Katherine, since they held adjoining properties and would be neighbors until they died. No one who held land in Reigny-sur-Canne sold their legacies outside the family.

Emile had continued to refine the sound from his amplifier, drowning out conversation with electronic squeals and hums as he adjusted the knobs on his secondhand equipment. His drummer, a car mechanic who hung out at the *pétanque* court most days, practiced his cymbals. The bassist, a young guy Katherine didn't recognize, sat calmly, surveying the audience. Mme Pomfort pantomimed her verdict with hands over her ears.

Emile had set his silver-and-red accordion at the edge of the small platform, which happened to be close to where Jean leaned against the bar. Emile was eyeing Jean nervously as he tuned his electric guitar. Katherine shook her head as Michael came back, put the thick stemless glasses down, and turned his chair around to straddle it, cowboy-style.

"He's afraid Jean will make off with the accordion," she told Michael, dipping her head in Emile's direction. "He's convinced Jean broke into the château and has been worrying for days that Jean is on a one-man burglary rampage."

A particularly discordant lick from the stage froze Michael. "Oh boy," he said, refusing to look at the stage.

Penny was having a hard time getting Yves's attention as he made a great show of charming the new resident couple, and now she left his side, moving over to where Emile was bent over a speaker. He looked at her, grinned broadly at something she said, and held up his index finger. Darting over to his pile of equipment, he brought back a tambourine, thrusting it at her with what Katherine could only describe as a leer. Ironically, given his former profession, he had a missing molar that made him at this moment look quite piratical.

Suddenly, standing up straight, he settled his guitar over his torso, planted his legs in a crouch, rolled his shoulders forward, and, with the help of his little band, launched into the approximate tune of a deliberately nasty Rolling Stones hit. Michael coughed to cover up a snort of laughter. "I'm not sure I can make it through one number."

"That's what the wine is for, darling," Katherine said.

And if that weren't enough, Penny now leapt up and stood next to him, tentatively waving the tambourine around as she struggled to find the beat.

Emile ended with a flourish and gave a jaunty bow. There was sketchy applause, which he interpreted as a request for more, and he responded by sailing enthusiastically into the first verse of an American pop song made infamous by its white-booted singer-songwriter several decades ago. At that moment, a hand grabbed Katherine's shoulder and squeezed. "Hey there, kids." She jumped, and the ruby-colored wine slopped over the lip of her glass.

J.B. and Betty Lou sank into the remaining chairs at the Goffs's table, looking around at the crowd and beaming. Betty Lou propped her guitar case next to Michael's and said, "When are we on?"

Michael said not until Emile had left the stage unless they wanted to perform as a trio.

"Can't miss an evening of homegrown talent, right, darlin'?" J.B. said. He looked around for a nonexistent waiter. "Shoot, I gotta get up again? What're you drinking, guys?" he said as he struggled to his feet, the Hawaiian shirt this time fire-engine red with large white flowers, possibly more noticeable than Penny's silk dress in this crowd, especially because it was paired with hippie-era sandals.

J.B. made his way back to the table in a few minutes, having managed, in spite of his inability to do more than point, to commandeer a plate of bread and sliced sausages, charcuterie. "So, what's going on with old Albert's death?" he said, popping a torn chunk of baguette into his mouth and speaking loud enough to be heard over Emile's guitar. "Have the cops been over to see you, Kathy? I hear they're making the rounds."

Katherine wished he hadn't brought it up. She pitched her

voice low. "I don't know much. Adele says the investigator's been back to talk to her and Sophie again, but I hate to pester her for details. She really is undone."

"Poor thing," Betty Lou said. "They'd been married for a long time, I expect. Although, I have to say, he was kind of controlling, if what I saw at your party was typical."

"Old-fashioned," Katherine said.

"She have any part in his business?" J.B. asked.

"I don't think so. He never talked about it to us."

Emile ended the song to raucous applause from the Polish table and immediately plunged into another number. Michael turned back to the table. "He's got another guitar up there and he keeps nodding at me. I either need a lot more wine, or to leave before he asks me to come up and play with him."

Betty Lou laughed. "Happens a lot. You say your voice is shot, or your hands are, or something. J.B., offer the guy a glass of wine and get him over to the bar and off our stage, okay?"

"In a minute, honey." J.B. was still probing. "Are the police checking into any Gypsies hanging around, or that nasty piece of work who runs the trash yard? Seems to me he might've been looking to rob the old man."

Katherine looked around. Jean, owner of the used-parts business, such as it was, seemed to have focused his scowling attention on Emile. "J.B., you need to keep your voice down," she said. "He's right over there."

"Hell's bells, none of these good people speak a word of English. Believe me, I've tried. Try getting directions to a decent restaurant, right, honey?" Betty Lou lit a new cigarette and shrugged. "Seriously, Kathy, I expect the cops are checking out the locals. Who else could it be?"

"You're the one who told us he was named in a big American magazine as a rich man, J.B. Anyone could track him down here. That wouldn't be hard, and I'm sure the people who live here would prefer it was an outsider."

"So you think it's a stranger?" J.B. looked at her thoughtfully, drumming his pudgy fingers on the table. "Did you tell that to the policeman?"

"Of course not. I haven't a clue who it was if there was even anyone to blame. I try not to think about that." Which wasn't precisely true, she admitted to herself. Lately, she had caught herself looking at people as though she were fitting them for a killer's personality. The middle-aged woman who cleaned for Adele once a week? Shifty, just because she had a limp and a lazy eye? How insulting and ridiculous, and what motive other than Albert's probable grousing about how much he paid her? The Danish businessman who had rented a house for the summer and whom she saw prowling around the forest near Château de Bellegarde, supposedly bird-watching? What did she think he was up to other than trying to find the overly enthusiastic birds who woke her every morning at five? But she couldn't help it. If Adele was reporting correctly, the police were inclined to believe someone had been in the château with Albert that night and might be implicated in his death. If she believed Jeannette, she had to include J.B. in that list, but that made no sense. Jeannette must have been mistaken. There was no reason for the American to be sneaking around Albert's castle in the middle of the night.

For an instant, she considered introducing J.B. to Pippa, if only to give the young writer someone new to question, but something stopped her. What was it about J.B. that seemed at times too intensely interested in Albert and his business and the possibility that someone had actually killed the old man?

Pippa had some of the same not-quite-proper level of curiosity, but then she was a writer desperate for material. J.B., however, asked too many questions and seemed far more eager for answers than made sense for a short-term visitor, and there was something that bothered Katherine about the way he kept at it.

"Well, here's another thought," he said now. "What if Bellegarde knew something about someone here in town, say another German, and was going to tell all? Collaborators or something. I heard there's a lot of old war grudges alive and well."

Where had he picked that up? Katherine wondered. It would have to have been someone who spoke English—Penny, perhaps, in an effort to keep any suspicion from attaching itself to Yves? If it was her, that woman was making trouble in her clumsy attempts to protect Yves. She decided to find out, if only to suggest to Penny that it wasn't such a good idea.

"Michael and I are trying to mind our own business, which is hard to do since we're—well, I'm—also trying to support Adele and Sophie. They are utterly alone up there in that big, cold place."

"Counting their money, I'll bet." J.B.'s grin was laced with something harder. Katherine didn't understand him on that score either. Was he really going to be a good fit for Michael? Did she have to worry privately if he, too, would find a way to take advantage of her husband?

"I really don't know," she said, putting as much finality into her voice as she could. J.B. was annoying her tonight and, much as she liked Betty Lou and hoped Michael was about to be recognized for his talent, she was counting the days until J.B. and his family left Reigny.

Emile had reached the final chorus of a summer anthem

of thirty years earlier and was crooning in what he intended to be the voice of the lead singer, if the star sang off-key with a rustic Burgundian accent. Katherine noticed Pippa still sitting in the corner, eyes fixed on the Don Henley wannabe, mouth open in what was either awe or horror.

Katherine was about to suggest it was a good time to leave, but J.B. stopped her with a hand on her arm. "Well, if it wasn't someone who snuck into town pretending to be a tourist," he roared over the sound, "it must be one of the local lowlifes."

Unfortunately, Emile's ending chord faded away just then, and J.B.'s words fell or rather blasted into a sliver of quiet. The Poles, oblivious, began their hooting and clapping, but Katherine could feel the eyes of the neighbors on them. Betty Lou barked cheerfully at J.B. to mind his own goddamn business, and said this would be a good time for a diversion.

Betty Lou gave her husband a look that sent him over to congratulate Emile and practically pull him off the stage. Michael and Betty Lou grabbed their guitars and climbed up the steps to a sudden shower of excited comments that papered over any collective insult J.B. had made. They put their heads together for a couple of minutes, then Michael pulled the inadequate microphone to the space between them, and the two brought their chairs in close. The audience was quiet, curious. When Betty Lou sang the opening lines of the Rolling Stones's "Wild Horses," Katherine was suddenly riveted. If she had ever known, she had forgotten that the woman had a glorious, husky voice, aching with passion and meaning.

Then Michael joined in, singing a tender harmony and playing so sweetly that Katherine found she was swallowing around a lump in her throat. Oh yes, he was good. Oh yes, he deserved a chance. Her vision blurred with tears she would not shed. Screw the Leopards if they tried to stop him this time.

The people in the café must have felt the same. There was a collective holding of breath, an intense kind of listening. The bartender stopped pouring wine, the Poles stopped drinking, and Emile looked as though he might faint from awe. When the music ended, there was an instant in which time stopped, and then wild applause, whistles, and people banging beer bottles and stomping their feet.

Betty Lou elbowed Michael and winked. Michael looked around, a slow smile breaking across his face, his color mounting. Katherine realized that to him this had been an audition.

They did one more song, then quit, over loud requests of "Encore, encore!" Katherine, getting ready to leave with Michael, who was still being congratulated at every table he passed by, noticed that Penny was flushed and self-conscious, apparently deep in conversation with Emile while sneaking peeks at Yves every few seconds. He was looking around with alcohol-glazed eyes, having run out of things to chat about to the young man with the big ears and his wife.

Katherine darted over to Penny. "I know you met Betty Lou at my lunch. The man with her is J.B., her husband and manager. Have you met him already?"

"Oh, is that who it is?"

Penny wasn't a good actress. So she had bumped into him somewhere and had unloaded her anyone-but-Yves theory. For all her jumping around onstage as Emile's new tambourine player, she seemed unhappy. Another lovers' quarrel to be made up later? In any case, Penny wasn't in a confiding mood.

"Did you see that Pippa is here? Over in the corner, by herself. She might like company."

Penny cast a careless look around but didn't seem interested.

"Come by for coffee tomorrow?" Katherine said, unhappy at Penny's coolness.

"If I'm in Reigny," Penny said, nodding and turning back to her musical mentor of the moment.

"Darling, you were out-of-this-world wonderful, you and Betty Lou," Katherine said to Michael. "And now I want to go home." She had caught up with him at the bar. "Penny's mad at me for not taking Yves's part in this police business, plus she's making a fool of herself trying to get Yves's attention and he's getting drunk and who knows what he'll say or sing. J.B. is upsetting everyone by talking about Albert's death like that. Look at Mme Pomfort. She's about ready to hit him with her bag."

"I doubt she understands half of it."

"That's not the point. He's loud and—"

"And you don't like him." He tilted his head and gazed at her, his expression neutral.

"It's not that," she said, dropping her voice to a whisper. "I've been working so hard to fit in, to be accepted, you know? And I feel like I have to apologize for him every time he opens his mouth."

"Baby, you take on the weight of the world and there's no reason to. If someone has to ride herd on him, it's Betty Lou. So, you liked our arrangements? Didn't I tell you she has a helluva voice?"

"Yes, you did, and yes, I liked—no, loved—it tonight. I'm so proud of you." She squeezed his arm and his answering smile traveled into his eyes.

"Let me find the men's room. Be right back," he said.

In light of everything J.B. and Betty Lou had done for him, Michael wasn't about to criticize the producer, especially if the idea of a recording was becoming more likely. But, said a little voice in her head, what if Jeannette was telling the truth? What if J.B. had been at the château later than the police realized? No use thinking about it now, she decided. Instead, she went over to Pippa's table, tucked into a far corner.

"I'm soaking up atmosphere," the young woman said. "This is wonderful research." She giggled. "Not so much that peculiar Frenchman's playing, actually. He's rather awful, don't you think?" Her hands fluttered in front of her face. "But he may be a friend. . . . I'm so sorry if I . . ."

"No, I agree. Emile wants to have a big spotlight in the fête, and I think this performance is supposed to nail our support."

"Will it? I mean, does one have to accept every bloke who comes along?"

"In little Reigny, Pippa darling, there aren't enough candidates to turn anyone down. And it'll be fun, you'll see." Saying good night to Pippa, she turned toward the door. "Uh oh," she muttered to herself. "The evening's not quite over."

CHAPTER 23

Jeannette was leaning against the wall near the door. Brett Holliday stood next to her. Jeannette looked miserable and Brett wore the same unreadable expression he always did. Katherine felt guilty for her sharp words to the girl. She made her way toward them, thinking she would try to make it right, but she had barely reached them when J.B.'s voice rang in her ear.

"Well, well, the younger generation has decided to join us. Want a beer, boy? And you, young lady? You probably grew up drinking vino. I read somewhere"—he turned to Katherine with another wink—"French babies are weaned on the stuff."

Before Katherine could argue, he said, "Just kidding. A soda for the young lady, coming up."

Jeannette refused to meet Katherine's gaze, looking down and picking at her nail polish, pink with sparkles tonight, and Katherine couldn't say anything about her anonymous note with Brett standing there. "Jeannette, I'm thinking of starting the painting of a nymph by a stream, the one where you'd wear that puffy skirt. I'll pay you, of course," she added quickly, unwilling to get tangled in Jean's argument again. When

Jeannette looked up, it was at someone else approaching their little group, her father, and his first words made it clear he was in a foul mood.

"Madame," he said, slurring his words, "I said you leave my girl alone, *non*?" Of course, he spoke in French, which, along with the volume of his words, meant everyone in the café could hear him now that there was no music. "You think you can ignore a father's protecting his daughter?"

Brett looked startled and his cheeks got pink. Katherine noticed but was caught up in her own embarrassment at being called out here, with Mme Pomfort and the rest of Reigny as witnesses.

Jean would have said more except that J.B. rejoined the group, holding a couple of bottles in one beefy hand. Katherine realized he had no idea what Jean was saying, but could certainly pick up the tone.

"What's this now?" he said, thrusting the bottles at his son and Jeannette. "Let's watch our manners, fella." He put his hand on Jean's arm, a mistake. Jean turned around and attempted to punch J.B. in the stomach. Between his off-balance movement and J.B.'s ample padding, it had no practical effect. But it drew every eye to them and caused the Polish contingent to jump up and crowd over to the space by the door, eager to see whatever might happen next.

Mme Pomfort and her friend rose from their seats in unison and hurried past the troublemakers and out the door with their chins high in the air. Katherine flinched at Mme Pomfort's meaningful look in her direction. There, the town's social judge seemed to say, you see why we can't possibly accept you as one of us? You insist on including that family in your circle of acquaintances.

To her surprise, J.B. didn't seem angry at Jean's attack. Instead, he roared with laughter, patted Jean on the back a few times, and turned to the bridge construction crew. "Nothing to see here, boys." They looked confused for a minute. "Drinks all around, on me," J.B. shouted to the bartender-farmer, whose English improved on the spot. With lots of hand-waving and calling back and forth in several languages, the room settled down and good cheer returned. Penny and Yves took the stage and began their a cappella version of "Will You Love Me Tomorrow," which was good enough to claim the audience's attention.

J.B. turned back to the group by the door, which now included Jean, who held on to a fresh glass of something that caught and refracted the light. Brett spoke for the first time. "Dad, I'm ready to go. Are you and Mom finished?"

"Son, the evening is just getting started. Am I right, sweetheart?" he said, talking directly to Jeannette and putting one finger on her forearm. She pushed her curls away from her face and glanced uncertainly at him and then down again.

"Mister," J.B. said, turning to Jean with a big smile, "you have one lovely young lady here, a real knockout."

Jean, who wasn't sure enough of his limited vocabulary to know what the word meant but worried it had something to do with their previous scuffle, said, *"Non, non, monsieur. Un malentendu, seulement."*

J.B. rode over his words. "Yes, indeed, a heartbreaker, right, Brett? I know the type." He turned to Katherine with a chuckle. "Fell for a few of these oh-so-innocent little girls myself back in the day, before my Betty Lou."

"Really," Katherine said. "She's hardly more than a child." Even as she said it, though, Katherine noticed that Jeannette was wearing a bra you could see through the fabric of her top, pink lip gloss, and a midriff-baring camisole of synthetic lace, perhaps chosen to please Brett. She did look more like a contemporary teenager tonight and less like the unself-conscious free spirit whose open face and mobile expressions delighted Katherine when the girl posed for her.

Suddenly, the sprite pushed away from the wall and, tossing her hair back, said to Katherine, "I am no child, and you do not speak for me. I will not model for you, I don't care how much you pay. Modeling is boring for me." She spoke in English, but her tone and the look she gave Katherine were enough to wake her father from his increasing stupor. He muttered to Katherine that she should go away and mind her business.

Her eyes swept the room in embarrassment and she saw Pippa's expression of keen interest before the young woman averted her eyes. Great, she thought, next thing I know I'll be a character in a crime novel.

Yves and Penny finished their ballad and there was general applause plus a loud "bravo" from Betty Lou. As they exited stage left, Emile bounded up stage right, accordion pressed to his chest. He began to play a familiar French cabaret song, and many in the room sang along with him, stamping their glasses gently on the tables in rhythm.

J.B. was still touching Jeannette lightly on the arm, looking into her face. Brett was flushed and he obviously didn't like whatever was happening. He turned abruptly and slammed out of the café door.

This is ridiculous, Katherine thought. J.B. is coming on like a lecher, the girl's father hasn't got a clue, and Jeannette is so angry at me that she's oblivious. Her first impulse was to insist on walking the girl home, but Jeannette only stuck her lower lip out when Katherine tried to get her attention.

Hell with them all, she thought, blood rushing to her

head and making her temples pound. She turned and went back to meet Michael. "I'm ready to go," she said, and he nodded.

No one turned to wish them a good evening as they left except Betty Lou, who waved with her usual absentminded good humor, and J.B., who cocked his head and winked as they passed. "If that man winks at me one more time . . ." Katherine let her sentence trail off as she and Michael started up the hill in the quiet and dark.

"Give it a break, Kay," Michael said, tension in his voice. "Let this ride until I've finished the recording and the tour, okay? Then, if you don't like him, you don't have to see him. I promise."

"Michael," she began tentatively, "I know this is a terrible thought, but I can't help but wonder if J.B. is a little too interested in Jeannette. He talks about her like she's sexually active, and I'm quite sure she's not . . . yet."

"No way. I've known a lot like him, sleazy talk but nothing more. He's harmless, especially in this tight little community and with that guard dog of a father."

"Maybe," she said, "but Jean's interest in protecting her is more about seeing if she's worth money to us rich Americans."

"You don't mean he's pimping her?" Michael sounded dubious. She told him about the modeling tempest at the river. "See, that's what I mean. I doubt he would go further."

She wasn't as sure and might have said more, but there was a crackling in the shrubbery in front of Mme Robilier's house, and Katherine turned to look. Nothing. But there it was again. "Brett?" No answer. Maybe she had imagined it. She was tired and her head hurt. All she wanted was home. If Brett was hiding, it was probably because he was hoping to catch Jeannette for a quick kiss later, or at least that's what Katherine hoped. Jeannette didn't want her help or advice. No one did. Fine. She'd paint the scene without a model; she had plenty of experience working from figures in art books if need be.

The dogs stirred themselves, bumping into each other and their humans as Katherine called in the cat and Michael locked up. They had almost fallen asleep when the sounds of a wailing electric guitar reached them, wafting up from the café. "Life in a picturesque little French town," Michael said into his pillow. Katherine, soothed with a prescription sleeping pill she rarely needed, only made a comforting noise, then fell into sleep.

She needed to get a decent night's sleep. The *vernissage* was tomorrow. She had barely finished the last painting in time and was sure the whole affair would be a massive flop. If Penny wasn't coming, would there be anyone there other than herself and Michael?

CHAPTER 24

The opening was bound to be a tremendous success, the two women who owned the gallery assured her. Madame Gigot assured her they had put posters up all over town and sent e-mails to their entire list of local art lovers. Katherine wasn't fooled, and, their shrill compliments and repeated exclamations aside, there couldn't have been more than two dozen people there, and not all at one time. She had put on her most ingratiating face, had left her vintage clothing at home and worn a little black dress, à la mode in West L.A. ten years ago, and rationed herself to a single glass of courage as she waited.

The paintings, spaced out so luxuriously on the white walls, looked different, more significant than when they sat on rickety easels in her cluttered studio, although a faint scent of varnish hung about the last couple she had finished. She was in love with them all, she realized, and hoped perversely that none would sell. She caught herself up short, remembering how precarious their finances were. No, she hoped they all would sell. She would paint more of these bucolic scenes with lambs and milkmaids and gold-touched clouds, but always with that little hint of something not quite *comme il faut*, as it should be, that she hoped made them more than pretty, made them a little dangerous.

Katherine had planned to bring Jeannette, who loved seeing herself transformed in the paintings of her, and was disappointed that the girl hadn't been at home when she stopped by to invite her. J.B. and Betty Lou breezed in, still dressed in casual clothing no Frenchman or -woman would wear, still blithely unconcerned about how thoroughly they stood out. They were effusive, loud, and adamant about the brilliance of her paintings, so much so that Katherine winced and felt obliged to say how disappointing the series was.

Partway through their visit, Sophie sidled in, immediately walked over to a painting as far away from the Hollidays as possible, and stood within a few inches of the canvas as if inspecting it for bugs.

Penny had come after all, but only for a quick look, congratulatory kisses, and the explanation that Yves was waiting in the car because there was nowhere near enough to park. "We're going to stop at a vineyard near Chablis and then race up to Troyes. There's a modern art museum there, did you know?" And with that, she was off.

Well, yes, Katherine thought, sipping her wine with great deliberateness. And there's modern art here, too, darling, in this room, if you and Yves cared a fig for art and were willing to walk two blocks to see it. Providentially, Mme Gigot pulled an elderly man over to be introduced, and Katherine pushed away her bad mood.

Several vineyard operators came in, hearty, tanned couples who, Katherine figured, came to all the openings as a break from the hard work of managing vines all year. She was sure the wine she had supplied would be privately scorned by them all, but since she had to pay for it, hell with them. She smiled broadly, however, marshaled her best French, and was surprised—no, shocked—when one couple purchased a large painting of a girl dancing alone under a tree. When the little red dot was placed beside it and the couple had shaken her hand several times before departing in a chorus of congratulations, Katherine had to sit down. My goodness, she thought, I've sold a painting in France. My work, she heard herself explaining to an unknown audience in some future setting, is in collections in France. Well, she'd have to sell at least one more to make that literally true, but it would surely happen now.

She looked up from her reverie in time to see Sophie approaching. "These are so charming, Mme Goff," Sophie said. "I am sorry Maman was not able to come herself, but I trust you understand."

"She's better?"

"Oh yes, but there is still much to do, and she tires so easily. I'm commuting from Paris at the moment, so difficult, but what can one do? You know, I am the head of the company now?"

From unhappy rabbit to CEO, a more impressive transformation than Cinderella's. Who would have thought?

"Later, when our lives return to normal, I would like to talk with you about doing a piece for Château de Bellegarde, if I might?"

"Of course. In fact, I had already begun to think about a double portrait of your parents before this . . . happened," Katherine said, stumbling over a desire not to say baldly that the young woman's father had died.

"Precisely what I was thinking," Sophie said, clapping

her hands and, wonder of wonders, smiling. "We'll talk later, *bien sûr*."

There didn't seem to be much to say after that, and, congratulating Katherine, the young woman turned to leave. J.B. had been watching her from the other side of the room and bounded over, grabbing and shaking Sophie's hand and explaining who he was in tones that suggested this was her lucky day. Katherine saw the young woman take a few steps sideways to escape his attention, and she tried to signal to Michael that it would be a kindness to rescue Adele's daughter. But Michael was listening to one of the owners, who was in the middle of a long tale that Katherine heard only wisps of, something cheerful to do with ice storms and bad roads in the Pyrenees. Sophie ducked out of the gallery and J.B. followed. They stood on the cobblestones, a striped awning in front of a religious bookstore across the narrow street serving as a backdrop as it filled and emptied in the stiff, swirling wind. J.B. was providing his own gusty sales pitch, she was sure.

Katherine resisted the urge to save Sophie from her rude countryman. Michael was right, she could not assume responsibility for every American who blundered around, making acceptance difficult for those who merely wanted to live quietly among the French. Luckily, there weren't too many J.B.s to apologize for. She turned away from the scene at the door and marched over to hear more about winter in the mountains of the Midi.

The vineyard owners' was the only purchase during the opening reception, but the gallery owners proclaimed it to be a wonderful omen for the two weeks the show would be up. They assured her they would contact their regular customers to tell them the work was selling quickly and that Mme Goff's paintings were the next thing, what one must have.

Michael grinned his approval at her as he loaded the unopened wine and the cheese platter in the trunk of the Citroën. He suggested celebrating by eating at a nearby bistro, but Katherine was exhausted and wanted only to get home, feed the animals, and spend a quiet hour reading Balzac.

CHAPTER 25

A fine mist was falling when Katherine left Mme Robilier's stuccoed house with its freshly painted pale-green shutters the next afternoon. She had accomplished what she came to do. The rival gardener to Mme Pomfort would contribute her prized yellow roses to decorate the table at the entrance to the tent where people paid a small fee for the show and received their programs. "The place of honor," Katherine had said, and Madame had nodded solemnly. Much better than festooning the stage itself, which was bound to be dusty and tangled with amplifier cords, she said, hoping her comment would never make it back to Mme Pomfort's ears.

As she passed the church garden, that keeper of Reigny's social order stood up from her low stool next to some tomato plants that were resisting her demand for order and propriety. With one hand on her back and a handful of weeds in the other, her posture still managed to signal the degree of Katherine's insult in calling on someone with such suspect ancestors. They exchanged *"Bonjour, Madame"*'s with no warmth, and Katherine reminded herself to have Michael arrange a firewood delivery from the farm in another town before he left on tour.

She trudged past Jean's messy courtyard and heard a rustling sound from the old oak tree that spread its ancient branches over the roadway. Jeannette dropped gracefully from her concealed place among the branches and, to Katherine's surprise, fell into step with her. To her greater surprise, Katherine felt her heart swell with, well, perhaps it was pride and perhaps it was affection. Katherine knew they were still visible to the disapproving old woman in her garden, but she decided she didn't care. Jeannette was worth a dozen Mme Pomforts, and if the girl was trying to make up for her outburst the other night, Katherine was happy to welcome the child back. Jeannette needed someone on her side as much as she did.

"Comment ça va, cherie?"

The question didn't elicit the same list of symptoms in the teenager as it had in Katherine's older neighbors. Jeannette shrugged and was silent. But her arm snaked around Katherine's waist, and they walked in a more companionable silence than they had in a week. After a hundred yards, Jeannette ventured a question. "When is old enough to have sex? Is it like the movies?"

Katherine stopped in the middle of the street. "I have no idea what movies you mean, but I promise you, you're not old enough." She noticed Jeannette was dressed in her normal tomboy attire today and the sparkly polish was already fading. "Is it Brett? Is he bothering you?"

Jeannette shrugged. "No," she said, hesitating, "not exactly."

Katherine wasn't sure what "exactly" meant, but the look on Jeannette's face said she was in the throes of suffering as only teenage girls can experience. "Listen," she said, facing Jeannette and holding both her arms. "You're only ready when you love someone so much that you don't even have to ask yourself the question." She struggled to make sure her French was good enough to drive home her point. She couldn't be sure Jeannette would get the message if she delivered it in English. "But, trust me, that's a ways off. And you never, ever have to let someone convince you if you don't want to, okay, *d'accord*?"

Jeannette nodded, even managed a small smile, the first Katherine had seen in a while. Impulsively, she hugged the girl. Mothering wasn't something she'd had much of when she was Jeannette's age, or practice in as an adult, or, honestly, much desire for given how unhappy the role had made her own parent, but right now she felt ready to do battle to protect this chick.

They resumed walking until the bend in the road where Katherine would go uphill. "Want some ice cream?" she asked.

"*Non, merci*, I need to go to the pool," Jeannette said.

"Pool?"

"At the old quarry. The little kids can't go there, but Brett and I sometimes swim."

"Isn't it too chilly today, with the rain?"

"*Oui*, but I have to go there for something." A look passed swiftly over her features, but it disappeared before Katherine could be sure it was there, and she kissed Katherine noisily on both cheeks and vanished from view down the dirt road to the quarry.

Katherine had almost reached her gate when the Hollidays' SUV passed her. J.B., at the wheel, stared ahead intently and didn't acknowledge her wave or even seem to see her. The car's noise faded as it disappeared from her sight. The phone was ringing and she hurried back inside. Michael was in

Auxerre at the music store and it might be him calling to see if she needed anything while he was in town.

"Hi, sweetie," said Betty Lou, in her warm contralto voice. "Can I speak to Mike?" Hearing that he wasn't there, she opted to leave a message. "J.B. has got it in his head that tomorrow's the day we leave for the Riviera. Honestly, that man is too much. But we did promise Brett we'd head to the beach sometime, and I guess this is that time."

Katherine wondered if they knew Brett and Jeannette were edging toward something they shouldn't. If so, taking a break wasn't a bad idea, although Jeannette would be devastated.

"Tell Mike not to worry. We'll be back in a couple of weeks to finish the sessions. Who knows, I might even have a little more zip to my voice if I hit it big in the casinos." She laughed. "And J.B. won't mind. I hear the young ladies wear nothing but thongs on the beach, and I don't mean shower shoes. Lord knows how we'll keep Brett from staring at them, though. The life of a mother," she said, and rang off in high good humor.

Katherine was restless after the call for some reason. Of course Betty Lou wasn't gambling with their money. She and Michael hadn't even written the check. Michael would have some time to ease up and shuck off some of the stress he'd been feeling as the CD and the tour began to take shape. This was all happening so fast, and they hadn't talked about the big issue—his having to deal somehow with Eric.

Another item on her list was a talk with Jeannette about sex before the Hollidays got back. She was pretty sure Jean hadn't faced up to that particular challenge and didn't have much faith in what he would say if he tried. The child seemed to swing between high spirits and despondency, the agonies typical of teenagers throughout the ages, she supposed. The girl's face as she kissed Katherine good-bye was open and trusting again, and that meant the world to her.

As she remembered, though, another face came to mind, J.B.'s as he drove past, and the sense of urgent purpose in his driving. She had a sudden image of J.B. drooling over the girl at the café. Without thinking too much, she grabbed the dogs' leashes and called for them. A walk down the hill would be good for all of them. There was no SUV parked at the café, or along the street, so perhaps he had been intent on an errand farther away. She peered as far around the down-hill bend as she could. Pippa was out for a walk too, her mop of red hair distinctive even at a distance. Katherine realized that she had seen a lot more of the young writer since Al-bert's death, doubtless because the police who were knock-ing on doors, the rampant gossip and speculation about plots and motives, had fired her creative juices. Katherine retreated, pulling hard on the dogs' leashes. The last thing she was in the mood for was being waylaid by the ardent crime researcher.

The quarry pool? If Jeannette wouldn't feel she was in-truding, perhaps that would be a new adventure for the dogs. Michael had never mentioned a pool during his dusk walks. As she ventured down the dirt road, not entirely sure where she was headed, she heard a voice raised and another weeping in the distance beyond a fork in the road. There was a trodden path up a short hill that looked more direct. As she reached the summit and looked over the tops of the greenery, she saw Jeannette, her back to a break in the rocks and, below it, water that reflected the gray of the clouds. The girl's bare arms were tightly crossed over her chest, and she was shaking her head. Whoever she was talking to was hidden from Katherine. Brett, come to say he was leaving?

"*Non, non,*" the girl said, loud enough for Katherine to hear, and took a sudden step backward.

CHAPTER 26

Katherine looked around for a way down that would advertise her presence so she didn't appear to be snooping, but it was too overgrown with dense, tangled brush. She would have to backtrack. She turned and was halfway down the path when, through some branches, she saw the SUV.

"Cock tease," he had called her in gross language, hadn't he? "A heartbreaker," in more conventional terms. But the characterization had been the same, and now Katherine was afraid J.B. hadn't been talking about her effect on his son. She hurried down the narrow path, stumbling over a large rock, pulling on the dogs' leashes when they stopped to sniff something, and found she was short of breath when she got to the quarry road. If J.B. was threatening the girl . . .

Jean was walking, slowing up from the other road through the rocky outcropping, wiping a dusty arm across his brow, looking the worse from a night of heavy drinking and a day of stone cutting.

"Jean, *vite*, come quickly. Jeannette may be in trouble." She pulled on his arm. He seemed not to understand. The dogs, sensing her anxiety, began to bark and look around in confusion for the cause of the trouble. From down the road,

Mme Pomfort walked slowly over to the church wall nearest the commotion, peering at them.

"Come with me. *Urgent, tout de suite.*" She was calling forth her French, which, perversely, was disappearing when she most needed it. She hoped the commotion wouldn't push J.B. into doing something that would put the girl in danger, but she didn't know what else to do. She'd feel like an idiot, of course, if J.B. was only there to let her know Brett was leaving town. But Brett was perfectly capable of doing that himself, even if he had to skate over on that rickety board of his to find her. What if there were some other reason J.B. was meeting Jeannette?

She spun back in the direction of the quarry pool, pointing.

"Madame, what is this?" a voice called. Mme Pomfort was sailing toward them, a trowel in one hand and a bunch of wilting leaves in the other, a malicious gleam brightening her dark eyes.

"Jeannette. I think Mr. Holliday is . . . is . . . trying to . . ." She couldn't say it, but it was clear Madame had an idea. The expression on her face underwent an extraordinary change.

"*Vitement,*" the old woman said to Jean, ordering him to hurry in a hissing voice not to be disobeyed, and pushed him in the direction Katherine had pointed to, giving him some instructions that were uttered too fast for Katherine to understand. He took off at a fast walk. When Katherine looked back, Mme Robilier had trotted up to the intersection of the paths, doubtless eaten by curiosity, enough to overcome her dislike of her foe. Reigny was normally so quiet, so completely placid that any stirring of leaves and dust was an event to be milked for all its drama. The two women spoke quickly to each other in high, excited voices, and Mme Robilier nodded before heading for her house at a fast walk.

"She will call the sheriff," Mme Pomfort said firmly. "Now, let us see what's happening to *notre petite* Jeannette." Untangling a leash that had wrapped itself around Katherine's leg, she marched ahead toward "our little Jeannette" with Fideaux, who, perceiving power where it manifested itself, was sufficiently impressed to trot along beside her without stopping.

By the time Katherine and the bearlike Gracey and the rest of the small rescue party reached the quarry pool, J.B. had backed up, and Jeannette was under her father's protective arm, crying softly.

"Easy, pal," J.B. was saying, holding his arms in front of him. "There's nothing going on here. Tell him, Kathy," he said as he turned and saw her coming. "The man's behaving like I'm some kind of criminal. Tell him to back off." He attempted a grin, but it faded when he saw the look on Katherine's face.

"*Verge,*" Jean snarled, using a French term for "dirty old man" that Katherine knew only because she had used it once to describe the weedy grass at the edge of her yard, causing Emile to sputter because he thought she was referring to him. Fortunately Yves had been there at the time to provide the vocabulary lesson.

Now, she strode up to J.B., made braver by the dogs, who had picked up the cues and were giving the producer their fiercest looks, and by the presence at her back of the woman who, at her angriest, resembled the Wicked Witch of the West. "What are you doing here, J.B.? Why have you been bullying Jeannette?"

"Come on, now," he whined, "what's the matter with the bunch of you? I came over to let Jeannette know Brett won't be around for a few weeks. Big deal." He ran one hand through his hair and looked hard at the girl.

Jeannette peeped out from her father's protective shoulder

and said through her sobs, *"Non, non*, Katherine, that is not what he say to me."

"Is he threatening you?" Katherine said, feeling herself grow a couple of inches taller as righteous anger overcame her. Gracey, in her large, shaggy blackness, began to growl. Katherine came closer to the producer. "J.B., have you come on to this . . . this . . . child? Have you touched her?"

"Touched her? Get a grip," J.B. said, his voice an octave higher. "You mean do I have a hard-on for her? What a joke. Are you crazy?" All evidence of the friendly business partner was gone, and in his place Katherine saw a stranger who had some kind of agenda with Jeannette that she didn't understand.

"Jeannette?" she said, and everyone looked at the girl.

Seeing that she was physically safe with her father, the intimidating Mme Pomfort, and her friend Katherine all there to protect her, Jeannette wriggled from her father's grasp and pointed to J.B. as she spoke to Katherine. "He know what I saw. He tell—told—me not to say what I saw or he make trouble for me."

Mme Pomfort stepped forward to stand in front of Katherine. She still held her trowel, which she used as a pointer, first poking it toward J.B., then toward Jeannette. "Child, you must tell us what you saw. *En français.* This is not a time for secrets, *tu comprends*?" Katherine wondered if she was imagining that Madame's voice softened at the end of her question. Mme Pomfort, who had been unwavering in her dismissal of the entire family only last night?

J.B. made a move as if to advance on the girl, but the dogs, having figured out what was required of them, barked in unison and stood at sharp attention. Mme Robilier's voice, as out of breath as if she had run a five-kilometer race, came from behind them. "We took the keys from his car. My Maurice has them, don't you, dear?" Her husband looked a bit disheveled, as if he had been roused from a nap, but he patted his pocket and smiled at them from where he and Mme Robilier stood.

J.B. looked around. Truly, he was cornered. His bulk made the notion of running up and over the hill on the narrow path impossible. Jean was flexing his considerable biceps, the old woman with the trowel looked ready to use it, and Katherine was blocking the road.

"Tell them, Jeannette," Katherine said, not taking her eyes off J.B.

"Brett's father, he was at the château late the night Monsieur died. I saw him from the woods."

"For Pete's sake, the police know I was there. I was meeting with the guy around dinnertime. This is nuts." J.B.'s face was turning a dangerous shade of purple.

"What happened?" Katherine said when the girl faltered.

She started talking faster now, in French, which Katherine struggled to understand. "I told you, he came back later in the night, when everyone was sleeping but me. I saw his car parked at the bottom of the driveway before I had to get home."

There was a gasp from Mme Pomfort, and Jean gave his daughter a sharp look, but no one spoke, not wanting to stop Jeannette's account.

"But before he got in his car the first time he went there, I saw Brett's papa throw something into the woods."

"The gun," Katherine said triumphantly.

Jeannette looked surprised. "No," she said, in English this time. "No, I see—saw—something shiny and I find it later."

"Of course," said a new voice, in ringing tones. "The murder weapon."

Everyone turned toward the speaker. Pippa, a walking stick raised like an exclamation point, returned their stares, her shining eyes focused on the music producer. "I knew it."

"Murder weapon?" J.B. said, incredulity in his voice. "No one's been murdered. Have you lost your minds?"

Katherine was confused. "What did J.B. throw into the grass?"

She turned to look at Jeannette at the same time J.B. bolted forward. Jeannette screamed and stepped backward toward the pool as Jean leapt toward J.B. This time, he knew better than to aim at the fat man's stomach. Instead, he pulled his arm back and punched it hard into J.B.'s face. The fat man crumbled onto the gravel at the same time the assembled women heard a screech and a splash as Jeannette hit the water.

Because they couldn't hear anything else above the noise they were making, yelling in two languages at once over the sound of two dogs barking, they missed the sound of the gendarmes' car turning with a skid into the quarry road, known formally as the sinister-sounding Rue d'Enfer, or Road to Hell. The car stopped behind the SUV and two uniformed young men tumbled out and hurried over to the little crowd. Maurice Robilier looked as confused as Katherine felt, but then he always looked confused. Jeannette had a thick rope in her hands and was climbing out of the pool like a monkey, hair streaming wet. Jean stood over J.B., as did Mme Pomfort, whose trowel was aimed in the general direction of the American's throat. Pippa stood a small distance away, taking pictures with her smartphone.

"Oh lord," Katherine said, waving her hands at Pippa to get her to stop, "that's all we need. We'll be on the Internet before supper."

The sheriff's battered van arrived right behind the gendarmes' car and he trotted over, talking on his cell phone and gesturing at his invisible audience.

To a gendarme's question about what was going on, everyone swiveled and started to speak at once. One gendarme stood over J.B., while Jean slunk as far away from the law as he could and still be present. Mme Pomfort was only reluctantly persuaded to aim her trowel somewhere else. Pippa tried to explain something, but her English rendered her account useless and the policeman trying to take statements waved her off. The second policeman was on his phone, presumably calling for advice. The dogs, however, could not be similarly persuaded to stand down. Their lives had little excitement and this was too good to give up.

Another police car with a flashing blue light, driven by a woman in uniform, crept along the narrow dirt road and came to a stop. Lieutenant Decoste, the policeman who had drunk tea on Katherine's patio only a couple of days ago as he worked to unravel the threads of rumor and fact presented to him by these same residents of Reigny, stepped out of the car, a puzzled look on his face. From what Katherine understood of his staccato explanation to the gendarmes, he had been on the A-6 from Auxerre to Avallon when he heard about the incident. No one was to leave without his permission, he said, before turning to the gendarmes for a report. He nodded as they spoke in undertones, then turned to the assembled villagers.

"Now," he said in a stern voice, "what do you have to say?"

This time, Katherine noticed, Mme Pomfort was not insulted but thrilled to be at the center of the police investigation. She would have stories to tell for months. Whenever Pippa edged forward and opened her mouth, Mme Pomfort stepped in front of her to block her way. Mme Robilier could hardly get a word in edgewise but was trying, lugging Maurice forward every few minutes until a gendarme finally noticed him waving J.B.'s car keys and accepted them with a polite bow. The sheriff paced a little ways off, still deep in his phone conversation.

The lieutenant finally turned to a brooding J.B., who had gotten back up and was touching his bruised cheek gingerly with a handkerchief. "This is grave, Monsieur," he said in English. "You are being accused by these people of causing the death of M. Bellegarde, of killing him. What do you say?"

J.B. shouted, loud enough to be heard in every house in Reigny, "I didn't kill anyone, dammit. Why the hell would I? He was about to lend me the money to buy my Memphis studio. We had a deal."

This last probably made more sense to Katherine than it did to the police, but could it be true? If he wasn't creeping around trying to sexually ambush the girl, what was he doing here, threatening her? Because he'd definitely been doing that when she arrived on the scene. And he had just lunged at her.

The policeman looked hard at J.B., then turned toward Jeannette, who had been silent. "And you, young lady, what is this evidence you found in the grass to prove M. Holliday killed him?"

Jeannette edged over to the rocks bordering the pool, knelt in the grass, and then brought something over to the lieutenant, looking guiltily at her father, who had lit a cigarette and was watching closely from a distance.

"What's this, then?" the policeman asked, holding the shiny object up. "A key? To what?"

Jeannette shrugged. "*Je ne sais pas.* I don't know. It's what he threw in the grass, that's all I know. I found it. When I showed it to Brett at the café the other night, he said not to tell anyone. Brett told me to throw it in the pool when I wouldn't give it to him. I thought I might find out what it opened. . . ." Her voice trailed off and her father stirred at his observation post. Best not to say too much about her hobbies.

"So that's where it was. Brett told me you had it. Damn him, anyway. Look at the mess he's created." J.B. ran his hands over his head as if to stimulate his brain into an explanation that would end the suspicion.

"Brett?" the lieutenant and Katherine said at the same time.

"My son, who doesn't have the brains he was born with," J.B. said glumly.

"Brett? Are you saying Brett was involved?" Katherine said, totally at sea.

An anguished voice from the bushes above the clearing startled everyone. "Let him go. My dad didn't do anything." A dozen heads swiveled as one and watched Brett Holliday slither down the hill, holding his skateboard and scattering pebbles and twigs before him.

"And you are?" the policeman said, his voice somewhere between annoyance and curiosity.

"This is my son," J.B. said, looking at Brett through squinted eyes. "Don't say anything, boy. This doesn't involve you."

"It does." He gulped and looked down at his board, picking at the frayed edge. "Sorry, Dad, this is all my fault." He looked up at the policeman in charge. "I . . . I killed the old man, but"—his voice broke—"I didn't mean to, honest. He was grabbing at me and I guess I panicked." The boy turned his head back and forth between his father and the policeman as he spoke.

J.B. groaned. The gendarmes moved closer to the teenager,

the elderly women moved farther away, and Katherine realized what had been nibbling at the edge of her consciousness.

"I took an old gun and some other stuff, just for fun. I was trying to put the bullets back in the case when he came out of a room and into the stairwell. I didn't think . . . I mean, he yanked my jacket and I swear he was going to shove me down the steps. I just pushed him away. I didn't know he'd fall. . . . I didn't know he was dead. . . ." His voice trailed off.

"But I saw your father," Jeannette said into the sudden silence, unwilling to consider her first boyfriend in such a terrible light. "It was his car."

"Well, I was driving it. France is stupid. Back home, I'm allowed to drive." He glared at the girl, relieved, Katherine thought, to be mad at someone other than himself, and worried sick about what his father was going to say about all this.

"No, that was me," J.B. insisted.

Jeannette stuck out her lip. "It was dark," she snapped.

"*C'est merveilleux,*" Decoste said, clapping his hands together. "Marvelous, two confessions to the same crime. What more could I ask?"

J.B.'s shoulders sagged and he shook his head. His voice was robbed of its usual bluster. "Look, I came over later, after Brett told me what happened. The old guy might have come to by then, for all I knew. I thought if I got rid of the key on the property, any investigation would stop there. I was shocked to hear Albert had died when I came over the next morning."

"You went back?" Brett said. "Dad? I thought you didn't understand it was an accident."

"We will decide if it was truly an accident, young man," the policeman said, fixing Brett with a look that made the teenager go pale. "Why did you come here now?"

J.B. tried again. "Officer, he doesn't know what he's saying. We have a right to a lawyer. Son, don't say anything."

"Excusez-moi," the lieutenant said in a commanding voice, holding a hand up in J.B.'s direction. "I repeat, why did you come here today, young man?"

"Because," Brett said, pointing toward Jeannette, "she has the other old bullet, and I thought if I put it back with the rest of them and told her to keep quiet about it, no one would figure out it was me. But I never thought anyone would try to blame my dad. And I didn't know where she hid the key until the other day."

Katherine murmured under her breath, "An old bullet casing. Why didn't I recognize Jeannette's good luck charm?" Pippa heard her from a few feet away and raised her eyebrows, but Katherine shook her head. Maybe later, much later.

Jeannette stared at Brett and then at Katherine. The confusion on her face mirrored Katherine's thoughts. She reached into her pocket and brought out the brass piece. *"Cette chose?* This little thing?"

The policeman strode over to the girl and held out his hand. "The key and the other object, *s'il vous plaît.* Ah, it is an old percussion cap—an antique bullet, you see?"

The clearing erupted into a handful of conversations, a small babel of languages, each one trying to untangle the skein of confessions. Above them, ringing with British certainty, Pippa's "I knew it," which Katherine thought was disingenuous in the extreme given that Pippa had ten minutes ago pronounced with equal authority that J.B. was a killer.

The gendarme in charge had had enough confusion too, Katherine guessed. He held up his palm again and all talk ceased. Then he dismissed Pippa, Mme Pomfort, and Mme

Robilier, along with Maurice, to their disappointment, and ordered J.B. into one police car and Brett into the other. He instructed the sheriff, pried from his cell phone, to escort Jeannette, assuring an alarmed Jean that it was only to provide her a lift home to change into dry clothes and then to come to the police station at Auxerre, where she could tell them exactly what she saw and who said what. Did Jean wish to accompany them? When the sheriff gave him a nasty look, he demurred.

The policeman nodded as if he had known that would be the father's answer. The girl would have a female police officer and someone from the social services with her during the interview, he said, and assuming she was telling the truth would be delivered home shortly by their good neighbor, the sheriff. He raised an eyebrow and looked at Jean as he said it.

The stage began to empty. The uniformed policemen left first, looking impassively forward, J.B. sitting in the backseat of their little car, waving his hands for emphasis as he told them something. The policeman ducked into the front seat of the chauffeured car with a drooping Brett slumped in the back. The sheriff, visibly annoyed at the interruption of his phone conversation, backed his van out. Jeannette peered through a passenger window at her father with a combination of childish appeal for protection and an ingenue's thrill at her starring role.

Before he left, the lieutenant told Katherine and Jean that he would have to speak with them again after he had taken a statement from the visiting Americans. Katherine realized she had better do something about J.B.'s car when she noticed Jean eyeing it appraisingly. "May I call his wife and have her pick it up? After all, you don't suspect her of anything. She's a famous singer, you know?" He looked confused. "Well, not really famous, more well known, if you understand. Country music?" When he merely stood there, staring into her face, she decided it was probably best not to say more. He might decide Betty Lou was worth investigating, and then where would she be with the fête coming up soon?

The lieutenant must have had a similar thought because he said, loud enough for Jean to hear clearly, "The sheriff will bring the car keys and then you may move it to your house, *d'accord*? Okay? I know nothing will happen to it in the meantime." He looked at Jean directly to drive home his point.

When he finally drove off, Katherine turned for home, only to be accosted by Jean, who, to her complete shock, grabbed her roughly and kissed her on both cheeks.

"*Merci, Madame*, you saved my daughter," he said gruffly, "my only girl child, who looks like her mother but has twice her brains." After which, wiping his arm across his watering eyes, he shambled away toward his house, from which Katherine could hear shouts of excitement from Jeannette's brood of siblings, doubtless getting a look at their sister being delivered home by the dreaded sheriff.

The message light was blinking when she stumbled, exhausted, into the house. As she collapsed on her chaise and the dogs nosed around their food bowls in hopes of a snack, she pressed the button. It was Adele. "The strangest thing has happened. Sophie called from the office to say Albert's lawyer has been on the phone to her, wondering why Albert never came to his office to sign some loan papers he had authorized. She wondered if I knew anything about it since the deal was with that horrible man who showed up the day poor Albert died. I've left a message for the lieutenant. It seems that your

American friend entered into some kind of agreement with Albert to build a music studio in America. Too strange for words, but Sophie says my husband has made a few similar loans over the years and makes money from them somehow. But American music? How very odd."

CHAPTER 27

The next week was consumed with speculation and rumor, delivered to Katherine by Emile in tortured gossip that was invariably false, or by Mme Pomfort and Mme Robilier, who wanted to relive the day in concert during their visits to Katherine's house. As they sat on the patio sipping lemonade and fanning themselves against the midsummer heat, the two women replayed their heroic actions on that fateful day when they and their neighbor Katherine rescued *la pauvre petite* Jeannette from the clutches of an evildoer and his dangerous son. As results of the investigation and the court's decision to treat the case as something a good deal less than murder were reported in the papers and via the *supermarché* clerk's daily delivery of gossip, the clucking became louder. Reigny's judge and jury, Mme Pomfort, had a little of Mme Defarge in her and would have voted for the guillotine. Mme Robilier was more generous, saying more than once to Katherine that the poor boy had such a dreadful father it was no wonder his judgment had slipped.

"Slipped?" Mme Pomfort said in shock when Madame ventured that opinion one day. "Pushed a distinguished

SUSAN C. SHEA

aristocrat and leader of society down the stairs? Surely, my dear friend, that is not precisely what you meant?"

Mme Robilier assured her in a soothing voice that it was indeed not what she meant, not at all, and that Mme Pomfort had been brilliant in giving the gendarmes her account of the events. Once Reigny's acknowledged queen bee had been properly soothed, the women settled back into their companionable rehashing of That Day.

Pippa also came to sit under the pear tree, announcing to Katherine that she had gotten several wonderful ideas for her stories from the events. "I was wrong about the murder, of course, but that hardly matters, does it?" She beamed at Katherine, who privately thought that it mattered a great deal. But she forgave Pippa's declaration as being the kind of comment a mystery writer might be likely to make.

"I missed the most important clues," Katherine said to Pippa as she sipped her *café crème*. "I almost recognized that little thing Jeannette was carrying around, and the girl told me herself, more than once, that she had seen J.B. late that night at Château de Bellegarde. I didn't take her seriously."

Pippa admitted she hadn't quite given up on the idea of a genuine murder at the old castle. "Perhaps I shall have to write something spectacular, eh, a real murder with blood and gore?" she said thoughtfully. "I'm really quite chuffed, you know?"

A visibly upset Betty Lou, on one of her frequent stops at the Goffs's house, confirmed what Brett had admitted. She had known nothing until the day it all came to a head. Her son confessed to her that he had noticed the key to a gun closet sitting in the lock during a group tour. Instructed by his parents to visit Château de Bellegarde as a summer history lesson of sorts, it had been easy for him to slip back up

248

the stone steps and take the smallest pistol, a little pile of empty brass percussion caps, and the key, figuring that when the owners found the key missing, they would think the theft could have happened at any time. It was for fun, a way to pass the long summer without his friends around. Betty Lou's voice had hardened at Brett's idea of fun. But the gun had turned out to be old and rusty, not worth keeping, and Brett had brought it back while he and Jeannette were skateboarding one day and tossed it into the shrubbery while the girl was coasting down the driveway. Then came the terrible night that he had tried to replace the bullets and wound up knocking Albert down the stone stairwell.

After Albert's death, when Brett came looking for Jeannette at the quarry to get the last percussion cap back and stumbled on the scene with the police, he realized that the alternative to confessing was the possibility of his father going to prison. "I would have had a heart attack if I'd been there," Betty Lou said, her voice gravelly. "But I'm proud of him for telling the truth."

"If you'd seen all of us making fools of ourselves, you would have attacked us instead," Katherine said.

"J.B. was devastated for Brett of course, but he was just signing a big deal with Albert. He wasn't thinking straight." Betty Lou lit a cigarette with shaking hands and inhaled deeply. "He decided to toss the key Brett still had on the property. If it was found, there'd be no way of saying how it got there, you know? How was he supposed to know the girl would be skulking around at two in the morning?"

"Didn't he think to call an ambulance or something?" Katherine tried to keep her voice neutral, but it had been bothering her once the story emerged.

"He wasn't sure what had really happened. Brett was

upset, and it didn't sound like that hard a fall, he told me. He could have been stunned, could have woken up a half hour later. J.B. told me he decided to go over first thing to find out." Betty Lou's voice wobbled.

Katherine looked over at her and saw tears dripping down her face. The singer took a packet of tissues from her bag and, after blowing her nose and scrubbing at her eyes, said, "Sorry. I cry a lot these days. Sometimes, I'm not sure who I'm crying for. The poor old man for sure, and his wife, who must hate us all. And for Brett, of course, my baby, who keeps making bad decisions. For J.B., who knows he did so many things wrong." Her voice trailed off.

Jeannette, Katherine found out during one of their painting and modeling sessions, had seen a great deal. She had seen Brett throw the gun into the shrubbery. She meant to come back for it, but then Monsieur had died and there were gendarmes everywhere. She had found the little key that Brett's father tossed late in the night. Jeannette explained that Mr. Holliday was not a good thrower and the key had landed right next to the paved driveway. Then, when Katherine told her the old man hadn't been shot, she felt better, *comprenez*? Katherine understood, surely?

Katherine did understand, sort of. "He was her first boyfriend," she said to Michael, when he admitted that the whole affair was like a jigsaw puzzle missing half its pieces.

"So Brett's not going to be tried for murder?" said Michael, despondent over the loss of a manager and a career comeback that hadn't even begun.

"No, apparently he'll get off with a stern lecture and the forfeiture of his visa for some time, which will break Jeannette's heart. J.B. lost his visa too. Betty Lou says the court was harder on him because he was setting a poor example for his son."

"I still don't understand why J.B was going after the girl when you found him."

"Oh, darling, because Jeannette finally told Brett about seeing his father throw the key in the weeds, and Brett told his father." She paused for breath. "And then Brett realized he needed to get the bullet thing back and ask her to keep it a secret so it couldn't be traced to him. . . ."

Michael stuck a fresh cigarillo in his mouth and rolled it around with his teeth. Katherine looked at him, trying to measure how much she had confused him. He picked up his guitar and, after playing a few quiet chords, looked up and said, "And J.B. wanted the key so badly at that point?"

"Betty Lou says J.B. thought getting the key back and per- suading Jeannette not to say anything might keep Brett out of trouble. It got out of hand when I misunderstood what was going on. I'm still embarrassed."

"You saw what you saw, Kay, and you did the only thing you could. I'm proud of you, baby, and that's the truth." He looked up at her and her heart swelled. Michael wasn't big on compliments.

She took a deep breath. "That makes me feel a little bet- ter, although I'm afraid J.B. will always remember Reigny as that place where he got falsely accused by some hysterical woman."

"He'll be fine, although I'm not surprised he will be even less welcome in France than his son. He's a tough character. You have to be in his business. And anyway, he's no saint, leaving Albert's body there for his wife to find. I don't much like that. Come here, woman." And he stopped playing long enough to ditch the cigarillo and kiss her full on the lips when she walked over to him.

She was fairly sure she had explained it correctly. Adele wasn't close to forgiving "that American hoodlum," but she had been relieved to find out no Gypsies had broken in and murdered her husband. Sophie was all business about the contract with J.B., which she intended to sign now that the company belonged to her. After all, J.B. hadn't killed her father. According to Adele, whose tone of voice betrayed some disapproval, Sophie was turning out to be a businesswoman first and foremost, a little like her father. Katherine privately thought Sophie was rather coldhearted, but maybe she took after her father that way too.

Brett was gone from the scene. Jeannette was torn between the agony of lost love and anticipation of the amazing story of herself as heroine that she could tell when school began.

In such quiet moments as Katherine had now that she was so completely part of Reigny-sur-Canne's social life, she scolded herself for being blind to the truth of everyone's behavior. She confessed as much to Penny as they sat under the pear tree, sipping Chablis Grand Cru that Penny had brought, left over from her dinner. "Why save it for something special when nothing around here ever is?"

Katherine, the glass at her lips, paused to consider the vaguely insulting edge to the comment, then drank. Penny, she told herself, didn't mean it quite that way. She nibbled at the squat peaches and goat cheese rounds she had bought at a good price in yesterday's market in Avallon. "Aren't the peaches delicious? I wish I'd had them at my *vernissage*. Did I tell you I sold a painting that day, and the gallery has sold another since?"

"I'll be able to say I knew the great artist Katherine Goff when," Penny said, and raised her glass in a toast to her neighbor.

"I had to race through the finishing touches on my shepherdess painting for the show. I think I'll go back and see the paintings in the wonderful light they have in that gallery. Do you want to come with me? We could go shopping for antique linens. I know a wonderful store tucked away in an alley. The proprietress won't yield on price, but it's too good not to try, and sometimes I find a little something that has a blemish or a tear in the lace and she'll discount it for me."

Penny laughed, but there was something in her voice that made Katherine look closely at her. "Wish I could, but I'll be packing and closing up the house."

"But why?" Katherine cried out in surprise. "The fête weekend is almost here, and this is the perfect season. It's not yet cold and the wind isn't blowing. We need you to sing with Yves also. Don't forget your duet."

Penny made a loud noise of disgust. "I can't forget fast enough. Really, he is so juvenile. And frankly, other than you and Michael, there's no one here of any interest. I'm thinking I may sell the mill house and get a pied-à-terre in Paris. Or perhaps in Rome, where it's warmer. You could come visit."

Her decision didn't make any sense until a week later when Sophie showed up with a lemon tart and a satisfied smile. Her mother was feeling much better and was considering hiring someone to conduct tours of the Château de Bellegarde again. There were so many tourists at this time of year, and one did not wish to disappoint them, you know?

Would Sophie escort people through? "Oh no," she said. She had too much to do at the Paris office. "But I will be here for the fête, and Yves and I have decided to sing some folk music. He's teaching me now. 'The Man of Constant Sorrow' is *triste*, so sad, isn't it? That's what I came to tell you, in part. We would love it if Michael could hear us rehearse and perhaps accompany us at the performance."

"I didn't know you sang," Katherine said. I didn't know you and Yves . . . she thought, but the moment sped by as the woman chatted on. Her color had improved drastically and she was wearing, wonder of wonders, a charming little sundress, *très chic* and definitely not from the flea market piles Katherine scouted for her own clothing.

When Yves stopped by next, obviously to gauge his reception now that he had changed singing partners, Katherine asked him the question that had been bothering her so long. "When Albert died, you were supposedly in Paris. But Emile was sure he saw you in Chablis. You two have lived for a long time in the same town. I sincerely doubt he would confuse you with a stranger."

Yves pushed his hair off his forehead and looked at her, his eyes bright and challenging. "Ah, so you are our Miss Marple, then?"

"Hardly. That's Pippa's territory. I got everything wrong and will never live down my horror at accusing the man who was going to become Michael's mentor of pedophilia. But tell me."

"You must tell no one, understand, my dear Katherine? No one."

She nodded, curious. Since it wasn't murder, there could be no harm in a small secret.

"There is a doctor there, a specialist, I needed to confer with."

"You're not sick, are you?" Katherine said with a small gasp. He certainly looked the picture of health.

To her amazement, his face bloomed red and he mumbled into his lap, "I wanted to reverse a decision I made many years ago. In case, you know . . ."

"In case what?"

"What if I want to become a father, *tu comprends*?"

Katherine threw herself back in her rattan chair. Of all the speculations she had made, this had not been on the list, would not have been for a million-dollar bet. She was, for once, genuinely speechless and could only look at the local rake with an open mouth. Finally, she gathered her wits. "And?"

"I go for the surgery next month. But," Yves said, reaching to tap her hand, "you will tell no one, *d'accord*?"

"*D'accord*," was all she could say, and she kept her face serious until he had driven off and she could begin laughing so hard tears sprang to her eyes.

One morning, while Katherine was painting an old wooden plank to look like theater footlights and Michael was hammering some signboards to advertise the fête, Pippa called out from the gate, "May I come up for a bit?" and bounded up the steps. Twisting her hands together in what looked like ecstatic prayer, Pippa said, "I've got it, you know, the idea for a story? It will be set right here in Reigny, and the château will be where my murder takes place. I'm awfully excited. I've already written several rather smashing scenes."

"Oh dear, are we all in it?" Katherine said, straightening up and rubbing the place at the small of her back that ached from a summer of gardening and painting.

"Well, yes and no. I mean, it's made up, of course. No one is for real. Terribly fun. I'm writing away like a demon."

"Aren't you afraid Adele will be bothered to find herself in a made-up story about her husband's death?"

Pippa laughed. "It will be in English, and one thing I have learned rather quickly is none of the French I've met care a drop for anything not written in French. Anyway, I shall use a pen name, and I've already decided what it will be. P. L. Vickers. The Vickers is my grandfather's name. That way, no one will know a woman wrote it. Will help sales tremendously, I should think. Do you like it?"

For the next couple of months, Katherine and Michael talked around the abandoned music project and tour, but gently. It had to be stinging for him to get close once more and lose a second chance at success. When the court had made its determination that Brett was guilty of giving in to panic but not of desiring to kill Albert, and J.B. had managed to convince the same court that he didn't think Albert had had more than a stumble, the producer had gone back to the States with his wife and son. The studio at Reigny was shut up and Katherine had no idea what had happened to the recordings. Sophie commented that plans for the new studio in Memphis were proceeding, and some big bands had already agreed to create new songs there.

Katherine wrote a short note to J.B., attempting to apologize, but was not quite sure it came off well. She had a desire to explain herself that, after several tries, she realized only sounded defensive. He was not a dirty old man, and there it was. Had there been a priest, had the little church in Reigny been a real church and not a falling-down relic, she would have gone to confession. But it wasn't, and she couldn't, and so she sent an abject apology in a letter and did her best to forget the most embarrassing episode since she performed a spontaneous and none-too-steady tap dance at a movie star's party in Bel-Air years ago.

She had been agreeing to everything Michael suggested, trying to make him feel better any way she could, which included buying the best soup bones for the dogs and the chocolate "escargot pralines," snails in any edible form being a sort of mascot for Burgundy, that were his only evidence of a sweet tooth other than American sodas. She even went with him to a tedious farm sale forty kilometers away in a dusty crossroads town even smaller than Reigny. "What on earth do you need from here?" she asked at one point as Michael ambled among tables piled high with vaguely menacing and rusting tools and pieces of equipment. He had no ready answer but hummed quietly as he picked up odd-shaped bits and pieces, even uncovering an old but serviceable pair of heavy garden shears that she had to admit were exactly what she needed for the shrubbery on the road below the garden gate.

They would be all right. She had earned her place in Reigny-sur-Canne, ironically, by standing up to Mme Pomfort, who had liked her better for it. The fête had been a success. But their days would be quiet, and dreams about larger excitements than the annual fête had to be put away.

So, she was shocked when Michael turned from the computer one evening, when she thought she had reined in her ambitions for herself and her husband, to say, "Well, I'll be damned. Listen to this, Kay."

J.B. had sent him a music file with the first dubbed versions of the songs they had recorded in France, asking Michael what he wanted in the way of added tracks to lay over them. He had some studio musicians standing by. He made no reference to Michael's hysterical wife. Betty Lou had recommended someone she'd heard about who was a genius at arranging tours, and would be e-mailing him to run through a package of dates to choose from.

Michael read out loud: " 'Given the crap my son put us all through, and the good deal I have with Sophie Bellegarde's company, I'm going to front this, Mike. I have faith that you and Betty Lou will make a go of it, with or without your fantastic new arrangement of "Raging Love." ' "

Katherine was stunned. "I didn't know you recorded it. Are you sure?"

"Hell's bells, Kay. I can't say I admire J.B. personally after what happened, but as a business partner, he knows his stuff. He pushed me to go back to my old song and refresh it as a duet. I'm going for it. Before they left, J.B. told me his lawyer thinks the song rights can be worked out. I've changed a few of the lyrics and we're doing it as a ballad. We'll see, but I'm not going to roll over so easily this time. What do you think? Am I an idiot?" He grinned at her.

"Never that, my love." She smiled and looked at the magazine in her lap, willing the tears in her eyes not to spill over. "All will be well, darling, I feel sure it will."

From her perch in the pear tree, Jeannette saw Michael smile at Katherine, a wide smile that made him even handsomer than usual. She could hear accordion music wafting from Emile's house next door in the cool night air of early autumn, and saw the cheese-making couple walking hand in hand toward the café. She picked a late pear, realizing as she bit into it that it was too far gone. She put it in her pocket rather than toss it. She wouldn't want her friend Katherine to think she had been spying. As she shimmied down, she narrowly avoided stepping on the yellow cat, waiting under the tree for the humans to open the kitchen door and let it in for the night, to safety, a last meal for the day, and a soft place to sleep. It had been, Jeannette thought, yawning widely as she headed for home, the most interesting summer of her life, with her first boyfriend turning out to be so *tragique*. The other girls in school treated her with new respect and the boys looked at her quite differently than they had last year. And Brett had written to her to say he was sorry for frightening her. It had been a most interesting year, *bien sûr*, for sure.